INELEGANT MACHINES

INELEGANT MACHINES

D. A. HAMLIN

Published in the United States of America by
QUEER SPACE a REBEL SATORI PRESS imprint
www.rebelsatoripress.com

Cover design by Sven Davisson

ISBN: 978-1-60864-413-1

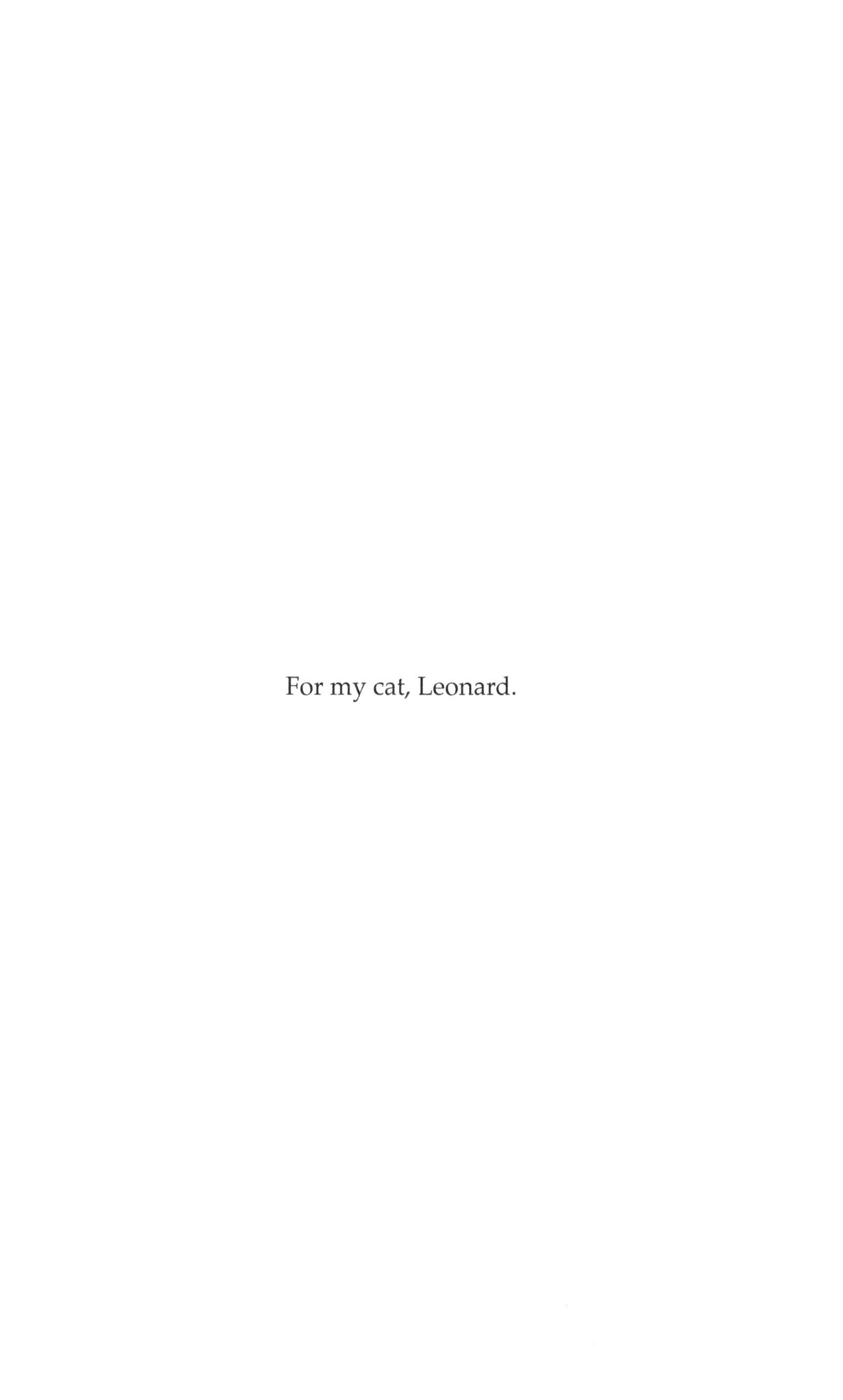

For my cat, Leonard.

CHAPTER ONE

The lights hummed in a rhythmic, pulsing cycle like a sickly heart. A glass pane stretched floor to ceiling, thin yet indestructible, creating an undeniable barrier between the onlookers and the object on display. Shallow scratches marred the glass, etched with the faint echoes of past terror.

On the opposite side, James Henderbeck sat in a metal chair, hunched forward with red-rimmed eyes and trembling hands, curling in on himself as if trying to disappear. Julian knew the facts: a forty-two-year-old tram technician, father of three, widowed, buried in debt. He'd memorized every detail on the tablet in his lap, but watching Henderbeck now, he saw a frightened man in the state-detained object—primal agony in every ragged breath he took.

The clock on the wall ticked away in agonizingly slow seconds, filling the silence with a faint click. Julian clenched his stomach as he glanced to his left: a woman with garnet red nails scribbling on a tablet; a man blinking lazily. Every movement on the other side of the glass, every shift of Henderbeck's shoulders or twitch of his hands, jerked Julian's attention back. He scribbled down messy notes, illegible to anyone but himself.

As the clock counted back to seconds, Julian held his breath, unable to break his gaze from Henderbeck. When it reached zero, Henderbeck crumpled forward, his body folding under some invisible weight. His fingers twitched. His face twisted in a silent, last plea, and then the cold settled over the room.

The impersonal voice echoed, "James Edward Henderbeck, declaration of death at 8:56 pm, January sixth, 2187. Debts: 1,945,045 civiks. Paid."

The woman with red nails swiftly gathered her things and slipped out of the sterile room, but Julian remained, staring at the mirror. His reflection, a young man with dark curls and hollow, weary eyes, fingers nervously tugging at the hem of a worn black blazer, sat where the prisoner's chair should have been.

Two men in scrubs entered and hauled Henderbeck's limp form away, his head lolling back, mouth open in a final silent scream.

Julian wiped a stray tear, blinking away the blur as he rose, slipping out the door in the woman's wake. He choked on the air around him as guilt wrapped thin, spindly vines around his throat.

He hurried out through the barren lobby and past two guards before escaping out onto the street. As she walked away, he caught a glimpse of the woman's bright red nails. She disappeared into the crowd, swallowed up by a city that consumed all. The lights hummed throughout the night, lining the streets and casting shadows down alleyways, stretching out long fingers down narrow corridors. Above him, a building reached dull metallic talons towards the sky, straining to mingle amongst the smog. Lights glimmered in the sky like stars, but their flitting motions betrayed them as they passed by one another. Snowflakes descended from looming clouds before slamming against buildings in the wind.

Warm bodies surrounded Julian as he navigated through the thick mob. A man slammed into him with a broad shoulder, sending him stumbling. He slipped below a low-hanging shop sign, forcing his way between two older men. A flick of red in a scene of gray caught his attention. As he scanned ahead, images of the lifeless man, of Henderbeck, melded with the blinding lights. On the surface of his working eye, Henderbeck's irises dissolved into the same lifeless gray as everything else around him. It replayed in his mind time and time again.

Red. Doorway.

The woman vanished through the bar's entrance. The glowing neon tubes above his head labeled the establishment as the "Rusted Donkey." The "t" no longer glowed, illuminated only by the reflection of the surrounding orange letters. Outside, the smell of smoke permeated the air, and a man in a brimmed hat perched against the wall with a cigarette pinched between two fingers. It dangled at his side as he blankly watched it burn to a nub. As the ash built up, he flicked it without ever raising it to his lips.

The bar was a compressed room, longer than wide, with a bathroom off of the end. Smoke slinked with spindly fingers from beneath the door to the bathroom. The walls were a deep orange, almost brown, though that could have been from staining, Julian thought, but the crisp white molding that framed the walls indicated otherwise. Scattered around the walls hung paintings with bold brushstrokes against white canvases. Rather than forming recognizable images, the colors collided with one another to form abstract shapes which blended with one another. The lights above the bar itself hung low, casting shadows over two hunched figures. While surveying the room, he noticed the woman with the red nails lounged in a green velvet chair tucked into the corner of the room, a cigarette between full lips. Her red nails contrasted against her pale skin, and as she continued to write on her tablet, the dim light caught on her stacked gold rings.

As Julian approached the woman, he hesitated, taking a quick breath before taking a seat at a diagonal from her.

"Should I call for Enforcers?" she asked without looking up from her tablet.

"What?"

"You followed me here. If you don't turn around and leave within the next thirty seconds, I'm going to have security remove you from here and hold you while I wait for Enforcers to arrive."

Two men in casual yet clean clothing posted by the door caught his eye as he glanced over.

"I'm a student at Robers University, and I was wondering if I could interview you," he asked.

"No," she replied bluntly.

"Look," he started, eyeing the security in his peripheral. "I don't need your name or anything. I just want to ask you a couple questions. It won't even take five minutes."

He leaned forward, bracing his elbows on his knees.

She smirked, glancing up only with her eyes from her tablet. "I'm asking you kindly to leave."

"As a paying customer, I have just as much right to be here as you."

She let out a breathy laugh, "You couldn't afford a drink here even you were old enough."

"What do you drink?"

"Something that will make you go away," she replied, returning her full attention to her work.

Before he could quip back, he was at the bar, hand planted on one of the stools.

"Two gin and tonics," he said.

The bartender nodded. Julian cast a glance back at the woman, catching the way she tapped the toe of her white pumps against the dark wood floor. Pulled back from her face, her hair draped over her shoulders, and the light of her tablet reflected off of the lens of her wire-framed glasses.

"Sir, should I put this on your tab?" the bartender inquired, gently sliding the drinks across the counter.

"No, um, I'll take care of it now. How much?"

"Five-hundred," he said.

Julian steadied his hands, scrolling through his watch before pressing the surface to the sensor on the bar. With the vibration, Julian let out a silent thanks. Julian crept carefully as the liquid threatened to jump from either glass. Gently, he set the glasses down one at a time onto cork coasters. He took his own drink, raising it to his lips, hesitating as he waited for her to follow suit. The potent scent hovering beneath his nose stung his nostrils.

"How do you think you're gonna pay that little stunt off?" she asked, waving over the screen of her tablet, which immediately went black.

Julian forced a smile, "If you don't appreciate my generosity, I'll drink both."

"Give me that one," she ordered, gesturing at the drink closer to him.

"Whatever you like," he agreed, setting down the drink to exchange it for the other.

She took the first sip. "What do you want from me?"

"To ask a few questions."

"What do you want from me specifically? What are you really digging for?" she asked.

Julian hesitated, taking an exaggerated sip from his glass. "I mean, I'm just an undergraduate, but I think I know who you are, or what you do at least. I certainly know who you work for."

"Why does that matter?" she asked.

Julian spoke carefully, "Don't you think it does?"

"Don't play that game with me."

"You're the one dancing around the question," Julian said with the glass nearly pressed against his full bottom lip.

"You said you already know the answer," she replied, gently swishing around her glass.

He let his chin drop, casting a gaze at her through dark lashes. "Sounds like we're both playing the game, then. So, if you answer my question, you deserve something in return. That's a game works, right? A move followed by a response or a transaction?"

She smiled meekly. "I want nothing from you. How often do you try that?"

The warmth surged into his cheeks. "I don't."

"I want cash. Four-hundred civiks per question, and I'll answer as many as you like," she looked him up and down, "or will that not work?"

"I'm not allowed to pay a source in association with a university assignment. They could expel me," he quipped. "If you don't want to help me, I already have everything I need. You're a debt collector for Lancut. What, you probably see that kind of violence every day? Probably wasn't even your first of the day? Your apathy is all I needed," said Julian.

Julian consciously relaxed the growing folds in his forehead, steadying his breath so as to not let his words quiver.

"Someone has to do it," she shrugged, returning to her notes.

Julian stood, steadying himself on the arm of his chair. His vision flickered with dark speckles, which slowly dissipated. With a swift motion, he drained his glass and then tucked his tablet back beneath his jacket.

"Have a nice evening—and thanks for the drink," she chirped as he walked away.

CHAPTER TWO

"I asked you not to leave these around," Syd sighed, picking up the mangled creature by the tail. Its lifeless body, still warm, lay trapped beneath the metal bar that pinned its neck to the wooden board at an unnatural angle. Its yellow teeth protruded from its mouth, blood dribbling from the corner. "They're just as scared of us as we are of them," said the man, his ginger brows furrowed.

"And they're just as hungry," replied Julian.

"We don't need to get these nasty traps."

"I'm open to suggestions," Julian muttered under his breath.

He fiddled with the button on his slacks before unzipping them. The dark fabric pooled at his feet. Quickly, he replaced them with a pair of heavy sweatpants, shivering as he did. Julian glared down at himself before carefully undoing the buttons of his shirt, pulling a gray sweater over his head. With care, he folded the shirt and slacks, tucking them into the bin amongst his other belongings. He nudged the bin with his foot further back into the cramped space, nestling it between another bin and the far wall.

Syd held the small creature in the palm of his cupped hand, cradling its fragile body. "Why do we have any more right to live than them?"

"We don't," Julian snapped.

"What has you in a foul mood?" Syd asked.

Julian pursed his lips. "It's January, Syd. I'm treading

water—"

"We all are," cut in Syd. "Did you want any rice? I put my leftovers in the fridge. You'll probably feel better once you get something in your stomach."

Julian stopped himself from spewing something regrettable.

"Yeah, I'd like some," he agreed.

His bare feet stung against the cold concrete floor as he stood before the refrigerator. The light glowed dully in the basement apartment as he took out a bowl covered with a damp cloth. Rice halfway filled the bowl, just white with no seasoning, but Julian eagerly fumbled around the drawer beside him. He scooped food into his mouth like a famished animal with his back to Syd. It stuck to the top of his mouth, soggy and overcooked. The rice clung to the back of his throat as if thick clay.. The spoon still quivered in his hand as he neared the end of his rations. Carefully, he separated out the rest into three bites, savoring each.

"How did things go?" asked Syd.

Julian failed to meet Syd's eyes. "As well as you'd expect from one of those government assholes."

"Didn't give you anything?"

He shook his head. "Useless. Just a waste of time and money."

"Are you okay from…" Syd stopped. "How was the rest of it?"

"It was fine," he said coldly. "It shouldn't be, but it is."

Syd remained quiet, opening his mouth before closing it once more, nodding his head slowly in solemn understanding.

Julian ducked his head, hunching to slip into the cramped nook beneath the stairs. He slumped onto his mattress, burying his face into his single pillow. Propping himself up on one arm, his vision blurred momentarily with darkness, and he sank back down with a sigh. With a limp motion, he reached for the door handle, seeking to close himself off from the man lingering outside in the dingy living room. His fingers brushed the knob, and he shifted onto one elbow to properly grip and pull it shut.

The faint glow of the lone light bulb illuminated his sparse belongings. Above him, a poster clung weakly to the ceiling. Its edges curled upward, held in place by old, rusted tacks hammered into the decaying wood. In sweeping, elegant letters, the poster read "Miami." Below, with its once vibrant pink feathers now dulled to a pale peach, a faded flamingo stretched its wings. Dust coated the glossy surface, clinging stubbornly to its sheen. If Julian stood, the musty scent of paper and neglect was quick to meet him, mingling with the stale air of his cramped refuge.

The surrounding walls radiated a creeping chill, yet the worst seeped through the concrete ground, permeating through his thin mattress and into his bones. His lithe body offered little shield from the persistent cold. He pushed two blankets to the edges of his mattress as a buffer. The walls were built from the same wood as the stairs, and the bulb hanging above his head swayed whenever someone walked up or down.

He slumped back onto his bed and closed his eyes.

Silently swearing, he told himself that he could not afford to give in to his exhaustion. It was never just a quick break. Soon enough, he would wake up to his blaring alarm and have to run out the door for his shift. He forced himself back up and tapped the microphone button. He watched idly as the words that fell from his lips appeared on the screen. After he heard a stirring outside of his door, he dropped his tone. As he rambled, his eyes fluttered shut, lids hanging heavily. Fog swallowed him as he sank into the makeshift mattress, drowningin the promising warmth.

Abruptly shooting up, he rubbed his eyes. He frantically

checked his tablet; he only lost a few precious minutes. Before he could slip back into the temptation of sleep, Julian put on a battered gray jacket on over his shirt, he brushed his shoulders, wiping away any dust. He pulled on a black hat that covered his ears, and he wrapped a knit scarf around himself, swaddling his face and neck until the soft wool brushed against his hooked nose.

Around him, two doors stood on either side of the staircase leading upwards. Someone had divided the ground floor of what was once a family home into two apartments and converted the small cellar into a barely livable space. Julian knew that if a fire broke out, there would be no escape, and the cold basement would certainly come to serve as his tomb. Inspections were rare, and those who could afford to own property in the city had the means to pay off whoever they needed just as easily. He envied the tenant living up the stairs who basked in the glory of a full floor to herself, yet he avoided said tenant in practice.

As he yanked open the door, the frigid air immediately pulled him into a realm where the wind bit at any exposed skin and wailed like a rabid animal. Snowflakes spiraled around him, pulled into the apartment building before he pulled the door shut.

In the night, tall lamps hovered like emaciated soldiers guarding over the city framed the streets. Few still produced light, but those which did cast long shadows of their posts across the cracked pavement, glinting off of patches of black ice. He hugged the side of the building with his body, keeping his left hand shoved in his pocket while he held out his right wrist, tapping the device twice to activate it.

He spoke aloud as he hastily walked down the street, shuffling through the windy night in shuddered movements.

Every few steps, he glanced down at the words appearing on the hologram before him.

"The debt-collector refused to speak to me about the issue. She was incredibly avoidant of any questions, actually. Instead, she wasted my time as we went back and forth about the ethics of her answering my questions at all. When I suggested that Lancut's methods were brutal, she did not refute by statement. Her lack of empathy was particularly jarring. When I brought up her position in the company, she told me that, quote, 'someone has to do it,' unquote."

Those words swirled about his mind as he walked, the dark plume surrounding them enveloping any other thought.

"Janette Swane, based on her online profiles," Julian continued to speak into the void, his watch capturing his words, "has worked as a debt-collection confirmation specialist for nearly a decade. It appears she worked for a call-center before this. However, connections to an uncle working within Lancut's asset repossession department may gave gleaned her an opportunity..." he rambled on.

He turned the corner, passing by a storefront with bashed in windows. Bits of glass clung to the edges of the frame like rows of jagged teeth protruding from the mouth of a beast. Julian couldn't recall a time since he moved to the neighborhood when the windows had been intact. If he shined in a light, he understood eyes would glare back at him with warning malice.

"Man," a deep voice cut through the wind. "What're you doing out this late?"

Julian raised his arm to his face. The man shone a flashlight into his eyes, melting away any identifying feature of the stranger in the pale white beam. While his face remained difficult to make out, the heavy boots and the dark red fabric of his pants gave enough away.

"Just walking, sir," Julian responded, quietly, keeping his eyes fixed on a deep crack beneath his feet.

"Who were you talking to?" the Enforcer asked, lowering the flashlight and clipping it onto his belt. The man wore a heavy jacket with a matching hat, both displaying an emblem of three stars framed by two wings.

Julian gestured to his watch. "Taking notes for an assignment—went out to work through my thoughts."

He tapped on the device until a small hologram cast the image of a document directly above it. As he waved at the air, Julian scrolled through his pages of writing.

"Remove your hat for me, and place your hands against the wall," the man barked.

He gritted his teeth while pulling off his hat, clasping it in a clenched fist as he pressed his hands against the cold brick. The officer removed a small device mimicking a cellphone from his belt, pressing on a button. In that moment, Julian's muscles seized up, entirely immobilized. Save for his eyes moving from side to side and his chest rising and falling, he was rendered motionless, unable to pull his hands from the side of the building or so much as wiggle a toe. A beep sounded, and the man pulled away the device, allowing it to display a hologram. Julian skimmed the document out of the corner of his eyes. His profile was short, reading his first and last name, height, sex and his front and profile pictures accompanied. A long number highlighted in red beneath drew attention from any other information.

Frowning, the officer started at Julian's feet, frisking along the sides of his legs before reaching for his abdomen.

"So, what are you really doing out here?" he pestered, feeling down Julian's arms. "Am I gonna find a little baggie if I take off your jacket? Am I gonna find a weapon? Or is it a wad of cash?"

The officer unzipped the younger man's jacket and ran his hands up Julian's thin shirt. He held his breath, closing his eyes while the man ran his hands over his waistband. "Or is that how you make your money?"

His face grew warm, and he sensed his skin on his cheeks bloomed red. Desperately choking to retort back, he could not open his mouth or move his lips. Suddenly, the grip paralyzing his body released, and he crumpled to the ground. His cheekbone slammed against the pavement before he could catch himself, and the bitter taste of blood bloomed on his tongue.

"Honest work," the Enforcer huffed, disappearing as quickly as he came.

As he lay on the pavement, curling in on himself, the sting of his bloody cheek was nothing compared to the numbness spreading from his heart to his fingertips. With shaking hands, he massaged over his temple. He brushed his fingers over the raised skin and the metal Disc beneath. He steadied his breathing, pulling back on his hat and brushing himself off. Julian sat up, staring at the flickering streetlight above him. As it flickered like a blinking eye, he imagined it was a being to worship, muttering a silent prayer.

The darkness of night was running out like sand through an hourglass. When morning came, so would mark another notch in an endless cycle.

CHAPTER THREE

Julian hauled a gray bin onto a stack, sweat slicking his back. With a quick slice of a razorblade, he opened the box, spilling its contents onto his worn table. Sorting clothes—pants left, tops right—he worked methodically, hanging items by size and design on a rack beside him. The table, cracked and bowed from years of use, bore the carved word "FORSAKEN." Around him, workers toiled in silence under cold, flickering lights, their movements mechanical.

A tall man's glare lingered as Julian ignored the burn in his raw fingers, focusing on his task. The manager's gaze shifted to a woman in gray pants—likely indentured. Julian glanced down at his own indistinguishable uniform, his thoughts numbed by the monotony of work. He avoided distractions, knowing mistakes meant instant replacement. Once, he'd witnessed Enforcers beat a man for defiance, dragging him away.

The bell rang. Julian logged his six hours and stepped into the freezing January air. His torn shoes soaked up icy sludge as he rushed along smog-filled streets, ignoring deep pangs of hunger. Ahead, his destination loomed—its polished glass and entrance a cruel facade for the cracks and decay within.

In the atrium, bustling students wound around one another, often brushing shoulders. The light fractured, catching on hanging crystal pieces from a chandelier at the epicenter of the dome ceiling. Painted a deep red, it cast the room in a warm glow. Carefully navigating the crowd, he strode into a wide hallway with six elevators. Three lined one side, and three stood across. After scanning his watch against the sensor, he crossed his arms once more, jamming his numb fingers into his armpits as he waited.

A hand clamped down on his shoulder. He nearly jumped, stumbling as he whipped around to find bright gray eyes staring back at him.

"Scare ya?" the other man asked, giving Julian another sturdy pat on the shoulder.

"One of these days I'm gonna slap you on instinct," said Julian. He managed a grin at the other man. The corners of his lips tilted down towards the floor in what his mother used to call an 'improper smile'.

Des kept his blond hair buzzed close to his scalp. His thin brows rose in a highly responsive manner, like a curious dog. His smile turned flat as his eyes fixed on Julian's cheek. For a moment, he raised a hand, reaching it towards the other man's face. Before making contact, Julian shyly stepped back, warmth rushing to his cheeks.

"Make love to some pavement?" Des asked.

Julian squirmed beneath his lingering gaze.

"Slipped on some black ice on the way home last night. I went to the doctor, and he insisted on putting some ointment on it, but it really wasn't bad," said Julian.

The elevator dinged, and the doors peeled opened. Students poured out in a stampede, and the two mans waited for the crowd to dissipate. They forced their ways into the cramped elevator beside two other students and a professor. His fingers still tingled from the cold. He clenched and unclenched his fists a few times, wiggling his fingers.

"Come have dinner at my place," Des suggested. "My father

is having over some kind of government bigshot, and I don't want to be stuck there alone. Dad's been twitchy about it for days."

Julian mulled over the invitation as half a dozen other concerns tainted his concentration. As if reading his mind, Des put a hand up.

"You'd be doing me a big favor, man," he patted Julian's shoulder, casting him a grin.

"I'm busy with my paper for Cruz," shot back Julian.

"I bet this guy has ties. He might get you in the running for the internship."

"The one I don't want?" asked Julian.

Des sighed, "Everyone wants it. If you want to be some bigshot, it wouldn't hurt to rub shoulders with these guys."

"They're corporate psychopaths," said Julian.

"Exactly."

"Fine, but you're driving me home," responded Julian.

"As if I'd ever make you walk?"

"I know."

The elevator dinged, and the two stepped out onto their floor.

"Meet ya in the library around four-ish?" asked Des, not waiting for a reply before setting off in the opposite direction.

Julian nodded in response, offering a weak smile before setting off down the hallway on his own course. With his backpack slung over one shoulder, he wove through the crowded corridor, his head swimming. When he slipped into a large lecture hall, he maneuvered his way to the front through a group of congregating students. He found his seat in the second row.

Beside Julian, a girl with a high ponytail filled the seat. She sat with one leg carefully crossed over the other. Her black winged eyeliner impeccably traced her eyes and swooped up. Her brows, jet black to match her pin-straight hair, complimented her rounded features.

Smoothing down his own pants with his calloused palms, he looked over the state of his clothing. He wore a brown belt that cinched his gray pants tightly just above his hips. Some of the fabric bunched up on itself around the waistband. He adjusted his sweater, tucking it into the front of his pants. Julian moved the excess fabric to the back. He swam in the oversized sweater like a child playing dress-up in his father's suit.

"How many tangents today?" scoffed the girl, Anna, next to him. She spoke without turning to him, keeping her eyes trained intently on the front of the room.

"And will any of them be relevant?" Julian responded.

The lights dimmed over the lecture hall, and the projection at the front of the room crispened against the white screen which swayed slightly from its fixture on the ceiling. Dr. Cruz paced across the front of the room; hands laced behind his back. He smiled out towards his audience, gesturing in an upward motion. The students uniformly turned to the left side of the room to face a flag with one red star and five wings, each blooming out from the concavities of the shape. The wings, a crisp white, angled to create an endless wheel. A deep navy background served as a canvas for the emblem, and the thin fabric slouched in the center, pinned from only the upper corners.

"I pledge loyalty," Dr. Cruz started, a myriad of voices joining him, "to the state of Lancut." Julian kept his lips flat, unable to so much as spit the words.

Beside him, Anna stole glances down at her phone, typing with her thumb.

"For the strength of the Union, which protects us, through service and loyalty, from indignity and injustice." Anna beside him mumbled along, rolling her head on her neck in a wide stretch. The voices around him spoke as one monotone force, the energy in the room dying, sucked from the air by their words. "A state of prosperity and greatness."

Once the last voice trailed off, coats and bags rustled as students dropped back into their seats like fallen soldiers. Julian sat back down, pulling up his notes for the class. Anna leaned over so subtly he doubted anyone else in the room noticed.

In a hushed voice, she flatly told him, "Be careful."

"I'd say the same to you."

"We live very different lives," she said nonchalantly, meeting his eyes.

Julian ducked his head down, digging through his bag, his fingers brushing purposelessly against old papers while his face burned.

Settling into his chair, he wrote the date at the top of his digital page. With a deep blue pen between two fingers like a cigarette, he awaited the professor's introduction. Julian bounced his leg incessantly, and his hand trembled even with his elbow planted on the desk. He lowered his pen to his page, but his first bullet point straggled into a jagged line.

Dr. Cruz's meek whisper carried through the amplified microphone pinned to his collar. "Grades aren't ready yet. I need another day due to the essay length—not that I'm discouraging thorough answers. So far, the exams I've graded are excellent. Except, of course, the ones that aren't." He smiled, scanning the class. "Let's discuss the reading. What stood out to you? Any surprises or unanswered questions?"

Julian skimmed his notes, waiting for someone else to speak. Matthew Pierce, from a shared freshman English class, spoke up. "The author highlights incentives for surveillance when profit is tied to crime but doesn't offer alternatives. Corporations and governments both prioritize profit, though for different reasons."

Dr. Cruz folded his arms, his frail frame almost shrinking. "So, do you think democracy and corporatocracy share the same flaws? Or that they merge without regulation?"

Matthew hesitated. "Not pure democracy, but real-world examples, yes. Corporations prioritize merit over charisma, offering stability. Surveillance supports these systems, just like traditional police enforce laws."

Dr. Cruz pressed further. "Are you saying neither system works without restrictions?"

Matthew nodded. "Exactly."

"Then let's consider the alternatives the author hints at. Any thoughts?" Cruz's gaze landed on Julian, who raised his hand.

"I don't think the reading critiques government directly," Julian began. "It suggests alternatives like addressing root causes of crime—debt forgiveness, capping rent, and reducing economic inequality. The current system rewards exploitation over collective good."

Dr. Cruz countered, "The author doesn't explicitly propose dissolving debt."

"It's heavily implied," Julian replied, fumbling. "Most nonviolent crime stems from inequality. Addressing basic needs may reduce crime more effectively than surveillance.

Anna raised her hand, interrupting Julian. "The author argues surveillance increases crime by catching minor infractions—traffic violations, public intoxication—that wouldn't otherwise matter. This pulls more people into the legal system, limiting opportunities and perpetuating crime."

Dr. Cruz nodded. "So, less surveillance might, paradoxically, lower crime?"

Anna smiled. "Exactly."

Julian's face burned as he looked down at his notes. The class dragged on, but his heavy eyelids betrayed his fatigue. Briefly closing them, he relished the quiet numbness, escaping the ache in his stomach and the weight of reality.

As the clock neared eleven-thirty, students began packing up. Julian slipped his tablet into his backpack, moving deliberately. Once the room cleared, he lingered near Dr. Cruz's station, waiting until the professor finished speaking with another student. When the moment came, he stepped forward, standing silently as Dr. Cruz jotted something on a scrap of paper.

"Ah," said Dr. Cruz, creases stretching out into a smile. "How's your paper coming along?"

"Henderbeck," he started, shoving his hands deep into his pockets. "He was executed last night. I was there."

The sides of the professor's lips fell slightly. "What did you feel?"

"What?"

"Before. During. After. What did you feel?" repeated Dr. Cruz.

Julian hesitated. "Nothing."

"I don't believe that."

"It's the truth," he responded. "Numb. That's what I felt."

"If I look at your notes, what will I see?"

Julian instinctively glanced down at his bag where his tablet held his scribbles. "It's not my job to report my feelings on the matter. I took detailed notes of the events. When something is clearly morally irreprehensible, that should be enough for people to conclude on their own given the evidence. I don't need to write an emotional ode to death."

"You're too focused on the big picture," remarked the

professor. "If you want to do anything worthwhile, you need to be persuasive. And if you don't want to process your feelings towards the situation, you should have chosen urban planning, or public transportation, or anything else, Mr. Harper. You're a bright young man, but sometimes you concern me."

"I—"

"Even now, you're rushing for an explanation. You're going to pull something out of thin air to explain your reasoning. Slow. Down. Or you'll miss key details."

Julian clenched his jaw, meeting the professor's dark brown eyes.

Dr. Cruz tucked his notebook into a cracked leather briefcase before returning his attention to his student. "I'm going to have tea in my office if you'd like to finish this conversation there."

"That's alright," said Julian. "There's an assignment I need to work on before my next class, and then I need to head straight home."

"Why don't you walk with me, then?"

Julian shivered in the cool hall, glancing in either direction. He caught Anna's eyes before she slipped out of the room.

"My mother has a terrible cold, and since she's stuck in bed, she asked if I would tutor my sister this afternoon, but I'll catch you during office hours tomorrow," he said.

"Okay, if you're sure. I'd appreciate reading your notes—including some post-event reflection," he added. "You're doing well, Mr. Harper."

He clung to the radiant sensation dripping from the professor's praise. Julian repeated the statement in his mind until the words ran together in his memory.

CHAPTER FOUR

"I'm about ready to pay you to write this damn paper for me," said Des, throwing a smile over his shoulder. "Name your price."

"You wish you could afford me," responded Julian.

"Oh, c'mon."

After the initial laughability, he asked, "Who's it for?"

"Dr. Lincoln. I don't think you've had her," Des responded. "It's basically a book report. You'd have it done in a couple hours."

"A couple hours? I'm a busy man. That's a lot of time," he retorted.

"Please, I'm begging you. Two thousand civiks, all yours, if you can do it by the eighteenth," pleaded Des.

His broad shoulders cast a blocky shadow in the sliver of sunlight jutting through the heavy clouds ever-looming overhead.

The snow swirled around the two young men, catching on their jackets before slowly melting into the fabric. Above them, the sky churned with gray clouds that dashed through the sky, rolling over one another like acrobats. Des gazed up at the sky, letting the snowflakes melt on his face. His blue irises appeared gray, with the reflection of the sky dancing on the surface of his eyes. Julian admired the other man's bold figure, the way his coat draped over his broad frame, and the fabric around his arms strained against Des' biceps and shoulders. His blond hair shone white in the pale light.

The black car cruised low to the ground. When Des tapped his watch to the back door, it drifted open with a wave of his hand. The taller man, ducking his head, climbed inside. Des took the chair at the far side of the car, gesturing at Julian towards himself. The shorter man carefully maneuvered through the wet roadside, shaking the sludge from his shoes before stepping inside.

"Take us home," Des commanded.

"Which house?" questioned a monotone voice.

"Oswald Street," he said, turning to Julian. "You'd think the tech would pick up on the patterns, but it doesn't."

"I guess most people have one house," said Julian plainly.

"Maybe," he shrugged with a nonchalance to his voice. It was a fleeting thought and nothing more. "But it should know that on weekdays I go to Oswald Street."

Julian suddenly remembered Des had said something to him, "That's why I prefer my own two feet. The fresh air is good for you."

"Yeah? Since when has there been any fresh air around here?" asked Des.

Julian shrugged. "Sometimes when it first snows or rains, there's that smell—and anyway, I always find my mind clearer after I walk around the city."

Des stared back blankly. "I'd prefer not to get mugged. Bet that's how you got that badge right there," Des nodded at Julian's cheek.

"Funny enough," he started, taking a breath as he mulled over his words, "I got this one walking up the stairs. We just had the hardwood stairs polished again, and it's always so slippery directly afterward. Especially with wet shoes," he added. "Caught my cheek on the edge of one of the steps. But if you'd like to hear a more interesting story, I'm sure I could make something up."

"You should have just gone with the mugging story," Des said. "Makes you sound less uppity."

Julian gave a sharp laugh. "You're right. I'd sound more modest if I said I got the shit beat out of me by the commoners trying to rob me for my precious belongings."

"Hey," said Des, a hint of defensiveness rising in his voice. "I never said that. The reality is, there are a lot of people out there who are real desperate right now, and you're a lot better off than them. Dad says a lot of people have been losing their homes. They can barely afford to eat right now."

"I know, I know," feigned Julian. "That's why my parents keep taking away my car access. They think I'm not grateful for what I have. They want me to move back in with them full-time or start paying my own rent as if I'm not in school full-time. They said I should get a job or something."

Julian let himself rest his head against the car window, the humming of the engine a barely audible lulling noise. They drove past gray buildings, many with tall glass windows stretching towards the grim sky. People in suits and heavy jackets rushed along freshly salted and cleared sidewalks, their breath lingering behind them in visible puffs. Julian much preferred the city at night when the neon lights illuminated his surroundings with bright colors otherwise stripped from the earth when humans forfeited nature for concrete. In the night, the abrasive dullness was replaced by the laughter from the bars and clubs, and warm light emanated from the streetlamps, soaking into the soul of the city. Even in the dead of night, lights shone from windows that disappeared up into the clouds, which swallowed any notion of stars.

At street level, a wide door raised, revealing a ramp that the car climbed down. Unlike a common parking garage, the walls were a clean, white drywall. Though Julian estimated the garage had space for over fifty cars, only a few were parked as if on display. Their car maneuvered itself neatly between two of the guidance lines, and the doors clicked open. When the air hit his skin, the overwhelming warmth stunned his face.

As he waited at the elevator, that familiar overwhelming heat assailed his face. When the doors peeled open, Julian followed Des inside. Des pressed his watch to the sensor in the wall before pressing on floor sixteen. Julian knew that Des and his family owned the top four floors. Floors sixteen through twenty were theirs to do with what they wished, and Des' parents gifted their son the sixteenth floor at the completion of high school education. Though Julian teased Des about why he still lived with his parents, he no more lived with his parents than most other students, rarely seeing Daniel or Maria Peterson unless utterly necessary.

As he walked out of the elevator, he stood with the same wide-eyed expression that overtook his entire body every time he visited, mouth slightly agape as he tilted his head up at the high ceiling.

"Want something to drink?" asked Des, quickly disappearing around a corner.

"I'll fix myself something. I mean, you invited me here. I can grab you whatever you want while I'm in the kitchen."

"Jenny can make us both something," said Des without hesitation.

"Jenny can make you something," he stopped himself. "Why don't you find us something to play in the meantime," Julian said.

"But—"

Julian shrugged off Des' remark, heading towards the kitchen before the other man finished his sentence.

The kitchen sprawled off one of the lavish halls; a well-lit space that boasted two ovens, a refrigerator and a large stone island at the center. Endless cabinets painted pristine white lined the walls, the gloss reflecting the light. In the sterile environment, the counters remained clear, and not so much as a houseplant added life to the space.

At the end of the room, Julian walked into a pantry rivaling the span of his entire apartment. Julian imagined that his eyes brightly glimmered, reflecting the colorful assorted packaged foods. While Des maintained a fondness for delivery services, once the restaurants closed for the night, he would drunkenly stumble into the pantry, taking down whatever chips or sweets he preferred in that moment, never limited in his options. In a high stupor, Julian watched him once open a can of corn, eating it directly with a spoon on the pantry floor. Though, primarily, when Des had too much to drink, or smoke, or huff, he would call on Jenny at odd hours of the night to cook him full meals. As of late, though, he had dropped this habit in favor of binging chips or other highly preserved goods.

Fumbling with the zipper on his backpack, Julian gently set the bag on the ground, squatting down by the canned goods. Quickly, he took three cans of pinto beans, setting them at the very bottom of the pack before zipping the bag and tossing it cooly over one shoulder. As he returned to the kitchen, he forced a smile. A middle-aged woman with hair pulled tightly into a bun glared at him. She wore a clean gray shirt and black slacks. At the counter, she held a crystal bottle of vodka. He watched her mix a drink with a smooth rhythm, barely looking down at her handiwork.

"How were classes, Mr. Harper?" she asked flatly.

"Fine. How was your day?"

"Fine. What happened to your cheek?"

"I tripped."

Ignoring her questioning glance, he turned on the coffee machine, grabbed a green ceramic mug, and lined it under the drip. Dark espresso mixed with steamed milk, and the bitter-sweet scent drew him in. Cradling the mug, he sighed as warmth spread through his calloused fingers. Without a word, he slipped past her and out of the kitchen.

In the living room the fireplace flickered with blue flames that gave no heat, and above, a slightly curved television responded to Des' gestures, scrolling as he flicked his hand. He sat down beside Des.

"Thanks," said Des when Jenny set down a glass on the table in front of him, not turning his attention from the screen. Once her footsteps were no longer within earshot, the man spoke up again. "I don't know what your problem with her is."

"I don't have one."

"It's not her fault," said Des.

"She didn't choose this, but she chose… this," he emphasized, gesturing around the room.

"She's working off her debts. We don't have room to say anything."

"I'd rather let them fry my brain and harvest my organs than be someone's slave," said Julian, plopping down on the couch next to Des.

"Oh, come on. She's not a slave," he said, a slight hint of irritation in his voice.

Julian's breath caught in his throat. "Not a choice I'd ever make."

Des gave a short laugh. "I'm not sure why you've even put this much thought into it," before Julian could respond he added, "You'll never have to worry about it. And I know, I know, you're going to climb that ladder and destroy the entire system. I hate it too, but, well, you know what they say about biting the hand that feeds you."

It starves me. It snatches the food out of my cold, trembling hands and laughs. If I bite down, I will nourish myself with the spilled blood.

"You're right," he managed, quickly washing down his words with a sip of his cappuccino. "I need to blow off some steam before dinner. What are we playing?"

"I don't really care," Des said.

"Me neither. Just something so I can zone out. I don't want to think," muttered Julian.

"Angel Apocalypse?" suggested Des.

Julian sipped his coffee, indifferent to whatever game Des queued up as long as it whisked him into another world. The goggles suctioned to his forehead, pulling him into pitch darkness before an animated environment bloomed around him.

Knee-high grass brushed against him in the breeze, some stalks vibrant green, others withered husks. Craters sprouted flora, overtaking pavement and collapsing buildings. Crows pecked at an unidentifiable corpse in the road. Julian glanced down: khaki work pants, combat boots, and a scoped rifle in his hands. Beside him, Des's avatar mirrored his tactical gear, machete holstered in a vest. Des's eerily lifelike face turned skyward toward the circling birds.

"Corner store, 2 o'clock," Des said, pointing. "I'll flank right; you take left."

"No way," Julian shot back, following Des. "You go first. I'll cover. There's probably a swarm."

Des grinned. "Fine, but when they circle us, don't blame me."

Julian sighed. "You're going to get us killed, but since you're hosting dinner..."

As they approached, an undead store clerk lunged. Des fired, the creature's head bursting into mist. "The dinner's for one of Dad's government contacts," Des explained, reloading. "Something about proving himself and his project to Lancut's government."

"Am I even supposed to be there?" Julian asked, slicing a zombie's neck with his blade before shooting another in the chest.

"My dad insisted," Des said, hacking through a growling creature. "Said you're ambitious. Hell, he probably likes you more than me."

Julian hesitated. Interacting with Martin Peterson always felt like navigating a minefield. The man's hawklike gaze seemed ready to rip away Julian's mask and shatter his carefully constructed image. Yet, Julian reminded himself, Des owed him: coaxing him into university after the gap year threat Mr. Peterson loathed.

Des would likely end up as a figurehead in his father's tech empire, Julian thought, despite his untapped potential. Des was smart, maybe even brilliant, but his apathy held him back. If only he tried, Julian mused, suppressing the rising frustration.

A glowing message interrupted: *"Please head upstairs within ten minutes."* Des waved it away. "One last round," he said.

Julian took out a zombie with a clean headshot, its body collapsing theatrically. Behind him, Des finished another with a machete swing. Blood sprayed as Des drove a knife into a creature's eye socket, twisting it free with a sickening squelch.

Then, the world froze and melted into black. Julian removed the goggles, blinking back into the pristine, white-walled living room. The spotless tile floor and sparse décor felt lifeless, like Des had never fully moved in.

Des was already ahead, swiping his wrist over the elevator sensor. Julian followed, brushing off his sweater as they stepped inside. A firm hand on his shoulder pulled him from his thoughts.

"It's just a dinner. Don't stress yourself out," assured Des. "You look good."

Julian forced a laugh, heart leaping into his throat. "I'm not stressed out. I just don't want to ruin this dinner for your dad. Doesn't have any bearing on *my* life."

Giving a smirk at that, Des started, "Well, I guess this has a bearing on *my* life, so I better come up with some good stories. I know I never go, but I'm technically on the debate team. Does that make me sound prestigious?"

"That's why they invited me," responded Julian.

"Ah, yes. Because you're the pinnacle of class," said Des.

"Once you're wealthy enough, you can afford to be a little trashy," Julian said as smugly as he could muster.

"That's not going to get you the internship," remarked Des.

"Good."

Des scoffed. The elevator dinged once the number read "twenty" on the small screen. When the ornately carved oak doors disappeared into either side of the elevator shaft, the expanse in front sprawling in front of him momentarily stunned Julian. Crossing the room with carefully planted steps, as if navigating a minefield, he held out his right hand. Mr. Peterson firmly gripped back, the lines of his face creased into a faint smile. Like his son, his blond eyebrows gave the illusion that he had none. His bald head reflected the broken fragments of light cast from the crystal chandelier fixed above them.

"Great to see you again, Mr. Peterson," said Julian. "I appreciate the invitation."

Peterson gave Julian a firm pat on the back.

"Glad you could make it. Des tells me you're interested in certain public policy, and I think you ought to meet my most influential client. Networking, my man, is everything."

Julian offered a perfectly procured smile. Not opening his mouth fully, he gave a toothless grin, careful not to expose his misaligned bottom teeth. "These kinds of opportunities are a great honor. Who is this client?"

"Mr. Edmund Sands himself," he said, slowly bringing a wineglass to his mouth, swishing the contents around the crystal.

"Oh."

Peterson smiled. Julian glanced around the room, noticing two heavily armed men in military kit stiff like statues at either side of the elevators. They kept their long weapons braced at their chests as if prepared to pursue an assailant within an instant. Their stout crimson caps balanced on their heads, out of place and ornamental beside the rest of the tactical pants and the thick vests they wore.

"Oh, okay."

"Yes, well, this has been a long time in the making. This dinner is nothing official, but it's in good taste to make your clients feel appreciated- special, trusted even. And nothing is as vulnerable as bringing children, the ones we protect most dearly, into the equation," said Mr. Peterson with a calm monotone lilt to his voice. "And, of course, I thought you would be great conversation for him. As well as keeping Des… in good taste," he gave a short laugh, nodding to his son, who appeared preoccupied, pouring something into a stout crystal glass. At the base, Julian estimated two fingers of whiskey swished around. "Anyhow, Mr. and Mrs. Sands and their son are already in the library with my wife. We'd best join them. It's in poor taste to keep the president waiting."

Des stood shoulder to shoulder with his father, the spitting image of the tycoon. They rose to stand half a foot taller than Julian. With identical statures, the two boasted broad shoulders and impeccable posture. Des lacked the lines of times carved into his father's face, but instead, freckles dotted over his nose faintly.

Both cleanly shaven Petersons led the way through a dimly lit white hallway and into a warm room. In the stark winter, the heat was nearly overpowering as Julian passed by a centerpiece which expelled flames from the base. Ovular, its glass walls prevented anyone from reaching into the fire, but its heat still radiated intensely from dancing orange flames, sometimes licking at the glass with blue tendrils. It danced in Des' light eyes when the two locked gazes. Julian, after years of stealing glances at the other man, still could not decide whether his eyes were blue or gray, their true color often overwhelmed by a deeper radiance that rendered Julian immobile and inarticulate.

The youngest person in the room was ten years his junior. Tre, or Edmund Taylor Sands the Third, scrolled through his tablet from one of the stiff gray sofas. His messy brown hair fell into his eyes.

Julian straightened his posture, practicing an inoffensive neutral expression.

"Mr. Sands," Julian approached the patriarch, "my name is Julian Harper. I'm a longtime friend of Desmond Peterson, and I was kindly invited to dine with the Petersons and your family."

"Nice to finally meet you," the man said, his gaze impaling Julian. The president's eyes burrowed deep into Julian's chest as if they could wrap invisible tendrils around his pounding heart.

"I'm a political science and journalism student at Robers with Desmond," said Julian.

Sands nodded, gesturing to a man who blended into the corner with his plain clothes. He lifted his glass, not acknowledging the man refilling it.

"Yes, well, Peterson mentioned your interests," said Sands. "Sounds like you're an ambitious young man with a good head on your shoulders."

Julian fumbled over his words at the compliment, looking away from the man he addressed. "I'm absolutely fascinated by how you've handled taking over for Mr. Price. I completely agree with the crackdown. How can you trust your staff to carry out orders if they have high debts themselves? They might sabotage tracking efforts," Julian carefully spoke, burying his contempt in ambition.

Tilting his head, Julian noticed the way Edmund Sands studied Julian's appearance, lingering on a stray piece of lint on the man's shoulder.

"Well, that was one component of it," Sands started. "I wondered how they were hired in the first place. I understand it was once ruled discrimination to consider debts and economic status when choosing candidates, but we've decided as a nation that the decision undermined our abilities to properly govern this country. If private firms are to abide by these new guidelines, the government should lead by example. I believe it's blatantly negligent to ignore such highly valuable information about a candidate. Are they responsible? Do they hold our values that we strive to embody as a society?"

Julian shook his head, letting the smile fall from his face, replacing it with a replica of pity for the man. "I know it was a

PR issue, but someone had to make the decision."

"PR," he laughed. "You're right. That was the real issue. Approval ratings dropped, but not for long. After the commotion died down, we're doing better than ever," he said.

"Had to be done, Edmund," said Mr. Peterson. "They were just looking for the latest person to blame their problems on instead of taking responsibility."

"You don't have to tell me," he huffed. "These animals are out of control. For god's sake, they were harassing my son," scoffed Sands. "It just reaffirmed my decision. They called me a killer for laying them off, as if they weren't the ones shattering windows and viciously attacking Enforcers in the streets."

Julian nodded. His body felt paralyzed in place as the words abrasively slammed into his chest. "They could just find other jobs," Julian managed. "I mean, I know a lapse of employment can mean automatic detainment, but you have to be so far in the hole already to qualify for that. At that point, you're just a drain on the system, anyway."

For the first time, Sands met his eyes with more than passing indifference. "A political science major who isn't a bleeding heart activist? I had my doubts when Dan mentioned inviting you, but it seems like you have an understanding of the bigger picture. How long until you graduate?"

"This is my last semester, sir," said Julian, suddenly wishing he had a glass to hold on to. His fingers tingled, the sensation pulsating with sudden nausea.

"And what are your plans afterwards, Mr. Harper?"

He waited, as if mulling over his decision. "I was hoping to go to graduate school to study law. That, or I'd be interested in completing an internship first, and then going. My parents want me to take a gap year, but I'd prefer to keep moving. I don't enjoy wasting time."

Des cast him a look.

"Are you applying for the Lancut Presidential Internship?" asked Sands.

Julian shook his head, "While it sounds like a great opportunity, I hoped to gain more experience in a smaller- non-governmental environment first- something more specific."

"If you change your mind," started Sands, "You'd be a competitive candidate. Applications are due by the end of the week, but I doubt that would be a problem for you."

"I appreciate that, sir, but I want to forge a more organic path."

"Sounds like you have a very promising future," replied Mr. Sands. "You have a drive that so many others your age lack. They become comfortable and complacent. Instead of draining the government's money, they just leach off of their parents. Almost as bad as the debt-holders, really."

"That's why Mr. Harper here is such a wonderful friend to our family. He's kept our Des working as hard as ever. Desmond is president of the debate team at Robers. Once he graduates, he's going to take an internship before he comes to work for me. I told him he could intern at Loget Tech, but he insisted he wants to work for someone else first."

Sands nodded at Des. "I can respect that. He doesn't want to just piggyback off of your wealth, Dan. Now, I must ask you about this study..."

Julian's attention wavered, vision falling out of focus. He stared into the far wall as if his eyes might roll out of his head and across the room. Smiling, he quickly excused himself, heading towards the bathroom.

Slipping into the large powder room, he let the door drift

shut behind him. Staring at himself in the mirror, he gripped the edge of the sink. He clumsily yanked open of the faucets, waiting for the water to run cold. Resting his fingers under the flow, he closed his eyes, honing his attention on the temperature, letting it envelop him. Rubbing his face with wet hands, he cleared his hair away from his eyes. The dark curls framed his jaw, resting on his shoulders.

"Suck up," whispered a voice.

Julian nearly jumped. "Oh, come on, man. I'm just playing the part."

"Of a ruthless freak."

"The system is ruthless," Julian snapped back. "Not me."

Backing up a step, Des put his hands up. "Hey, I mean, I know we have to keep order, but maybe Sands took things too far."

Shaking his head, Julian spoke. "You know who I am. I'm saying what I have to."

"It's a little scary, man."

"*You know who I am*," he repeated, catching Des' eyes this time. "I believe we need to overhaul the system. I do, and I don't agree with Mr. Sands. I think he's a maniac, but do you really want to disagree with the maniac? A very powerful manic. Where does that get any of us? We're supposed to butter him up for your dad. When you're sitting in your newest vacation house, you can thank me," said Julian.

"Julian—"

He spun around, the edge of the sink digging into his back as he cowered beneath the larger figure. "Don't. Don't start."

Des' eyes flashed with something Julian could not read, and Julian thought it may have been a hint of fear.

Pulling out a small baggie, Des frowned. "Fine, dictator. I know what'll make the rest of the night go by much quicker."

"Right now? Does this feel like a good time?" asked Julian hesitantly.

"Suit yourself," shrugged Des, taking one of the diamond pink pills out.

Julian put out a hand. He took the pill from his friend, slipping it into his pocket while Des dry swallowed his. "I'll take mine after dinner—once I'm not being watched."

"Fine, but I think they're about to serve dinner, so we should probably get back out there before mum and dad get suspicious," said Des.

The dinner table proudly acted as the centerpiece of the ornate room. A long table-runner made of woven silk thread adorned the rich mahogany table down its center. The candles were already lit in the dimmed room, meticulously placed every few inches. Taking a seat next to Des, Julian shifted in the uncushioned wooden chair. Windows took up the walls on two sides, overlooking the bright signs and passing headlights cruising the city at night. When Julian squinted, they all blurred together into an endless array of glowing color. Julian deemed the display more incredible than anything the Petersons could buy for their extravagant penthouse.

If he could buy back the privilege only to fully admire the view for a few moments, he would feel content. Julian assured himself that with time, he would no longer feel the deep loss.

As if penetrating his thoughts, Mr. Sands started, "Cornea transplant?"

Julian jerked his head to meet the man's eyes, a peculiar smile on his lips. "Yes, it was what? Three months ago? I'm still getting used to it."

"And so young," he shook his head. "Was it an accident?"

"Yes, sir, or sorts. It was an infection. I was volunteering and managed to get some sort of parasite. Before I knew it, everything was going fuzzy on that side," he said, gesturing to his left eye. "They tried to save my vision, but I only regained my vision with a transplant."

"You squint with that eye—just so you know," Mr. Sands noted. "I was considering the procedure myself. I mean, I don't have any story as fantastic as that, but things are getting cloudier with age. I'm not sure if I want to deal with the healing process."

"Oh, I'd definitely go through with it. It was just over two million, but worth every penny. The doctors had me taken care of with the pain meds. I will admit, though, it takes quite a bit to get used to. It's not fully healed yet, so sometimes lights are a bit blurry," he said calmly. "I requested the donor was young, so I should get some good mileage out of it. It was an extra hundred thousand, but I think it's worth it."

"Dead or alive?"

"What?" managed Julian.

Sands repeated himself coldly. "Was the donor dead or alive?"

"Alive. I insisted. They claim there's no difference in outcome, but the doctors gave in. Live donor with overall good bill of health. I understand it's about the quality of the cornea rather than the status of the donor, but still. Maybe there's something unnerving about the donor being deceased," said Julian, trailing off as a man rolled a cart up to Mr. Peterson's seat, serving him first.

On a blood red plate, a small piece of steak laid oozing at the center with asparaguses leaning up against it at a leisurely slant. As much as the hunger consumed him, bile rose in his throat at the conversation. He couldn't help but picture himself lying in his own red oozing fluids with a doctor glaring down at him. Recalling how he signed the papers—how the surgeon marked an "X" over the eye to be sacrificed before cutting into his healthy, youthful flesh.

"I'm not sure," piped up Des, earning a glare from his father.

"About what?" asked Sands, long taken away from their previous conversation.

"I just—I don't know—about live donors. That's it."

"No, I'm curious. I know plenty of your generation doesn't believe in it, but I don't understand why. Is it any different from selling your time rotting away at a job? We're all selling parts of ourselves. I put in sixty hours at the office every week," Sands responded in a monotone voice, tucking his napkin into his shirt.

Sands stared at the piece of rare, bloody meat below him with the eyes of a predator, pupils dilated. Looking away from the man, Julian balled up his napkin in his fists.

Watching Des' twitching lips, Julian wondered if Des would respond. Julian supposed he should interrupt before anything turned sour. After all, that was his job. That's why he was invited. When Des started, his voice was steady, but a slight quiver betrayed him.

"I guess it's just so permanent," said Des.

"You don't get time back either," replied Sands. "People have children at that age. If you can take care of a child at that age, I think you have the right to sell something that belongs to you."

Julian spoke. "I think it's an unfortunate reality, but in our current system, I think people should have the right to do it."

"We need to think about why people are making compensated donations to start with," said the elder Peterson. He continued, "In order to reach that point, you have to severely mismanage your finances. None of us have needed to take such action. With proper financial management, compensated donation wouldn't exist—deactivation wouldn't exist—indentured service wouldn't exist. But unfortunately, we live in a country where people think they should be able to act frivolously and then become upset when the bill comes. It just doesn't cost that much to live."

"The latest reports show," said Sands through a mouthful of food, "that most of them wait until the very last moment. They're about to be detained for debt, and in a last-ditch attempt, they donate. At that point, you're just treating yourself like a machine to be scrapped for parts."

Julian's hands trembled as he brought his fork to his mouth, a mound of the potato puree falling from his utensil.

Mind racing, he blurted out, "I wonder what your stance on prostitution is. Personally, if people are allowed to sell their bodies for parts, I don't understand why prostitution is illegal. It's far less permanent. And if people are working to repay their debts, I'm not sure why it's an issue."

"You're an opinionated young man," Sands mused. "Personally, I don't think much about it, do you?" said Sands with an air of curiosity.

Julian shrugged.

"Not particularly, but I think it's an interesting topic."

"It's bad for society," remarked Sands. "What kind of values is that encouraging? What does it produce? Are the whores creating a product beneficial to society?"

Interrupting before Julian could reply, Mr. Peterson piped in. "I completely agree. We need to be creating products that are going to push us forward."

"Said like a true entrepreneur," replied Sands. He addressed Des directly, "That's why your father is such a successful man."

Des just nodded, casting a glance at Julian. "Yeah, he's done a lot for all of us."

"Yes," agreed Julian, "Thank you for hosting this wonderful

dinner."

Julian stared down at his now half-empty plate. Cutting off another sliver of steak, he brought it up to his chapped lips. He chewed slowly and thoroughly, swallowing even as the meat threatened to stick to the back of his throat. His stomach still ached with emptiness, but he feared if he ate too quickly, all he already consumed would be for nothing. The potato puree was cold as he scooped the fallen heap onto his fork. He washed them down with a large gulp of water.

The child, Julian had already forgotten his name, picked up a hunk of steak, dangling it over the edge of the table. His father glared at the man as he let go, and the meat splatted on the wood floor. Sands shook his head, and the man giggled before returning his full attention to his tablet. Propping it up on the table, he hunched over until his nose nearly brushed against the screen.

Desmond's glazed over eyes appeared empty. He moved his knife back and forth on an asparagus already cut through, sending a high-pitched scraping sound from the blade scratching against porcelain. Julian gave Des a nudge, and the sound ceased.

"A wonderful dinner, and one with a purpose," stated Sands. "I look forward to doing business with you."

Dan Peterson hesitated. "I was hoping to show you some better models tonight and in the upcoming days."

"Not necessary," said Sands, spittle spraying from his mouth, "I have faith in Loget Tech. You've never done us wrong, have you?"

"I suppose not," agreed Peterson. "Our manufacturers are prepared to launch large scale whenever the time comes. At least let me show you the demonstration video? The marketing department would be disappointed if I didn't."

Inspecting the surrounding faces, Julian realized he was the only one still picking at his food. With half-empty plates, they spoke with fervor. Quickly setting down his utensils, he sat back in his chair, folding his hands in his lap. The man who served them quickly picked up his plate, carrying it through the far doorway and disappearing.

"Well, I'm sure my team would like to see it," replied Sands.

"If I could invite you for coffee in the study," said Mr. Peterson, standing up, gesturing for everyone at the table to follow. "I'll give you a preview."

In the study, the man who served them earlier prepared a large screen, eventually dimming the lights until Julian could barely see his hands as they rested on his thighs. Julian sat in an armchair with Des beside him. The other man clutched onto the arms of his chair as if holding onto a crumbling ledge. His dilated pupils told a story mirrored by his suddenly particularly pale complexion.

"I know that you're already familiar with the product. Well acquainted, really, but my team would skin me if I didn't show off their promotional video," said Peterson with a slight laugh. "Presenting, the I28-Vision."

The screen glowed deep blue, fading lighter and lighter until the image shattered like glass. Out of the blurred background emerged a small chip. A model of a human brain rotated, coming apart to reveal where a disc's rod intruded. Just below the skin, the small device anchored to the skull, pushing against the flesh above and bulging out less than a few millimeters.

A deep voice boomed around him, encompassing the small group, "The I28-Vision by Loget Tech," the chip clicked into the sensor, and the brain closed around the device. "Elevate and innovate. Using the technology already installed, this compatible feature allows for state-of-the-art security. By connecting to the brain's own mechanisms of sight, we can record footage through the very eyes of our people. Immediately uploaded, storage is never an issue." A rendering of a human eye emerged on the screen, dismembered into its individual components. The screen faded to black, and the lights slowly illuminated the room around them.

"You can tell your team that they sold me on it," said Sands. "You know I already hired people on my end, Daniel."

Dan Peterson wore a satisfied smile. "I'm glad. I'd like to start putting together a contract. If we play our cards correctly, we could have these fully installed within the next year. I believe we can include installation of the new chips into pre-existing Discs at mandatory stations. Obviously, we can integrate these into all new Discs manufactured. If everything goes smoothly, everyone born in 2188 will have them from birth."

"I appreciate your enthusiasm," said Sands, taking a glass from the servant tending to him. "I don't believe I'll have any issue getting this by my people, but you know there's going to be backlash." Edmund Sands took a sip of his gin before setting to down on a pale coaster. "That said, we'll make it happen. We need to take control over this nation again before it spirals out of control. People act most responsibly when supervised."

"Just to clarify, who would have access to this data?" asked Julian.

Mr. Peterson took a long sip of his drink. "We will distribute it to the relevant law enforcement agencies. This has the potential to bring crime to an all-time low."

"We can get this approved," said Sands. "I can promise you a hefty payout."

"A toast to Lancut: a crown jewel amongst savagery," Sands

raised a glass.

"And to a continued alliance in the name of greatness," replied Peterson.

CHAPTER FIVE

As if held back by an unseen force, Julian struggled to stand. He glanced down at the small square of gauze taped down in the crook of his arm. Head swirling, he clung onto the arm of the chair. Once he steadied himself long enough, he stumbled towards the front desk. The woman tapped away at her computer with long green nails. Julian switched his weight from one foot to the other, folding his arms over his chest as he took stuttered breaths.

"Full session?" she asked in a raspy voice.

"Yeah."

"Great. Five-hundred will be uploaded to your account by the end of the day as always. Would you like to set up your next appointment?" she asked.

He nodded, struggling to form words. "Yeah, uh, forty-eight hours, right?"

"That's correct. Same time?"

"Yeah," he replied.

He ducked his head and slipped out of the clinic, walking as quickly as he could on wobbly legs towards the University.

Rogers on a Tuesday morning hummed like a warming engine. Within the full thralls of the semester, students threatened to crush each other in the halls, shoving past one another rather than risk being marked tardy or worse, have a professor lock them out of class altogether. Julian practically stumbled into his last lecture, making his way toward one of the remaining seats at the front. No more than thirty people filled the small room with desks carefully positioned to create narrow walkways winding. The clutter created a maze-like arrangement. Sinking down, he nearly slid onto the ground. Gripping onto the desk until the moment passed, he steadied himself. Julian took out his tablet, sighing as he noted the battery percentage.

The class passed quickly. Though work loomed over his head, he first made his way through the halls, waiting for the elevator in the atrium. As a cramp twisted his stomach, he folded his arms over his body, resisting a wince. When the elevator dinged, he stayed in place; he stood dully. People around him flooded past him and into the elevator, one colliding their shoulder into his and sending him stumbling back. As the doors closed, he stood in place, vision swimming, creeping darkness encroaching in on him, infecting his vision from the inside out. He carefully leaned against the wall until the next elevator arrived. Quickly stepping in, he pressed on the fifth floor.

When the doors opened, he waited for those around him to clear out first before hesitantly placing weight back on his feet. Walking out into the hall, he turned left, heading towards the northern wing of the building. He passed a group of kids his age around a table tucked into a nook.

Dr. Cruz sat at his desk with his door propped open. Julian peeked around the corner, silently observing the professor engrossed in his work before slipping into the office. Setting down his backpack on the ground next to him, he lowered himself into one of the rusted orange upholstered chairs facing Dr. Cruz. He sank into the soft cushion, and for a moment, he allowed himself to close his eyes. When Cruz finally caught notice of him, his wrinkled face spread into a smile.

"Ah, Mr. Harper, how was your day?" the older man asked.

"Long," replied Julian. "But that's alright."

"How's your mother?"

"Fine," he said, quickly wracking his mind. "This morning when I left the house, she was doing much better. I imagine when I get back, she'll be back to the complaining, but it's nothing more than a runny nose," he forced a dry laugh. "I thought I could ask you if you've read my draft?"

The professor nodded, pulling up a projection to the side of the desk. "For a first draft, you're definitely on the right path. But my real question is why are you already so far along? What's the rush? These things take time so you can percolate on your thoughts. Really think about what you're writing. Did you do anything this past weekend except write?"

Julian shifted in his seat. "Oh, I did. I just like having things done early."

"Months early?"

Julian choked on his words, "I mean, you never know what could happen."

The professor cocked his head.

"Just—what if I got sick this semester? Or one of my other classes flooded me with work? I'd rather do it now while I have the time," he managed.

"Mr. Harper, you act like a madman running out of time, always assuming the worst is to come. You're a young man. While I admire your dedication, as your professor and advisor, but also as someone who cares for your wellbeing, I'm asking you to take a step back. I'll leave feedback on your draft in two weeks," said Dr. Cruz, idly scrolling through Julian's submitted draft.

Julian sat in stunned silence for a moment. "I—" he started, pausing. "Sir, I need this feedback."

"And I'll have it back to you," said the professor. "In two weeks. Do you fear your unexpected death before you can finish your work? That would be poetic, Mr. Harper, but you're not the ill-fated protagonist of a cruel tragedy."

Julian's face grew warm, and he feared his cheeks reddened. He hoped not to beg, get on his knees and grapple for his advisor's aid. No, he could take his paper to another professor for feedback. He stood up, tucking his hands into his pockets.

"No," commanded Dr. Cruz calmly. It was not an order with a threatening overtone, but the small man's authority did not allow disobedience. "Sit back down."

His heart throbbed in his chest, hands trembling as he looked down at the professor. He held eye contact as he lowered himself slowly back into his chair.

"Mr. Harper, I'm not sure what is going on, but I think it would do you well to talk to someone," said the professor.

"I don't know what you mean, sir," he responded, his voice barely quivering.

"I know you do, Mr. Harper. You're a bright kid. I don't know what's bothering you, but something is."

"Truly," feigned Julian, "There isn't."

Dr. Cruz studied him in silence for an uncomfortably long period. He cocked his head. "You look exhausted. Your statements in class have been erratic. Fueled by emotion rather than logic, and this bizarre hurry to finish your assignments is worrying. Julian, what's your plan once you graduate?"

"I'll go to graduate school."

"Do you need a letter of recommendation? It's a bit late to apply now, but not out of the question," said the professor.

"I was going to take a year off first," Julian fired back.

"Okay, and what will you do during that year?"

Julian gripped his thighs through his pant pockets, digging his nails in. "I'll find an internship somewhere. That's what my parents want me to do if they're gonna pay for grad school. They think it would broaden my horizons."

Dr. Cruz nodded slowly. "And what do they do again?"

"Who?"

"Your parents," clarified Cruz.

"Why does that matter?" blurted Julian.

Cruz shrugged. "It doesn't."

Julian waited for him to add anything. When he didn't utter a word, Julian stood up once more.

"Can I leave, sir?"

"Yes, you're dismissed," the professor said with a smile, no hint of his prior demeanor to be found in his warm eyes and inviting smile.

Julian quickly marched through the hall, putting as much distance between himself and the professor as possible. His mind raced, and he questioned what assumptions lurked behind that friendly facade.

"Hey," a voice made him jump. Turning around, Des slouched with the weight of a backpack slung over one shoulder, a mindless grin on his face. "What has you all jumpy?"

"Me?" Julian asked with raised brows. "I'm just a little tired. I'm heading home to take a nap. Afterwards though, I'd be down to get drinks?" suggested the shorter man.

"Sure," agreed Des, catching up to him as he neared the elevator. "Manny's Pub?"

"You know it," said Julian, slipping through the closing elevator doors.

When he trod out the front doors of the University, the dry winter air stung his chapped lips and exposed face.

Trudging along the sidewalk, he kept his head down, tracing the cracks with his eyes. They wove like spiderwebs, increasing in depth and frequency as he departed away from the University and towards his neighborhood. The soles of his shoes, worn down, barely lifted him out of sludge, and where the canvas of his sneakers met the rubber, the cold slop pushed up onto the sidewalk seeped in, soaking through his socks. When he reached the front entry to the apartment building, he let himself in, wiping his shoes on a sun-bleached gray mat in the doorway. Without looking, he pressed his watch up to the sensor on his door. Julian yanked the knob with his other hand, leaning into the basement entrance. Julian's shoulder collided with the door. Fiddling with the knob, he prodded the door with the toe of his shoe, giving it a light kick.

Julian frantically thought back. He set aside the civiks for rent that would automatically disappear from his account. He must have gone over-budget somewhere, but he could recall nothing outside of ordinary expenses. Tapping on the correct app, he logged himself in, scrolling through a list of purchases. The only purchase out of the ordinary was the drink he bought for the auditor after the execution.

Call your landlord. It must be some kind of mistake.

His eyes danced over the lines of small transactions for groceries and school fees before halting at an attempt to withdraw fifteen-thousand civiks for rent. The scheduled payment was marked with red letters as failed. His rent should have been twelve-thousand. He racked his brain for any reason for the extra three-thousand. Between himself and Syd, neither requested maintenance services, and the two rarely used the heat other than to keep the pipes from freezing.

Julian's fingers prickled with numbness, heart thudding in his ribcage, his stomach dropped. If rent went up for the new year, there was no way he could scrounge up an extra three-thousand. One-thousand, yes, but not three. If he had known, he could have picked up more hours. He could have done something. His skin burned hot, icy dampness in the corners of his eyes, forcing him to blink again and again. Leaning against the wall, he slowly sank to the ground, wrapping his arms around his knees like a small child.

He saw his mother's stern face through the distraught haze. What would she say right now, watching him whimper like a wounded animal on the ground?

"Hello," a voice snapped him from his trance, and he looked up through dark eyelashes. The petite blonde who lived upstairs stood above him. Scrambling to his feet, he forced a smile.

"Are you locked out?" she asked.

"Oh, yeah," he admitted. "It's alright though. I just need to wait for my roommate to get back."

"Do you want me to call the landlord so he can unlock it for you?" she asked, though when Julian caught her gaze, emptiness stared back from behind bulging eyes.

"That's alright. I wouldn't want to bother him," responded Julian.

The blonde stepped forwards, her warm breath close enough to feel against his face. "Are you late on rent again? I'm not judging… I just want to help you."

"I'm not late. There must be something wrong with the system," he replied, his voice catching in the back of his throat as he leaned back against the wall.

"It's nothing to be ashamed of. I'm sure once you graduate, you'll be just fine. Until then, you might need a hand. There's nothing wrong with accepting help. What's different this time?"

"Don't worry about me."

"I toured that apartment of yours before I moved into mine. To share it between two people? That must be awfully cramped. Nobody would choose that unless they had to, Julian," she said, her voice saccharin sweet, but she stared him down as if sizing him up to strike. The way her eyes flicked back and forth with small pupils, he imagined a cobra raising its head over a frightened mouse.

Julian stayed frozen in place.

"I'm fine. I just need to wait until Syd gets back."

The blonde, Jenna, crossed her arms. "Rent went up, didn't it? It's not an issue to lend you a few thousand. I'll give it to you. I'll give you enough to get to graduation."

At that, Julian hesitated. "Why?"

"You're a nice man. A talented man," she said.

"Oh," he said, eyes widening in recognition. "I-I said I wouldn't do that again."

"I know," she said. "You're a good student. A pure young man dragging himself up in the world, Julian." She tasted his name on her tongue, savoring the way he pulled back. "Sometimes you need to know when to accept help."

"I don't need money. There's a glitch in the system, and I'm going to wait for my housemate," he stated firmly.

She stepped back momentarily, crossing her arms over her chest. "Well, if you don't need any help, you're still welcome to stop by. I always welcome a guest."

"I-Okay," he managed.

Julian sank back down into the corner outside of his apartment, watching Jenna lightly make her way up the stairs, socked feet tapping quietly against each step. Staring at his locked door, he thought about the night ahead. Fumbling with his watch, he messaged Des quickly.

Even through the haze of exhaustion, he happily took the opportunity to leave his apartment, forfeiting any notion of a quiet rest. He waited outside of a bodega until the car arrived an hour later. Once safely inside, he leaned his head against the window, shutting his eyes as the car navigated the roads.

When he arrived at the bar, the sun had set, but people were still scarce. Manny's was a small pub with smoke-stained walls and a pool table tucked to the side. A dart board flashed every few minutes, beckoning drunken players to test their aim. Beside it, the drywall bore the small holes of shots gone awry. Des moved across the room with an effortless confidence that Julian admired. Julian watched his friend's defined muscles moving beneath his white tee-shirt while he himself hunched further into his black hoodie. As he took a seat at the bar, Julian leaned forward and placed his forearms on the sticky surface in front of him.

"You want anything to eat?" asked Des.

"Sure," he turned his attention to the bartender, "Do you mind sending an order for a cheeseburger with all the fixings to the kitchen?"

"Two," added Des. "You can put them both on the Peterson tab. And get us a couple of drafts."

"I shouldn't," started Julian.

"Why? School tomorrow? I thought you wanted to go out."

"No, I mean, I just want to get something in my stomach first," he said as the bartender turned around, offering each of them cloudy glasses of beer.

"Fine, let it get warm," Des said, taking a long chug. "With my week, I'm gonna get wasted on an empty stomach. I'm two points off from failing my fitness course. You know, I took it as an elective. How hard could it be? I just have to show up, get in the pool, and play the game, ya know? But it's never that easy," he muttered, taking another sip.

"Man, how do you mess that up?" asked Julian.

Des shook his head. "You know how those early classes are. It's fine the first couple of times, and then you're halfway through the semester laying in bed, snoozing your alarm, and when you finally wake up, you've missed it. Apparently, if I miss one more, I'm going to actually fail- unless I make some up, that is."

"Hey, for the right price, I'll show up as you," replied Julian.

Des laughed, "Yeah, you want to get up for the six in the morning makeups?"

"That's not so bad," he said, perking up his nose. From the back, the smell of sizzling meat wafted through a window and into the bar hall. "If I got a bleach job, they'd never suspect a thing. Anyway, who cares if you fail it? Just take it again next year."

"I'm gonna graduate on time. We're gonna get those degrees together," argued Des.

"Oh, come on. You'd love another year to screw off. It wouldn't be so bad."

Des shrugged. "You're not wrong," he said, raising up his glass before taking another gulp.

When the barkeep turned around, placing a dripping beef patty in front of him, his head swirled. As tempted as he was to jam it down his throat, he nibbled off a small bite mostly consisting of bun, chewing it thoroughly before swallowing it. He savored the sensation as his stomach accepted the morsel.

The night still clung to its youth when the crowds filtered in. After his meal, Julian ordered a shot of vodka, swallowing it down easily. As the sounds of voices rose in volume, so did the music, vibrating the glasses on the bar and the neon sign against the windowpane. After a few drinks, his body loosened, and the dread in his chest faded. Grabbing Des by the wrist, he pulled the other man over to the darts. Shoes belonging to countless patrons eroded away the wooden floor. The wear created a scuffed ditch on the ground to shoot from in place of a line.

"301 points on the board. First to get to zero," said Julian, lining himself up. Pulling his arm back, he flicked the dart forwards, landing on a plain twenty. The machine echoed out the number, calculating his score to 281.

"Watch this," said Des.

He made a show of licking his finger, putting it up in the air. Des made a triangle with his thumbs and point fingers, pulling in the shape towards his face and then pushing his scope back out again. Rubbing the dart between his fingers, he squinted, feigning a few test motions of his arm and wrist. When he finally released the dart into flight, it flew straight, embedding itself into the black border around the board. He put his arms up, turning to Julian before placing his hands on either of his friend's shoulders.

"Now, that's how it's done," Des proclaimed.

The machine spoke in a monotone voice, "Zero."

As the larger man leaned down, meeting Julian's eyes, Des steadied himself on his friend's shoulders. Julian stared into the great gray abysses, blurry with tears of laughter. His smile showcased his perfectly white teeth, all aligned in a genuine smile. Julian reached out a hand, nearly brushing against Des' shirt, warmth radiating off of the other man. He steadied Des, pushing him away gently. The man stumbled back, catching himself on a lone chair. Julian prepared to take his own shot. Lining up the dart in his sight, he launched the small projectile.

As it stuck with a thud just outside of the bullseye ring, he did not bother watching where it landed, eyes instead wandering to Des. The larger man shoved another short glass into Julian's hand. Hesitating, he looked up at the blond.

"Look," slurred Des, in what should have been a whisper. He nodded towards a girl with long black hair in two braids down her back. "Isn't she gorgeous?"

Julian's words caught in his throat, "I mean, yeah, she's very pretty."

"I'm gonna go talk to her."

"No, no, you're not," said Julian, gripping onto his friend's wrist with narrow fingers. "You're drunk."

"Why? You want to take your shot first?"

"I really don't," muttered Julian. "You just want to stick your dick in something, and this is going to end poorly."

"No, no," he waved, "I just think she's really pretty."

"If I got on my knees right now, you'd be perfectly happy jamming your dick down my throat," Julian spat, immediately recoiling at his own words.

A goofy grin crossed Des' face, "Is that why you don't want me talking to her?"

"No," Julian protested, "I'm just saying, you'd be just as happy with—what I'm saying," he stopped himself, leaning against the pool table. "Just go jack yourself off in the bathroom, and then you can see if you still want to talk to her."

"Don't be a buzzkill," said Des, tugging away from Julian's weak grip. He cast the other man a smile before sauntering confidently across the bar, cooly sliding onto a stool next to the girl. She offered him a polite smile, moving her lips to say something that Julian couldn't make out.

The dartboard's flashing lights faded to the back of his

mind, never truly holding his attention at any moment during the night. He considered sliding up beside Des, talking up the girl with him. As an uncomfortable feeling grew in his chest, he forced away the thoughts, approaching the bartender once more. Taking another shot, he sat down, checking his watch. If he hoped to manage even close to six hours of sleep, he needed to head home, but casting another look over at Des and the girl, her hand rested on the man's forearm.

Silver rings on her fingers glimmered in the dim light. Des gazed at her as if held in place by an unseen force. Forcing himself up, he hesitantly approached Des and the girl, careful not to stumble over any of the stools strewn about the joint. A tidal wave of words washed over his mind as he tried to speak, intertwining themselves with the rational script.

After an uncomfortable silence, he squeaked out a cough. "Hey, um, I have a lot of work to get done. I think I'm gonna head out."

Des stood up, pulling Julian into a tight embrace, patting him on the back. "You're a good friend," said the larger man at an uncomfortable volume. "I love you, man."

"Thanks," Julian stuttered. "Love you too."

When Des pulled away, he stole a part of Julian with him. Julian resisted the keening noise resting in the back of his throat.

The cold air forced a dose of reality through Julian's body as he ventured into the night. Casting one last glance into the bar, he pivoted his head away, forcing his eyes down to the sidewalk as he began his trudge. Digging through his pocket, he rolled a small pill between two fingers. Thinking back to dinner the other night, he remembered the dazed expression on Des' face; the face of a man with no concerns, just idle numbness. Rubbing the diamond pill between his pointer finger and his thumb, he considered saving it. Pushing any hesitant thoughts out of his mind, he placed the small pill on the back of his tongue, dry swallowing.

His fingers numbed before he could shove them into his pockets. The walk passed quickly as he pored over the events of the past few days. A strained laugh escaped his chapped lips as he thought back to dinner with Petersons and Sands. Julian was a stranger in a known land, an outsider let in by mistake, he thought, with the lies held together by fragile threads, ready to be wiped out of existence like a web in a corner. Perhaps he was a fly stuck in the spindly fibers, or maybe he was the spider. After all, it was his creation. A spider bound, trapped within its own silken creation, caught in a trap carefully wound to keep others out while smothering himself helplessly within.

When he pushed in the front door to the apartment building, he stopped himself. The warmth that now spread over him flushed away the terror that earlier overtook him. He checked his watch, considering messaging Syd to let him in. He refused to allow the lingering thought to take hold in his fading mind.

He walked up the stairs in a fog. The old wooden steps boasted a polished sweeping railing that spun into an intricate knot at the base. At the top, a singular door stood proudly, fitted with a brass knocker like something out of a movie. Steadying his swaying hand, he gripped the brass, giving three quick consecutive knocks.

The door cracked open, an eye peering through. The person shut the door, and Julian heard the fumbling of a metal and chain before the door opened all the way, revealing his neighbor. She sported pajama shorts that barely brushed her thighs and a tank top that hugged her chest. In the chilled apartment, her nipples poked through the thin fabric. Julian looked past her, into the dim apartment, ignoring the figure in front of him.

"Why are you here?" she asked innocently, with wide doe-like eyes.

"I—" Julian stammered, "I wanted to accept your invitation."

She approached him, resting a hand at the base of his neck. "What do you need from me?"

Julian looked over his shoulder and back down the stairs. Her fingers pressed into his skin, digging into his neck.

"My paycheck is running late," he said.

Jenna tilted her head, running her hand through her short blond hair. "And how can I help you with that?"

"Could I borrow three-thousand civiks?"

She nodded.

"I'll send the money to our landlord tonight. It should automatically renew your access," she started into the apartment, bare feet padding against the shaggy gray rug. "And you don't have to pay me back tonight if you're not up for it. I don't like it when it feels forced." She took out her tablet, swiping through pages of text. Tapping the screen a few times, she turned back to Julian. "All done."

Julian stood stiffly in the doorway.

"I don't like to owe people."

"But you already do," she remarked, an unnerving smile painted across her face. The dim lights shrouded her features in darkness, casting a heavy shadow over her brow to create dark hollowed pits where her eyes should rest.

"I—no, I don't."

"I mean, what did you do to get yourself into it? Cars? Gambling? Something salacious?" she questioned, a glimmer in her eyes. "If you want to live that life, you have to pay for it," she said, starting towards him. She gently took his hand in hers, pulling him into the apartment. The door drifted closed behind him, gently latching shut.

Julian's stomach churned as she shoved him harshly onto her couch. He planted his hands behind himself on soft green velvet, staring up at her. His heart pounded and his chest tightened.

"The innocence thing—I don't like it," she said coldly.

Julian's mouth was dry. "I—what do you want?"

"You can't play that role anymore. You already played that card months ago."

As she leaned in, he didn't pull back, allowing her to push her lips against his. Closing his eyes.

As he stumbled down the stairs an hour later, he leaned into the dulling of his mind, plunging into the depth of nothingness in search of sweet relief. He felt no relief when he scanned his watch and the door easily opened.

Lying in bed, his mind haunted him as his body struggled to keep his bloodshot eyes open. Fading in and out of dread and humiliation, he clung onto the brief moments reprieve long enough to slip away. When he slept, it was not a peaceful slumber, but it was preferable to the unrelenting ache of consciousness.

CHAPTER SIX

His heart leaped in his stomach when the knock on the door echoed through the apartment. Rubbing his eyes, he rolled off of his mattress, emerging out from his nook beneath the stairs. Stumbling through the small living space, he checked his watch. He had another two hours before he needed to leave for class. Julian plodded up the stairs, knuckles white as he gripped onto the rusted metal railing. His fingers fumbled with the chain-lock. When he cracked open the door, nobody stood outside waiting, yet an icy chill filled the entryway as if someone had only just left. Stepping into the common area, he half expected to see Jenna standing behind him, her breath warm yet chilling against the back of his neck. Instead, an unsuspecting paper envelope stuck to his door with a piece of yellow tape. With sweaty hands, he tore open the envelope, pulling out a letter.

Julian Arman Harper,

You are summoned to the North Street facility on April 17th, 2187, for bodily decommission. Your debt is currently set at 1,280,588.00. Based on our records, you do not qualify for any restoration programs. Please report at 5:20PM on the day of your appointment. If you see an error with this information, please contact the State immediately. Thank you for your compliance.

He quickly folded the sheet of paper, frantically glancing for somewhere to dispose of it. It felt like his fingers would burn as he held it, passing it between both hands before jamming it into his pocket in a frenzied motion. As he held the envelope, ready to crumple it in his palm, a slight resistance stopped him. Peeking into the envelope, he pulled out a second paper, this one bearing a seal depicting three stars framed in two wings. Cautiously, he detached the wax, unfolding the paper.

Julian Harper,

We would like to congratulate you on being accepted for the Lancut Internship. Edmund Sands invites you to attend lunch on this date, January 27th, at 1PM. A car will arrive at Rogers University to collect you twenty minutes prior to the appointment.

He stood statuesque in the entranceway, the letter still held before him as if the words could evaporate from the page at any moment. Edmund Sands knew where he lived, and, of course, he knew about the debt. He knew everything, Julian supposed. After all, working for the government, practically being Lancut, the man had access to such information. The nausea building in his throat threatened to overtake him.

Julian quickly took the first letter out of his pocket, ripping it in half, then tearing it again to make four pieces. He tore and tore, frantically ripping as the flakes of paper fell to the ground at his feet. He looked around, as if a neighbor might enter unexpectedly, and pocketed the scattered pieces of paper, stuffing them in haphazardly. Quickly, he scuttled down the stairs and into the apartment bathroom. Dumping the contents of his pocket into the toilet, he flushed. Julian dropped to his knees, the warmth in his throat rising. He heaved into the toilet bowl, but nothing came up. Hot bile burned the tender skin on the inside of the throat, never reaching his mouth before sliding back down.

After removing the other letter from President Edmund Sands, he read over the words again. He followed the lines of black ink, muttering the words quietly under his breath. The man already had a pool of internship applicants foaming at the mouth. Julian clung to the toilet seat once more, staring down into the basin, stained with the heavy mineral levels in the water. He sat back on his heels, knees digging into the rough cement floor. As he rubbed his eyes, he tried to clear away…everything.

He pictured Des' face, that reassuring smile suddenly distant.

"Hey, late night?" asked Syd.

Julian shrugged. "I went out with Des. You know how he gets plastered, and then I take care of him—kept me up all night. It was a good time, though."

"Good," said Syd, patting Julian on the back. He squirmed away from the touch. "You deserve some time to kick back. I'll be out late tonight. I'm staying over at my girlfriend's place, so the apartment is yours."

Julian nodded, gripping the sink behind him tightly. "That's great. Don't worry. I won't trash the place," he forced a smile.

"Hey, you could have Des over to the apartment. I know it's cramped when we're both here," said Syd.

Julian nodded. "Yeah," he managed, "I'm sorry to bail on you, but I really have to get going. I'm running late," he said, pulling his shoes on over two mismatched socks.

He wrapped his scarf tightly around his neck, pulling his hat over his head so that his dark curls still fell over his shoulders. Julian hesitated, glancing back at Syd once more before heading up the stairs.

With one eye, he peered out of the door, eyes trailing up the stairs to the other apartment before slipping through the doorway. Plunging out into the cold, the abrasive brightness of the sun assailed his eyes. Squinting, he shielded his face, blinking profusely. The air was still dry and crisp, and the wind still whipped against his exposed nose. The bright radiance of the sun was an unsettling hypocrisy. It taunted him, not blocked by a single cloud as it beamed down on him. It cast a long shadow on the sidewalk that followed with the same trudge as his own steps.

By the time he reached the steps of Rogers University, he managed a flat expression. The soaked knees of his black pants, though painfully cold against his skin, were barely distinguishable from the rest of the dark fabric. The patches hardened as the dampness turned to ice in the harsh winter conditions. He quickly hopped up the steps. The warmth of the University hit him with overwhelming relief, almost uncomfortable against skin, cold to the touch like porcelain.

"Oh, why are you all dressed up?" asked a familiar voice. Anna, her hair pulled into her signature slicked back high ponytail, joined his side, her puffed sleeve brushing against his shoulder. She flashed him a questioning glance.

He shrugged. "I'm not. Just wanted some extra layers. It's been cold in here the past few weeks," he said.

She raised her brows. "Too cold?"

"I'm always cold," he said. "I was meant to live somewhere warmer. I can't wait for next year to sit in some climate-controlled resort on the edge of the city."

"I thought you weren't doing the gap-year thing."

As he searched his mind, he recalled fading memories of his words to her.

"I'm not really sure anymore," he settled on. "There's just so much out there. I mean, I have time to do it all eventually, right?"

"Aren't you the one always saying there's not enough time in the day?" she hesitated. Julian's heart thrummed until she shrugged. "It's nice to see you finally took a chill pill," she chided with a stiff smile.

"Someone important told me I was rushing things. I'm trying to stop and smell the flowers," he said. "It's a beautiful world out there, isn't it? Even if I didn't have forever, maybe that's when you really have to appreciate it."

She halted in place.

"Are you good?"

He shrugged, tilting his head inquisitively.

"Oh, yeah."

"All of this stopping to smell the flowers bullshit makes me think you're either in love or going to kill yourself."

She halted, and he stopped with her in the middle of the atrium as students passed around them like water split by river rocks. Anna commanded an energy like a force field, halting anyone in their path from daring to insult her by brushing against her in a narrow hallway or huddling too close to her in an elevator. Julian envied the respect she commanded.

"I'm just trying to be more positive in the New Year," Julian said. "It's sunny out. I think that's done more for my mood than anything."

She stared at him with a blank expression before letting it fade into a faint smile. "Okay, well, I guess you must be a new man."

"That's what the sun does to people," he said, walking. She followed him, hurrying to catch up. "You should try it sometime."

She caught his eyes, her impeccable black winged eyeliner matching her dark brows. "Fine. After classes, we can walk downtown."

"I mean," Julian started. "I absolutely would, but I have a lunch meeting with someone, and I don't know how long it's going to last."

"Fine," she replied. "Maybe we can grab the last bit of

daylight and get an early dinner."

Des' arms wrapped around the girl at the bar, swaying gently as he made quiet conversation, his eyes fixed on her body. Julian reached out as if he could pluck the memory from the air, swiping it out of existence.

"I'd love to," he said before he could fully weigh the decision.

"That place on Allen Ave. I'll see you at five," she said, turning away, her ponytail swishing behind her as she walked in black kitten heels.

"Wait," he stopped her, "I have a lot of work to get done tonight, but I'd love to go out another time. Why don't we shoot for next week?"

"I guess I can wait," she smiled, her fingers dancing as she waved a quick goodbye, melting into the crowd.

After checking his watch, Julian quickly took the stairs, slipping between the herd of students and into his classroom. Waiting for the professor to arrive, Julian tapped through his watch. A new message popped into his notification bar. He read it silently.

I woke up feeling like shit this morning. I'm skipping class if you want to come over at some point.

Julian cleared the message away without responding, instead focusing his eyes forward as the professor, a short woman with hair trimmed neatly at her shoulders, settled at the front of the room.

Glancing at the door, he momentarily considered slinging his bag over his shoulder and bolting. Lancut would track him, and they might hunt him down themselves, but just maybe he would be the one to survive. He considered the fate of those who had made it to the border, only to be automatically decommissioned when they crossed the threshold—taken down as they finished their race.

Checking his watch, he swore to himself. He stood, brushing down his pants to smooth out the wrinkled fabric.

He waited at the elevator. At this time of day, few students wandered the halls. Unless heading to the library or to eat, there was little reason for people to loiter Classes ended, leading to a flood of students coming to and from, some entering and leaving the school entirely. Once the rush died down, Julian no longer needed to grapple his way upstairs or into an elevator, nor face the jabbing elbows and disdainful stares of those who also shoved through the crowds. When the doors dinged, he stepped into the elevator alone, pressing the button showing the ground floor. He strode through the ornate atrium and out of the main entryway.

As he stood at the base of the steps, he suddenly wondered how he was supposed to identify which car was there for him. He half expected Enforcer cars to pull up to haul him away. A deep green car slowly drove by, jolting as it climbed one of the speed bumps in front of the University. He watched it disappear down the road, eventually turning behind a building. It was as if out of nothing that the black car slinked in front of the school. Even with salted roads and the sludge pushed onto every curb, the car glimmered pristinely, its metal exterior free from a singular blemish. The tinted windows blocked his view inside, reflecting his own image back at him.

Hesitating, he gently pulled on the door handle. When it held firm, his heart jumped.

He leaped back when a tall man wearing a stiff black suit approached him. The man scanned his wrist against the car, and the back door drifted open with a hiss. When the driver motionedfor Julian to climb in, the young man did as he was told, taking his seat in the back. He pulled the seatbelt across his chest, letting the magnetic piece lock. The finely dressed man climbed into the driver's seat, resting his hands on the wheel. Julian wondered what purpose the man served. He only ever saw bus operators in such a position, where the drivers monitored the vehicle and occasionally manually overrode stops.

The car lurched forward, and Julian sank into the leather seat. He resisted the urge to ask the man where they were headed or who he was, staying silent and gazing out the window. Though the car's windows were opaque from the outside, his view was clear as they passed towering high-rises, far grander than the school or the crumbling outskirts. At a red light, pedestrians scurried by, but the car rolled forward, unbothered. The crossing traffic came to an effortless halt, waiting for the black car to pass before resuming, as if choreographed.

Before Julian voiced his thoughts, the man spoke in a flat tone, not bothering to look back. "The sensors allow us priority. No car will hit us. They automatically stop."

"I—How?"

"Edmund Sands requires priority travel on behalf of Lancut."

Julian just nodded slowly. "Does anyone else… How does someone get priority travel?"

"Lancut can approve or deny vehicles," the man replied.

Julian craned his neck as the tower loomed into view, a menacing spire at the city's decaying core, with roads like clogged arteries sprawling outwards. Four Peterson wings crowned the structure, stretching skyward, their jagged, blade-like edges glinting in the light. There was no need for a name on the facade; its sheer dominance was unmistakable. Julian tilted his head back, mouth slightly agape, as his eyes climbed the endless rows of reflective windows.

In Lancut, power resided in a single structure. The tower

housed all—committees, officials and the president's office perched high above like Mount Olympus, ruling without rival. The car crept forward through a procession of vehicles, passing passengers lost in their screens. As they neared the polished granite stairs, Julian watched blank faces flicker past, glances grazing the black car before returning to their devices.

The car stopped before the crystal doors. Sharp-edged and imposing, the doors rose at the top of the stairs, flanked by black obelisks polished to a mirror finish. The driver opened Julian's door without a word, bowing to avoid his gaze. Cold air bit at Julian as he stepped out, pausing at the base of the stairs. His reflection in the obsidian was rigid, wide-eyed.

The driver gestured him onward, and Julian climbed the steps, struggling to keep his gaze forward. Inside, a metallic chill filled the air. Footsteps tapped against the pristine floor, echoing faintly in the vast, barren space. The tower wasn't buzzing with activity like a university or office—it was eerily quiet. A few impeccably dressed figures moved through the lobby, their vacant eyes fixed straight ahead, passing each other in silence.

Julian's gaze wandered to the high ceilings, their polished stone mirroring the room below. When he glanced up, his reflection stared back—insignificant and swallowed by the tower's grandeur.

The driver stopped in front of three quick steps leading to an elevator with a wrought-iron cage for a door. "Mr. Sands is awaiting you on the top floor," he said, leaving Julian alone in front of the daunting doors.

As Julian waited for the elevator car to arrive, he wondered if he would walk through those doors and never return. He never considered the prospect of an elevator ride as anything other than a round trip, but he concluded that was no more than an assumption and not an assurance of his fate.

He thought of Des, giving a slight laugh. Julian wondered what would happen if he died right there, never getting the chance for any explanation to his oldest friend. Maybe the other man would assume he had run away, escaping away with a stash of civiks. A twinge of guilt twisted in him. After all their time together, never had he told Des the truth. Everything Des saw was a filtered, carefully curated facade.

He tapped on his watch, scrolling to Des' contact. As he considered what to type, he momentarily stopped on the steps.

He stepped onto the polished wood floor of the elevator. His heart raced in his chest as he looked at the lack of buttons. The doors slowly closed, trapping him behind ornate metal bars and confining him to an artfully crafted cell, subjected to silence other than the dull hum of the hoist motor. Slowly, the platform rose, pulling him up through the shaft. With his back to the far wall, he closed his eyes, his thoughts consumed by the image of Edmund Sands, a gun in one hand and a pen in the other. He held out the weapon, nestling it between Julian's eyes.

Before the image in his mind pulled the trigger, the elevator dinged, interrupting the stream of images bombarding him. As he slowly proceeded onto the polished marble, the view pulled the air from his lungs. Stepping forward hesitantly, windows surrounded him that stretched towards the sky. If it weren't for the fog, Julian would have thought they were brushing against the clouds. Small dots of light below illuminated orbs of fog like holy spheres of unconfined energy. He noted the padding of his boots against the white marble floors, suddenly conscious of the city sludge clinging to the soles.

"Good afternoon, Mr. Harper," spoke a familiar voice.

Edmund Sands stood a few inches taller than Julian, his

peppered hair and beard outstanding features of his otherwise unremarkable appearance. He wore a navy-blue suit with a white button-down. In his left hand, he held a clear glass. Julian smelled something savory in the air comparable to the scent of seasoned meats he smelled wafting from the expensive city restaurants. Swiveling around, he traced the smell to a small table pushed against one of the tall windows. A red tablecloth covered the rectangular surface with two white ceramic plates carefully place across from one another. On each plate were two slight cuts of steak stacked with care. He snapped his attention back to the man in front of him, scrambling to take the hand Sands offered him.

"It's great to meet with you again," said Julian, mustering a smile even with his clenched jaw.

As he shook the man's hand, his own calloused fingers passed over the soft palm of someone who rarely touched anything but paper and pen, never picking up a mop of his own or needing to mar his knees on the ground.

"I apologize for the short notice, but once you waste enough time making a decision, why waste time on moving it forward?" said the man, walking away. Julian quickly followed, jogging for a moment to catch up. "I hope I can make up for it with a decent meal."

Julian hesitantly stood at the table, waiting for Sands to sit first. A man dressed in a black suit came forward, pulling out a seat for Sands, then pushing it back gently behind him. Once Sands sat, the man, who Julian assumed was indentured, unrolled Sands' napkin, draping it over his boss' lap.

Julian glared at the steak in silence. Its red interior, once appetizing, was suddenly nauseating. He watched the way the meat jiggled ever so slightly when Sands' knee bumped against the table. Some cream-colored puree was carefully painted around the edge of the plate. Julian noted that the meal was nearly identical to what the Peterson's served. Picking up the outermost fork, he waited for Sands to slice into his meal first before daring to scoop a tiny portion of the puree onto one tong. The man's lips slapped against one another, and Julian saw the shredded flesh between Sands' teeth.

"You're a hard worker," said Sands eventually. "And ambitious. I was shocked to learn of your stock."

"Sir," Julian said, feigning an expression of confusion with wide doe eyes and a slight frown. "I have political aspirations, but I'm not sure what you mean about anything else."

Sands smiled. "I sent the letter to that tenement. As if I don't understand exactly what- who you are."

Julian paused. "I still don't think I understand."

Suddenly, the polished tone dropped. "I don't like liars, Harper. I hate liars, but I am willing to overlook it because you seem like a clever man. Ruthless, even."

"Sir, I'm not sure what you want from me."

"I want to see what you're capable of," he said, flipping seamlessly back to a friendly demeanor. "I know about your debts. I know how your poor mother killed herself, and how it all fell on you. All of it is just tragic. A real sob story. Yet, you're not soured to the system. Maybe you have the occasional outburst, but deep down," Sands gripped his chest dramatically, "you understand why we have it. You're the kind of person it was designed for—for you to climb to your potential. The system benefits us all, no matter where we stand. We are inelegant machines meant for greatness."

"My desire to ascend in society outweighs my aversions to our hierarchical system," he said, his voice quivering.

"You don't want to die."

The words plunged into his chest like a barbed dagger, deflating his lungs. "No, Sir."

"And you won't sell yourself into servitude—not that you could, anyway. You're far too in debt for that. You know you don't qualify. But your will to live is admirable."

Julian remained silent.

"Maybe you don't love the system, but you don't want to die. You've already sold yourself," he said, hesitating. He looked over Julian, starting at the man's feet and slowly panning up, hovering his eyes at his crotch before meeting the young man's gaze. "I know you sold your vision. You try to compensate, but you can't see from your left side."

Julian hardened his gaze. "I take care of things myself. After all," he said from behind a false smile, "I'm always looking for opportunities."."

"So patriotic," Sands said enthusiastically. "You stand for everything this nation values. More than the Peterson man or anyone else in that university. I couldn't understand why a bright young man like you wouldn't apply for the Lancut Internship until I looked at your records and saw that you didn't qualify. Your debts would have flagged you immediately. Instead, it would go to someone like the Peterson man. Someone entitled. That's what I like about you. You're not lazy and entitled like him."

"I wouldn't say that about Desmond Peterson. He's very bright. A loyal friend."

"No," said Sands. "I chose you because I want you. I want to offer you an opportunity. You'll never have to sell your soul to anyone. You'll be a free man. No debts."

At that, Julian sat paralyzed, eyes wide and lips parting as his mouth hung agape.

"What kind of opportunity?"

"I want you to work with me on the launch of the new Loget Tech I28-Vision. You understand what fear does to people. It eats them up inside. They'll do just about anything to worm their way out of it. You are more familiar with this than anyone on my staff ever will be," he laughed. "That's the one drawback of the mass firings you so heavily praised. You're going to sell this device as the solution to their woes. Their compliance will be of their own free will, not just a government ordinance. After all, this is a democracy. We could force people to comply, but wouldn't you rather guide them to the correct conclusions? Gently nudge them to make the decision themselves?"

"Sir," he whispered. "What does this mean for me? Will I still be able to study at the University?"

He nodded.

"You can finish your degree while you work for me. Once ninety percent of the population has Vision installed, your debts will be forgiven; completely cleared from the system. Ignore that date in April. I can push that back as long as you need to meet that goal," he said, shoveling another bite into his mouth. "But don't think that means you have forever. This is a business."

"My debts will be completely forgotten?"

"Gone, and I'll make sure you have a salaried position lined up. You'll never worry about rent or food another day in your life. You'll be with your friend, Desmond, on your way to whatever lavish getaway his parents are shipping him off to. You'll meet with me and a team a few times a week, but otherwise, nothing changes for you."

Julian nodded slowly as he mindlessly prodded at his unfinished steak. While his stomach ached with hunger, the flesh beneath him felt all too familiar.

He chose his words carefully "I appreciate your offer, but I'm not sure I'm best suited for that particular project. I—" he stopped. "Just based on my qualifications. I also fear I wouldn't be able to put forward my best work with my debts looming."

"Here, I'm offering you an internship- the internship your classmates are threatening one another over. It's everything you could ever dream of, but that's the job. You're perfect for the project. Otherwise, I would have chosen someone else," he replied. "Even if you weren't in debt, interns don't get paid a regular wage. You're not being treated differently than anyone else I considered."

He hesitated. The dread knotting in his stomach crushed him."I'm interested in taking a position, but I think I would do better work without distractions.."

"You'd like me to pay your debts before you complete your task? That would be me giving you free money without you earning it. I want you to stay motivated, Mr. Harper. After all, your drive is the foundation of why I selected you. Do you have any idea how many candidates, ones who actually applied, will be crushed?"

Julian hesitated. Freedom in exchange for a few meetings a week for maybe a year. No debt. No fear. No pain. A ticket to the government. An opportunity threatening to pass him by if he did not reach out and snatch it. Perhaps the expense on his morals was a great one, but not so much as the expense of his debts.

"If I'm going to work for you, I won't have time to work my other job."

Sands nodded. "I'll arrange for you to receive a stipend for rent and groceries."

Julian sensed the bile rise in his throat as he uttered the words. "I'll do it."

CHAPTER SEVEN

Papers. Enough papers to drown in lined the desk in a white cubicle. A black pen perched atop the tall stack. Julian did not read the small text, just signing on every highlighted line. If Edmund Sands was going to screw him over in the fine print, well, that was the whole point. Edmund Sands now owned him in all but title and held his fragile indebted life in his hands like a glass ornament that he might crush and eviscerate in a thoughtless moment. Once he smudged ink on each physical document, an Enforcer posted at the door handed him a tablet. Without reading, he signed the same contracts in digital form. Hovering his finger over the screen between pages. He glanced over his shoulder at the exit and the burden of choice gnawed on his soul.

Shaking the thought from his mind, he signed a last time, returning the tablet to the expressionless Enforcer.

At the tip of his tongue, questions begged to roll off. He understood the Enforcer acted as only muscles and a warm body, but he wanted to blurt out an endless stream of concerns. When his stipend would begin- who he was allowed to tell, and when? Thoughts raced through his mind as he dizzily followed the man in crimson uniform back to the elevator.

When the elevator reached the first floor, the room echoed with boisterous noise from the bustle of after-lunch traffic. He obeyed instructions, leaning against one of the marble walls by the southernmost doors, awaiting a car to return him to his apartment for the evening.

An Enforcer patrolled the area with one hand planted on his firearm. His uniform fitted tightly to his body with a black bullet-proof vest over the top. On his head, he wore a helmet that fastened under his chin, tightly securing it in place. Julian noticed how well the Enforcers melded into the background, their eyes searching the crowd, yet standing like statues in waiting.

He thought about Des in his massive apartment in a building brushing the clouds, windows stretching to reveal an incredible skyline. His far shorter tenement, as Sands called it, was nothing to brag about, but when he shut the door to his space, it was all his own. When he lay down for the night, he felt the walls squeezing in on him in a comforting embrace. He could not imagine finding that sense of reassurance in a vast penthouse, but to invite over guests- to invite over Des. The idea tantalizingly hung in front of him. After always visiting the other man's house, he might invite Des over, perhaps even paying for a chef that night to cook them something nice. He pictured Des' pleased grin as a man dressed in a fine tuxedo placed their dinner on an oak table. He would line the table with candles and maybe some napkins folded into those triangles that stood up on their own. A smile floated to the surface, and he let out asigh.

As he retreated from his thoughts, he stared back through the window. Dark eyes met his through the thin glass. The young woman on the other side stood close, fogging the outside window with her breath. She dressed in a loose black coat, hair covered by a knit hat of the same color. Still smiling, he gave her a nod, and she smiled back at him. He waited for her to pass by like any other pedestrian out for a quick lunch. She wasn't dressed to informally to work in this district, and he doubted she was his driver. Maybe she was just passing by, sharing in his relief for just a moment before disappearing back into the sprawling city. In one of her gloved hands, she held a small device. She broke their eye contact, tapping the screen four times.

The sound resonated through the atrium with a crack. Looking to the ceiling, one of the great black stone tiles split down the center, hurling towards the ground. Julian threw himself to the floor, shielding his head with his hands as he pressed his face to the ground. Shots rang out in quick succession, and he clenched his eyes shut, pushing himself further towards the door- towards the woman who had disappeared. As his hand brushed up against the glass door, he opened one eye, blinking away the dust. Bracing himself up on one forearm, he turned back. Shattered glass shimmered on the ground like fresh snow. It settled over fractured stone chunks that dug into the floor. They jutted out like a jagged mountain range, cutting through the heart of the building.

Julian ducked once more as thousands of shards hit the ground, ricochetting like shrapnel. A group of masked figures filed into the shattered front door, long guns held firmly in gloved hands. Julian only ever saw the Enforcers carry those. Scarves or makeshift masks covered their faces and heads. Aside from skin peeking out to reveal their complexions, their hair was their only distinguishing feature between them. One of the figures was stocky yet muscular with dirty-blond hair swaying at his shoulders. He marched ahead of the others, head on a swivel before he waved the others on. His heavy boots pounded against the ground.

Julian pushed himself further into the corner, yet he leaned into the action despite the wailing voices. A woman screamed, clawing at her leg. A piece of stone protruded sharply from the gash, gushing blood. It soaked the white fabric of suit pants, spewing out from the wound. She clamped down on it, and the blood rose up between her fingers.

The man at the head quickly stepped over the debris to fix himself at the center of the room.

"Everyone," he barked, his voice distorted not only by the mask covering, but by a voice modulator. "I want everyone to hold still. Stay exactly where you are, and someone will guide you against the far west wall. Hands on top of your head, do as you're told, and nobody here will die."

Julian held still, watching the way the man conduct himself as if the world would move with a gesture of his hand. He slung his rifle over his shoulder. Standing at the center of the room, two of the figures pulled away from him, disappearing down a hallway. The man tore off his goggles, eyes scanning over the room. In the light, his irises glowed like amber, and his thick brows lowered with authority. Julian counted eight members of the group, excluding the leader. Two of them disappeared out of a side door, and two stayed on either side of the man in charge. The other six dispersed through the room. As they separated from one another, each kept their weapon fixed on the tens of people in business attire, most of whom cowered against debris.

As Julian glanced up at the cracked ceiling, Julian's heart pounded as he studied the deep fissure directly above him. The ceiling did not moan under the stress of damaged supports. He looked behind him; the glass door lay shattered in thousands of miniscule shards show like crisp snow soaking up spilled blood. Slowly sliding backwards, he dragged himself towards freedom. He grit his teeth as the glass dug into the palms of his hands, embedding into his calloused skin. With his feet, he pushed himself back without putting any more pressure on his bloody hands.

"Where are you going, you little shit?" the man in charge strode towards him.

Julian scrambled on hands and feet backwards towards the empty doorframe even as the man pointed the barrel of his weapon at Julian.

"Still trying to get away? There's no getting away. Don't you know where you are?" The man shoved the end of the gun into the side of Julian's cheek, pressing in. "You want me to blow your brains out?" he asked.

Julian, with wide eyes, halted in place. He didn't dare speak, but he also didn't want to shake his head and risk startling the gunman.

"Got nothing to say?" The man prodded at his cheek with the end of the barrel, pulling at the side of his lip with the metal. "I asked you a question."

Julian did not open his mouth.

The man towering above him had already fired. The bullet had already ripped through his thigh. The sound slammed into him first, reverberating in his skull, and then the searing, electric pain tore through his body. He gasped, then screamed, the shriek tearing from his throat before he could stop it. He stared, wide-eyed, at his shredded flesh, unable to make out the wound through the gushing blood. His head pounded as he struggled to look away. The leader of the group lowered his gun with a huff, letting it hang at his hip, swinging slightly.

"Please," he didn't even realize the words passed over his lips.

Shame washed over him even as the pain demanded his unwavering attention. Blood gushed to the surface, staining an ever-growing orbit in his torn pant leg. The man, with crumpled eyebrows, stared down at him as his vision swam.

"That's what I thought," he said, pushing the barrel of the gun towards the gaping wound.

Julian let out a high-pitched whimper that erupted into a scream as the metal nudged the edge of the torn flesh, prodding.

"Now, you're going to get up, and I'm gonna bring you to the west wall. You got that?" said the man, crouching down to his level as if Julian were a disobedient child.

Julian nodded quickly, the throbbing blood in his ears muffling any sound around him. The man's firm grip was a vice around his left arm, yanking him forwards. Unable to gather his feet underneath him, he slammed onto his forearms on the stone floor. The agony radiated up his arms and through his shoulders.

"Get the fuck up," the man barked, gripping Julian's face with one hand, roughly jerking Julian's eyes up to meet his.

"I—I," his voice caught in his throat.

"You what?" the man mocked.

"—Walk. I can't—can't get—" he began, but the man cut him off by ripping one of his arms out from underneath him and dragging him harshly by the bicep across the floor.

His head hung back weakly, and he watched as his own blood smeared in a trail behind him. His thigh burned, and he let out another cry as his back made impact with the wall, forcing him to sit up. The bullet hole wept. Blood drained from his face, and for a moment, he feared he would lose consciousness at the scene unfolding before him. Julian screamed as the man planted the heavy sole of his black boot on the wound, pressing down.

"Be grateful," the man muttered, "I'm stopping the bleeding," he pressed down harder, and Julian's vision flickered, the edges tinged with dark static creeping inwards.

A man with wide eyes fell next to him, collapsing onto his knees, hands on the back of his head with his fingers laced together. He stared down at Julian's leg, immediately looking away. When the man towering above him finally released the pressure, the sudden rush of blood back to the wound seared, and Julian's breath caught in his throat. The man with the gun muttered something to the tall woman next to him, also dressed in a mask and goggles. With whatever he said, the woman nodded, jogging away, rifle held carefully with both hands as she did.

The man with the blond hair looked down at him, pitying eyes meeting his. Julian reached out an arm. He was not sure why he did it, but he yearned to reach out, to brush against the gloved hand of his captor. Another shot rang out. His eyes shot down, expecting blood to gush from a wound in his chest, or stomach, or perhaps between his eyes.

"Put your hands in the air," commanded an unfamiliar voice.

Julian swiveled his head, as did the man above him. An Enforcer, dressed in his crimson garb, stood without a weapon. As Julian glimpsed the small device in the Enforcer's hand, he braced himself. His body seized up, freezing into place. The man next to him still whimpered, though his legs no longer shook, unable to so much as tremble. The blond man smiled beneath his mask. His face pulled up in what could only be a grin, eyes glimmering the blown-out lighting. He walked across the shards of glass and debris lightly, as if moved by the forces of will.

He pointed the barrel of the gun at the Enforcer. "Who am I? Tell me who I am?"

The Enforcer stared down at his screen, unable to conjure words.

"I was dead, but I've been Reborn," he said, and then the shot rang out.

The Enforcer gripped his chest before crumpling to the

ground. The shooter leaned down, snatching the device from the man's unmoving open hand.

"Stay," said the man. Julian's hands were still frozen in a vise around his leg wound. His vision flickered, and then darkness overtook him.

CHAPTER EIGHT

The gown fell softly against his skin. It was foreign after the heavy coats and layers of the harsh winter. He tried to scratch the fabric away. A warm haze enveloped his mind, drowning it in a fog that he stumbled through blindly. With a flutter of his eyelids, the lights were too bright to make out anything other than the white walls. An ache in his lower body cut through the mirk. Sloppily, he retraced his memory.

His leg.

Peeling away a blanket, the bandaged appendage remained. He nearly cried with relief. Heavy gauze covered his thigh, and he didn't dare try to move his leg. Willing his toes to wiggle, he sighed. Only now did he notice the IV in his hand, with a line running to a bag dangling from a metal stand. He assumed the clear saline was mixed with a cocktail of drugs for pain and infection. Julian lifted his hands to his face, tracing over the lines of his forehead, gently settling on a forming scab across his cheek. He wondered how discolored the welt was, but without a mirror, he could only wonder.

His stomach dropped. How much was this going to cost him? How was he allowed here, anyway? This facility, these painkillers…With his debt…

He remembered the face of Edmund Sands staring at him across the table, and the deal. His heart lurched. He sold himself to Lancut Industries after everything he said. Everything he stood for, gone down the drain, and for what?

Closing his eyes, an overwhelming weight settled on his chest. For a moment, he wished he might hold his mother's hand, look into her dark eyes and beg for reassurance. He would hold on to her like a worn plushy a child clutched in weak hands. Gripping longingly onto his thin blanket instead, he clenched his eyes tightly shut, for a moment a sensation of overwhelming solitude consuming him. He ached for the reassurance—the embrace of another to brush the hair from his face and tell him he would be alright no matter the truth.

He fell back again, hit with a wave of dizziness. As he let his head fall back against the pillow, the world came back into focus, no longer swimming on the surface of his eye. Julian couldn't decipher what moved in the corner of his vision, dismissing it as his own shadow.

"Hey, man," said a voice softly. "You've been out for a few hours."

A chair leg squeaked deafeningly against the ground, and Des hovered above. He felt the other man's warm breath on his cheek. Des sat back in the chair, offering a faint smile as he looked over at Julian.

"Hey," Julian managed back, suddenly noticing how dry his throat was.

"You got yourself real messed up," said Des. "You're lucky you didn't bleed out once you lost consciousness. At least that's what the nurse said," he corrected. "And what the hell were you doing in the Lancut Tower?"

"What..." Julian trailed off. "What happened?"

"It's everywhere," said Des, shaking his head. "My dad said that they've had an increase in cyber-attacks from a terrorist faction, and apparently, there was a small data breach. He hasn't told me much more; didn't want to scare anyone. Apparently, the terrorists went for information. Didn't take hostages or kill any of the executives. Dad says they got a bit of data, but we're not supposed to tell anyone. But, I mean, seems like you're already involved in this."

"Whatever terrorist organization this is—it's fear mongering. It's a myth," rasped Julian, the lights suddenly far too bright. "I mean, it's real, but it's nothing more than a concept; people scattered about, whispering about the same idea."

"No, it's not," said Des. "Not anymore at least." Des looked as if he were about to say something more, but he closed his mouth. "They stole a bunch of records."

"How? They're not an organized group?"

"They are, Julian. The Reborn," Des said. "They stole a ton of debt records. Either they didn't have time to get very far, or they just focused on the lower thirty percent. Seems like they weren't too worried about who the wealthiest were. They also took a few other files, but nobody knows why yet. Or what they were even looking for."

Julian scoffed, "We already know who the wealthiest are. It's the poor who are hiding in plain sight."

Des made a face as if he were about to say something, before looking away.

"I just... I don't know what they're doing with it. It's not like they erased the data, not that it's possible. It's backed up, but they have it too now."

"Who can get to them first?" asked Julian.

"What do you mean?"

"Doesn't matter," he said, rubbing his eyes. "The bastards shot me. Right through the leg. Stings like a motherfucker. Did anyone else get hurt?"

Des shrugged, "Official statement says three were injured,

and one death. You and two others were hurt in the crossfire, I guess. They used a small electromagnetic bomb. Some kind of pulse damaged part of the building. Knocked out security systems long enough for them to manually saw through any locks and get to the physical data storage."

"So that's why their Discs didn't work," mused Julian.

"What?"

"There was an Enforcer. He's the one they killed. He immobilized us all, but it didn't work on any of the gunmen. They just stood there."

Des stood silently for a moment. "The report didn't mention anything about that."

"Yeah, then they shot the Enforcer. We couldn't move, but they sure as hell could," said Julian, recalling the unnerving sensation of losing all ability to so much as move a finger. "But they were fine…" Julian trailed off, lingering on the implication. "How?"

"I—I don't know," said Des. "That shouldn't be possible. Unless they're foreign militants…"

"They didn't have accents. One of them talked to me," he said, recalling sharp amber eyes boring into him. "I mean, I guess they could be foreigners."

"And you're sure their Discs didn't work?"

Julian nodded. "I swear. I don't know how they did it. They were all wearing masks and goggles. I have no idea how they're going to identify any of them."

Des nodded slowly. "I'm glad you're okay. Really, I was terrified when they said you were here. I came as soon as my dad found out who the victims were. Names haven't been released to the public."

Julian mustered a smile despite the pain slowly trickling back into his body. Hopefully, they would give him more painkillers soon.

"Yeah, I'm glad too. I'm all alone out here. My mom and sister are out of town. Who knows if they've even gotten the news yet?"

"I'm glad you didn't wake up completely alone. I know I'm not family, but still," Des said quickly, as if trying to expel the words as soon as they came to his mind. "What were you doing in Lancut Tower?"

Julian smiled, "I figured you already knew, with your dad and all."

"Hey, he doesn't tell me everything."

"Edmund Sands offered a position in rolling out your dad's innovation. I got that internship," replied Julian. "I guess he took an interest in me the other night at dinner. I hope he doesn't expect me to start tomorrow," he smiled, gesturing down at his wound.

Des was momentarily silent.

"Congratulations," he said with a half-hearted smile.

"Yeah, I, um—I think it's gonna be a good opportunity," said Julian. "The past couple of days have been a blur. Did you ever end up going home with that girl from the bar?"

The other man shook his head. "Nah, she was way too wasted. She basically stumbled into a car half an hour after you left."

"So, I guess I really didn't miss anything," he said.

Des shook his head. "Wouldn't say that. While you've been off in dreamland, things have gone into a panic. Only authorized vehicles on the road. Curfew in place for the next few days. I don't know what's going to happen next."

"We wait."

"We wait," agreed Des.

Julian couldn't shake the wild eyes Des stared down at him with. He admired the way the other man's jaw tightened, and his eyebrows scrunched as if he were holding too many thoughts at once. It was a rare expression for his friend, given his choices tended to be between drinks and colors of overpriced sneakers; whether to take the flashy car or the maneuverable faster one. Julian sighed, looking down at the man's hand, the way it gripped the rail of the hospital bed. Each tendon rippled under the man's soft skin.

He quickly jerked his gaze up at the sudden appearance of a woman dressed in light blue scrubs. She wore tightly fitting nitrile gloves, pushing a cart with her.

"I'm going to redress the wound," she said. "I'm going to ask that your friend steps out of the room."

Julian smiled. "Why don't you head home? I'm sure I'll see you at school tomorrow. I'm a fast healer."

Des shook his head.

"C'mon, man. You know I can't leave you here all on your own. That's just not right. How 'bout I wait for you, and when you're ready to go home, you can come back to my place, so you have someone to make sure you don't fall or something?"

"Nah, I sleep better in my own place," he said. "You probably have homework to get done, anyway."

"Nothing I can't do here," replied Des, gesturing to a backpack on the floor beside his chair.

Julian scrambled to counter.

"All of my clothing is at my place."

"You can borrow some of my old stuff. I haven't cleared out half of the junk I grew out of when I was sixteen."

Julian feigned an indignant expression.

"What are you saying about me?"

"I—I just," started Des.

"I'll think about it if you let the nurse do her job," he blurted, watching the woman stand with a cart, eyes darting between the two young men. "Only until my mom and sister get back tomorrow."

Des nodded, backing out of the room. The nurse approached Julian, pushing a titanium cart ahead of her. She peeled the blanket back from Julian's leg.

"On a scale of one to ten, how is the pain?" she asked in a soft voice. She was no older than Julian, he supposed, or maybe a couple of years his senior.

"It's fine. I'd like to go home. I can re-bandage everything on my own. Do I need to sign anything to leave? Can you tell me what my bill so far is?" asked Julian. The questions poured from his mouth, one after another, the words nearly slurring together.

"Mr. Sands insists that you only receive the best treatment. He wants you taken care of with the best precision," she replied. "What would you rate your pain at? Let's say a one is a slight discomfort, and ten in agony."

"Is he…" he hesitated, double-checking the status of the closed door, "taking care of expenses?"

She nodded. "He doesn't want you to worry about anything other than your internship. Now, I need to know how much pain you're in so I can treat you appropriately."

"It's like a four," he admitted.

The wound throbbed, but he managed to distract himself from the pain long enough to hold a conversation, so he supposed it couldn't be more than a five, according to any scale. As a concoction coursed into his bloodstream, his face immediately softened, and he lay back in the bed, allowing the warmth to run through him, blooming out of his slipping mind.

"What would you put your pain at now?" she asked.

"One," he slurred, taking a moment to piece together the word.

"Good. There's no reason for you to be in pain. Once you're out of here, we'll send you home with some pills to take the edge off. The surgeon who took care of your leg wants you here overnight. We'll bring you something to eat, and if you need anything, you can press that button beside your bed," the nurse said, slowly unraveling bandages that secured down rust-colored, soiled gauze. "We also checked on your organ functions. Are you aware that you're at high risk of eventual kidney disease?"

"Um," Julian managed, "I guess not."

"We can schedule a procedure to take care of that now. We can get you a high-quality replacement," she said disinterestedly as she tended to his leg.

"No," he blurted. "Absolutely not."

"It's standard—"

"I want to go home tonight," he protested, gritting his teeth as she peeled the gauze directly from where it clung to the now-stitched hole in his leg. It pulled off in short, stunted segments.

"We legally can't keep you here, but it would be against our advice. Staying overnight will not add any charge to you. Everything will go directly to the government employee account," assured the nurse. "And if you don't stay, we highly recommend you don't go home alone."

Julian shook his head.

"I have a roommate."

"Why don't you let your friend take care of you," she suggested, voice monotone as she carefully placed clean gauze over the stitched-up wound. Carefully, she secured it with a wrap, maintaining pressure throughout the procedure. Julian, with the flood of painkillers, barely registered her touch.

"I—I'll be fine on my own," he stammered, fighting the warmth inviting him to close his eyes again.

She dropped the subject, instead gesturing to the wound.

"You'll be walking with crutches for a while with that, but you should be able to return to school in a few days. You're going to need plenty of rest. The bullet went through clean, so that's the good news. It didn't damage any bone…" she continued to speak, but the warm glow in his mind clouded out anything she said to him.

He assumed the nurse was giving him instructions on how to care for the wound, or what to expect, but his mind wandered back to the attack. He was screaming on the ground, his leg gushing from a gunshot wound. Knowing now it was The Reborn, he would relive the agony if only to catch another glimpse into the moment. If he could shut his eyes and reopen them to the attack, he wasn't sure what he would do differently other than ask for answers.

He needed to speak to them, to understand who they were. If The Reborn were an actual organization and not some fictitious entity or a ghost story, he yearned to brush paths. His heart throbbed in his chest with exhilaration at the prospect, his curiosity over scoring the fear of the memory. Yet his mind continued to race, plunging him back further into his memories. He pictured the girl in the bar, Des laughing next to him, but as the girl turned to Julian, he saw Jenna's face. The scenes melded together, contorting into a vision of Des with a wide grin standing over him rather than the gunman.

A hand on his shoulder snapped him out of his terror. Des rested a hand on Julian's upper arm, staring at him with a concerned expression.

"The nurse said you're insisting on going home. They'll let you go home with me."

He wanted to protest that he never agreed to such an arrangement, but he resigned himself to a nod of agreement. "I don't want to stay here longer than I have to."

Everything swam as he forced himself into a sitting position on the bed. It was as if the lights were swaying with the figure above him.

"You sure you don't want to wait for your mom to get here?" he asked.

Julian let out an amused huff.

"My mom is far, far away, Des. We'll be waiting an eternity. I just want to get out of here. I don't like hospitals."

"Nobody does."

"I really hate them," he snapped.

Des said nothing in response, instead gesturing to a pile of carefully folded clothing on a chair in the corner of the room. "Well, if you really want to get out of here, you'll have to change out of that gown. Your bloody clothing is there if you want it, but I brought a pair of my sweatpants, if that's more comfortable."

"That's alright," he said, dismissing his friend.

"C'mon, man. You really think you'll be able to even get on anything other than sweatpants?"

Julian ached to fight back, but when he finally spoke, he whispered a resigned, "Thank you."

CHAPTER NINE

Julian lay in bed, staring at the clean white ceiling. No water stains, no cracks, just an unbroken expanse of drywall. He scrolled through his phone mindlessly, finally calling work to report that he was injured and would be out for at least a week. Their reply was curt: if he didn't show up tomorrow, he'd be fired. The line cut off as he stammered.

He set the phone down, feeling like he'd severed a lifeline. The freefall sensation that followed made his stomach churn, but he told himself he wasn't tumbling to his demise. No, he'd figure it out. He still had a plan—at least one more trick up his sleeve.

Checking his finances, he swore under his breath. Sands hadn't mentioned when the stipend would kick in, and his mind churned with ways to scrape together extra cash if it didn't arrive soon.

Julian had sworn he'd be back in school and resuming his life within 24 hours. He hadn't accounted for the difficulty of dragging himself there, let alone convincing anyone to help him defy doctor's orders. His crutches allowed him to shuffle between the bathroom and kitchen, but even in Des' sprawling single-story apartment, every step was a challenge.

That morning, Julian insisted he couldn't miss class. Des refused to call him a car. "I have to meet with a professor," Julian argued, but Des had already disappeared down the elevator.

By the time Julian made it to the parking garage, Des was long gone. Snow and wind greeted him as he ventured out. He nearly toppled over, adjusting to his crutches. His pace slowed to a crawl on unplowed sidewalks. The snow coated the ground in slippery sludge, forcing him to take minuscule steps.

Finally, he gave up and slouched against a building, glaring at his watch. Des' contact popped up as a suggestion, but Julian ignored it. The wind stung his skin, snow whipping into his face. He hardly managed to lift his arm to shield himself.

Through the storm, warm neon lights cut through the wall of snow. A glowing "Plasma Center Open" sign called to him, and he stumbled toward it. Inside, the sharp smell of antiseptic hit him as the automatic doors whooshed shut behind him.

The receptionist barely glanced up from her desk. "Sign in at the kiosk," she said flatly.

Julian shuffled to the machine, grimacing at the effort it took to navigate the touchscreen with his trembling hands. After fumbling through the registration process, he slumped into a waiting room chair, propping his injured leg on the opposite seat.

He watched the other donors. Most of the donors hunched over phones or scrolled on tablets with their faces illuminated by cold blue light. A few tapped their feet impatiently, clutching water bottles or prepackaged snacks.

When his name was finally called, Julian straightened up, steeling himself.

"Mr. Harper," the nurse greeted him. She looked him over, her polite smile faltering. "What happened?"

"Long story," Julian said, forcing a laugh. "I'm here to donate."

Her brow furrowed. "Are you still on antibiotics?"

"Yeah, but doesn't that make my plasma safer?" he joked weakly.

"Sweetheart, I can't let you donate in this state," she said softly, her pity cutting through him like a blade.

Panic bubbled up, and he scrambled for an argument. "Is there any way to sign a contract? I'll donate extra later—just let me—"

She shook her head, her voice gentle but firm. "You know the rules. We can't accept plasma if you're on certain medications, and with your injury—"

"I need this," Julian blurted, his voice cracking. "I need the civiks."

Her expression softened, but her stance didn't waver. "I'm sorry, truly. But I can't help you today."

Defeated, Julian nodded and shuffled back toward the exit. The blast of icy air hit him as soon as the automatic doors opened, and he hesitated, crutches digging into the snow as he stepped out. His watch buzzed, and he reluctantly answered.

"Hey," he said, forcing his voice to stay steady.

"What are you up to?" Des' tone was sharp.

"Throwing a party while you're in class," Julian quipped.

"Really? Guess you didn't throw it at my place," Des shot back.

Julian rolled his eyes. "And I guess you're not in class."

"No, I'm not. All the cars are still here, so I'm assuming you called a cab?"

Julian hesitated. "Oh, just went for a walk. Needed fresh air."

"What the fuck?" Des snapped. "I'm sending a car. Drop your location." The line went dead.

Julian sighed, letting his head fall back. He was sure this would earn him another lecture, but there was no arguing with Des when he used that tone. He sent his location and waited, shivering in the cold.

When Des arrived in his sleek red car, Julian climbed in, trying not to meet his friend's eyes.

"You didn't have to come," Julian mumbled.

Des didn't look at him. "Wasn't sure you'd actually get in the car."

Julian bristled. "Sorry."

"No, you're not," spat back Des. "You never are. You're a remorseless lying bastard."

Julian sat stunned, momentarily unable to speak.

"You're the one holding me hostage. I can't for the life of my figure out why you're doing all this shit—like you're obsessed with me or something," he blurted, instantly recoiling at his own words.

"For fuck's sake, Julian, I'm just trying to look out for you, and all you do is sneak around, trying your best to get rid of anyone who gives a flying fuck about you," he raised his voice, face becoming red, jaw clenching.

"You're crossing a line."

"You're a liar," Des fired back.

"You're right," said Julian as he threw up his arms until they hit the ceiling. "I said I would stay in bed, and I didn't. I'm an adult. I can take care of myself."

"You really think this is just about taking a walk?"

Silence settled over the car. Julian looked Des in the eyes, daring him to proceed, but his hands trembled by his sides.

"I don't know, Des, is it?"

"It's clear you think I'm just an oaf to keep around, but I'm not blind. Where's your mother? Why on earth would your own mother not visit you after you were shot?" he blurted.

Julian shook his head. "She was out of town. Then I didn't fucking tell her because I didn't need her up my ass like you."

"So why was I able to find her death certificate in the public records?"

The air deflated from Julian's chest. He turned away, struggling with the door handle of the car, which didn't budge.

Des gripped Julian by the collar, yanking the other man until their noses were only inches apart.

"You're ridiculous! You're ready to throw yourself out of a moving car rather than just tell the fucking truth. And then you turn around and work for the very system that destroyed your family. You're a sick bastard; you'd have to be a sick bastard to work for Sands."

"My parents are dead. What excuse do you have for your parents not wanting to have you as a son? They'd rather invite me to dinner as a buffer while you do God knows what pills in the bathroom. You have no fucking right to nose into my life like this," he cried.

"I know you don't mean that," Des warned.

"I'm trying to make your life easier. Can't you accept a gift? The entire world was made to shield people like you from the ugly truth. Wouldn't you rather have a polished facade than have to know what you're associating with? Do you want to know the things I've done? You'd puke up your five-course meal just hearing about it."

Des balled his hands into fists, and for a moment, Julian slid away from the other man. Instead, Des spoke in a low tone, "I'm done having the wool pulled over my eyes. You can suck up to Sands and Lancut all you want, but who does it help in the end? This making change from the inside bullshit? Do you really believe that? Do you really think I won't work for my father out of laziness? He's doing evil things. I've seen his work- seen what he has waiting for society. Project Richter—"

"Des, you need to stop talking about things you don't understand," Julian cut him off.

"What don't I understand? You want to climb the ladder? It's not a ladder. You're climbing over corpses."

Julian fought the urge to scream. "Of course I don't. Of course I fucking don't, but what choice do I have? Des, if I sit here hoping for revolution, I'll be executed in April. You think I wanted to make a deal with Edmund Sands? Do you think I want his balls down my throat? I don't, but I don't want to die. I'm afraid to fucking die. I'm not going to be some martyr. Sorry if that's not idealistic enough for you. I tried to keep things pretty for you, but you fucked that up."

"I don't know how you believed that I'd think any differently if you just told me the truth."

"You still don't fucking get it, and you never will. You were born with a silver spoon in your mouth."

Des spat back, "And what does that have to do with empathy?"

"That doesn't matter. That's the whole point. My debt is a character flaw to your people, and your paternalistic bullshit is worse than actually facing it. I'd rather be groped and harassed on the streets by your beloved Enforcers or denied from a job for my status than deal with whatever this shit is," Julian was gasping, tears rolling down his face. He choked on his words as he tried to force them from his throat. "I'm not an animal to rescue and train to your high society standards."

"I hate the whole fucking system, Julian," Des blurted.

"Okay, but you still get to sit in your penthouse while people sell themselves to survive another day. Does the idea of saving me alleviate you of guilt? If you can just save one, you've done all you can? God bless you, Des. You're such a good person. Will that help you sleep at night?" Julian managed before his words devolved to sobbing. "Just drop me off at my apartment. I'm going home, and there's nothing you can do to stop me."

"That's what you think about me? Really? After everything?" asked Des, a tremor to his voice.

Julian quickly pivoted. "How long have you known?"

Des looked as if he were about to boil over.

"Why the fuck does that matter?"

Julian didn't think before throwing his fist towards the other man Des quickly intercepted him, gripping Julian's thin wrist in a firm grip. Julian let out a hiss, for a moment fearing Des would snap his wrist, refusing to release his vice-like fingers. Thrashing with his full weight, Julian finally pulled free, losing his balance. He slammed his head against the car window behind him, and his vision faded for a moment. Julian sat back down and looked over at Des, who now had his hands carefully tucked away in his pockets.

Despite the snot running from his nose, and his now-bruised wrist he cradled, he could not stop himself.

"Please, Des. How long have you known?"

Des looked like he was going to dismiss Julian before he curtly replied, "Six months."

"And you just played along? Did humoring me amuse you?"

"It was none of my business," he said. "You said that yourself."

"Well, apparently you thought it was if you went snooping to figure it out. Searching for my mum's death certificate? If that was an accident, then I'd love to hear if you've ever done anything on purpose," said Julian, his voice still shaking, tears flowing down his cheeks and onto his lips.

The car slowly came to a halt, and Julian looked out the

window. There stood the meager building he resided in. Or, rather, the building whose basement he occupied. Julian paused briefly, then glanced back at Des. Without a word, he fumbled with the door handle, throwing himself out into the storm. He jammed his crutches underneath his arms before hobbling towards the doorway. Nearly collapsing through, he swiped his wrist against the sensor outside of the apartment door. The lock clicked, and Julian threw open the door, staring down the steep staircase.

He settled against the wall, planting his butt on the first step. Letting go of his crutches, he watched them slide down the stairs, clattering at the bottom. With his hands on the floor beside his hips, he carefully maneuvered his good leg, jamming his foot against the wood of the step below. In a slow motion, he lowered himself until he fully sat on the next step down. Counting the seemingly endless steps, he told himself he could repeat this action another thirteen times. Scooting down again, he lowered himself down another stair. He considered laying down on the stairs, giving in to exhaustion. By the time he reached the bottom, he panted, struggling to breathe.

He left his crutches behind and crawled towards his nook. Julian pulled himself onto his mattress, rolling himself onto his side, facing towards the wall.

After days of rest, he would go back to university on Monday, surely dodging questions about what happened, and then his work would really begin. Julian Arman Harper would have his debts cleared. He would be free.

CHAPTER TEN

The questions weren't half as distracting as the stares. In the morning, Julian thought himself paranoid, and then he chalked it up to walking with crutches. However, as he limped into the elevator, he knew eyes bore into the leg he carefully hovered above the ground. Their eyes followed up his torso, then at his sullen eyes and hollow face. He couldn't tell what exactly they were looking for, but the unspoken questions were written on the faces of anyone who accidentally met his eyes. He wondered how much they knew.

He kept his head down, the hair on his arms standing up as, around every corner, he swore he spotted the blond man.

At his lecture hall, he quickly made his way to the front. Even after only a few days, he was far more agile with the crutches than the week prior. He maneuvered into the correct row, lowering himself down next to Anna. She looked him over.

"And here I thought the rumors were full of shit," she said disinterestedly, returning to her notes.

He smiled in relief. "Anything to get out of class."

Dr. Cruz paced across the room one way before quickly turning on his heels and walking back across the room and back towards his desk. He repeated this twice before Julian returned his attention to his classmate. As always, she had pulled her hair back into a pristine high ponytail, slicked back with gel. Black-winged eyeliner sharply lined her eyes. Anna Huang took out her tablet, pulling out the slim accompanying pen to scribble down something.

"I can send you my notes," she offered. "I mean, you missed exam prep and the exam, but I can point out what was in the notes was on the test."

Julian smiled. "I appreciate that. I'm gonna stop by Cruz's office and try to bargain my way out of the exam altogether. Getting shot seems like a decent excuse."

She scribbled something else down. "I wouldn't bother. Easy exam. Use it as a grade booster."

He was unable to answer before the projector brightened the front of the room. Dr. Cruz stood at the center, his gray hair tousled as if he had just rolled out of bed. The slide in the front of the room displayed the same title as the reading assigned the night before: Lancut's Position on Unionization at the Corporate Level. As Dr. Cruz turned to face the flag, the students around the room rose. The sounds of coats and backpacks rustling filled the space. Julian gripped the arms of his chair, hoisting himself up slowly. By the time he stood, hovering his injured leg above the ground, the chant had already begun. Every student turned to the left, staring at the flag, the droning sound of voices melding together into a monotone recitation. They spoke in unison with the dean, who led the chant over the loudspeaker.

Julian struggled to maneuver himself up, eventually sinking back into his chair.

"—for the strength of the Union, which protects us, under faith, service and loyalty, from indignity and injustice. One Union, of the people, with free will and prosperity for all."

The students dropped back into their seats as Julian struggled.

The speaker crackled, continuing, "We would like to congratulate Julian Harper for his success in winning the Lancut Internship. I applaud all who applied, and I was assured by the president himself what a tough decision this was," said the dean, and the loudspeaker crackled once more. "Please give a round of applause to Mr. Harper."

Dr. Cruz brought two fingers up to his lips, letting out a sharp whistle and drawing attention back to the front of the room.

"Congratulations, Mr. Harper. On a note more pertinent to this class, I hope everyone got through today's reading. I'm well aware we're getting to that point in the year where the weather just makes us want to sleep, but we have to push through," Cruz began. "I hope a few specific points stood out to you. Before I get talking, I want to open this up to you. What, from the reading, stood out to any of you?"

Anna cooly raised her hand, waiting until the professor was certain nobody else from the quieter back rows had anything to say. Cruz nodded at her, and she began, "What I think really stood out to me was that across the board, unionized employees had higher wages than non-unionized, even within the same industry. I understand that while this may benefit workers, this would directly conflict with a company's rights to profits.

Cruz nodded in approval. "And what were your thoughts on the Rights to Profit Act?"

She glanced down at her notes, a look of hesitation coming over her face.

"Well, the reading describes it as the rights of a company to maximize profits, and it legalized a multitude of means to achieve such results. Infringing on a company's profits by striking or even pressuring for higher wages is a fireable offense, and might, in more extreme cases, end in arrest.

"But what do you think about this? I want you to analyze whether you think this is an effective solution for the economy in the long-term," Cruz said, reaching out into the air as he spoke, as if he were just about to grasp onto some tangible idea.

"The reading didn't get into that," she said cautiously.

"I know," he said. "Does anyone else want to take a stab?"

He made direct eye contact with Julian, who quickly glanced down at his blank tablet. He did not dare to raise his hand.

By the time class ended, Julian's hands, slick with sweat, slid easily over the armrests.

"How about finally getting dinner? Or do you have too many government responsibilities now?" asked Anna.

He hesitated, heart beating in his chest as he felt her keen eyes pass over him, darting just as quickly back to his uneasy expression.

"I have to talk with the professor. Can we talk later?" he asked.

Before she could respond, he stumbled towards the front of the class, stopping at a distance away from Dr. Cruz as he wiped his hands on his pants, forcing an empty smile onto his face that failed to mask the unease in his eyes. A man ahead of him talked to the professor quickly, as if he couldn't wait to deliver some crucial information. Despite Julian's efforts, he couldn't focus on the words, instead allowing the noise to swirl around him like gnats around a corpse. When the other student finally sauntered away, he approached the professor. The older man looked at him with a creased brow and a concerned tilt of his lips.

"I've been meaning to reach out to you, Julian. How are you healing?" asked the professor.

Julian shrugged as well as his crutches allowed.

"I would have been back up and moving earlier if it were up to me."

The professor hesitated.

"And how are you… otherwise?"

"Fine," he replied quickly. "Been worse. I wanted to talk to you about a few things."

Dr. Cruz nodded. "Why don't you walk with me to my office?"

The professor tucked his tablet into his bag alongside a red notebook, slinging it over his shoulder with more ease than Julian expected from the man's stature. As the professor strolled up the aisle, Julian struggled to keep pace with the graying man. Noticing his student lagging, the man shortened his strides, offering an apologetic smile.

They stopped in front of an elevator, pressing the button to go up. The staircase beside them loomed mockingly above Julian. He was shamefully aware that if not for him, the professor preferred to use the stairs, claiming it was the key to good health at his age. Julian figured that general wealth was the true key, but he kept that sentiment to himself.

When the two men stepped out of the elevator, the professor led Julian down a well-trodden hallway where footsteps had eroded the carpet. Turning into one of the small and windowless rooms, the professor gently lowered himself down into a rolling desk chair. He tapped the base of his lamp twice, and the bulb lit up, illuminating the small space. Julian took a seat, carefully propping his crutches against the wall. He crossed his arms over his chest, studying the professor as the older man rummaged through his desk drawers, eventually taking out a mint which he popped into his mouth, offering one to Julian. The younger man shook his head in decline.

"You don't look well," said Cruz in a matter-of-fact tone. "You should take more time off. There are more than just physical ailments to recover from."

Julian managed a pained laugh. "I'm not traumatized, if

that's what you're implying."

Cruz nodded slowly.

"I suppose only you can know that. I will admit that I have many questions, but first I'd like to know why you've sought me out."

Julian hesitated. "I—" he started, rearranging the words in his head. "I'm not sure what I'm doing."

The professor nodded. "Nobody does."

"But we all have to make decisions—decisions that have real consequences—serious repercussions, and I'm not sure how to know if what I'm doing is right," he admitted.

"What do you want me to say to you, Julian?"

Julian failed to hide the expression of frustration that twisted his face. "I'm not sure."

"You came here for a reason," said the professor. "I will offer you my advice, but I'm not sure you want it."

Julian rubbed his eyes. The lamp shone into his eyes, nearly blinding him. He never remembered it being so bright on past visits.

"I just need more time."

"Don't we all," replied Cruz.

Julian clenched his jaw.

For a moment, he considered spitting out the truth. He could tell Dr. Cruz why he accepted the internship. He feared the shame he held was all the indication he needed of right and wrong, yet there was also reality to consider. Life and death trumped all other factors, or for the time being, it needed to.

"I will admit, after our class discussions and your writings, I was surprised you accepted, or even applied, to work for Lancut," said the professor. "I'm assuming that's what this is about?"

"Yeah," he admitted. "And I didn't apply."

The professor offered a puzzled expression.

"And you don't feel good about this decision. But you did it for a reason, correct?" asked the professor. "You don't strike me as someone who would take that position lightly."

"I… I thought it was the best possible option for my future. Maybe the only one."

"The only one? Now, I don't believe that. We all have choices, Mr. Harper," said the professor.

"Maybe, or maybe we're all prodded and manipulated to stand exactly where they want us to."

The buzzing of his watch startled him. As he looked down, a call came from an unknown number. Struggling to get his crutches underneath him, he nodded at the professor as he ducked out of the room. He accepted the call, holding the device close to his face.

"Hello?" he questioned.

"This is Gina Teller," the voice spoke over the phone. Her lips slapped loudly as if she were eating something or perhaps chewing gum. "Mr. Sands is sending a car to the University that should arrive in fifteen minutes. He wished to inform you that this is your first official day, and you can expect your stipend for the week uploaded to your account as soon as you finish your first meeting.

The receptionist severed the connection. He stood blankly outside of the office, catching Cruz's eyes through the open doorway. The frown on his face underscored the deep lines of age which Julian previously failed to notice. Julian leaned against the doorframe, looking at his professor with growing unease in his stomach.

"I have to," he murmured.

"We all have choices," the professor replied in a detached tone. "And it sounds like you've made yours."

Julian shook his head.

"I don't have a choice," he said.

The professor didn't reply, sitting in his chair with fingers laced together silently as if waiting for Julian to add some justification.

"I don't believe that. We all have choices, and I trust you to make the right one," he said after some time.

"I'm going to climb to the top, and I'm going to make changes. You believe me, don't you? After everything I've said? Everything I've argued in your class?" Julian blurted desperately.

"I have more grading to attend to, and it sounds like you have somewhere to be. I hope your internship doesn't interfere with your studies."

Cruz turned back to his desk, riffling through the top drawer before pulling out a pad of yellow paper and a pen. He glanced back up at Julian, feigning a smile, as Julian turned his back.

The unease tightened in his chest, a knot of dread coiling around his heart. He moved slowly—not just from his pounding head or wounded leg, but the weight of something darker pressing down on him. Stumbling to the elevator, he descended to the ground floor. Sunlight streamed through the glass doors, scattering rainbows across the floor. Julian stuffed his hands in his pockets, aware of the fraying hole in the left one. Wiggling three fingers through, he made a mental note to repair it before losing anything important. As he leaned against the wall, he chewed his bottom lip until it cracked and the sharp taste of iron filled his mouth.

A man appeared, briskly guiding him to a waiting car. This one wasn't the same driver as before, but like the last, the man slid into the front seat, leaving Julian in the back beside his backpack. The city blurred past. Too tired to care, Julian rested his head against the window, eyelids heavy. Where they'd turned right last time, they now veered left.

Through the business district, men in sharp suits swarmed sidewalks, bustling between buildings. As the scenery shifted to low-rise residential blocks, the air changed. Concrete buildings loomed, their surfaces marred by cracks, like old, fractured bones. Farther out, ruins bordered the city—walls so damaged they seemed to lean on borrowed time. Forgotten structures left to crumble, too costly to save, were now shelters for squatters.

The car stopped in front of a plain concrete building. Dirt streaked the walls where they met the sidewalk, and windows only began on the third floor, leaving the lower levels blank and forbidding. The man yanked Julian to his feet, shoving crutches under his arms with unnecessary force. Squinting against the sun reflecting off lingering snow, Julian watched a solitary car pass on the deserted street. A firm hand directed him toward a narrow alley.

They walked for several minutes, turning into quieter, shabbier streets until they reached a heavy metal door. The man tapped a pin into a keypad, and a security scanner hummed to life, sweeping over Julian. Instantly, the Disc implanted in the side of his head flared to life, sending a jolt that seized his muscles. His legs stiffened, his grip on the crutches trembling, and he teetered, heart hammering. Then, just as suddenly, the paralyzing surge receded. Strong arms steadied him, setting him upright before the door swung open. A nudge pushed him forward, leaving him no choice but to comply.

Inside, pale blue drywall masked the concrete beneath. Dim ceiling lights cast a sterile glow as they moved down the corridor. At another door, the man entered a pin again. Julian braced, dread coiling in his chest. The scanner activated, and the Disc's grip clamped down with unerring precision. His body frozen from neck to toes. He could barely breathe as the man's hands moved over him, patting pockets, cuffs, and boots with detachment. Satisfied, the machine released him. Julian's hands shook violently on his crutches, knuckles white, the phantom pressure lingering in his limbs.

The conference room was stark. Gray walls, stale air and a massive screen dominated the space. Four people sat around a plain white table: two men and two women. One man, older than Julian by a decade, sipped from a mug of green liquid. He kept his black hair neatly braided, and it shimmered under the dim lights. The other man's sandy hair and unremarkable face seemed vaguely familiar, like an older version of mans from school he couldn't quite name. Julian's guard went up immediately.

The two women, nearly identical, sat close together, their ginger hair loose around their faces. They turned to appraise him in eerie unison.

The man with the braid stood up, offering a warm smile that turned the corners of his lips slightly downwards. There was something captivating about his singular dimple and thick brows.

"You must be Mr. Harper," he said, offering out a hand. "I'm Elex."

Julian took the man's hand, giving a firm handshake.

"Julian Harper. You're welcome to call me Julian."

Elex motioned to the others around the room. One woman piped up next. "Ella Martinez," she said matter-of-factly.

"Ina Martinez," the other woman added.

The last member of the group looked up from his tablet,

glancing at Julian with disinterest. "Timothee Agner. I'm the one who puts everything in motion. We make decisions as a group and then I make it happen. We maintain complete confidentiality here, and if anything leaks from this room, we will conduct a thorough investigation and prosecute the offender to the highest degree. Obviously, the security here is tight, and that's intentional. There are plenty of people who either have already expressed concerns or who will oppose this project. It's our job to make it happen anyway, and even better, make them like it. After all, innovation is what keeps this nation safe."

Julian nodded slowly. "Do we have a timeframe?"

Agner replied, "As soon as possible. And I suppose the sooner this is done, the sooner you get your proper job in some cushy office?"

Julian forced a strained smile, "That's the goal, sir. I assumed we would work in the Lancut building?"

Ina was the one who spoke up. "Initially, yes, but after the other day's attacks, we confirmed that anything that's not directly related to presidential business is to be conducted elsewhere. Don't put all of your eggs in one basket, so to speak."

Julian considered the pure practicality of the location. Rather than the sleek structures with sprawling windows, these were mostly constructed from scarred and crumbling concrete. Little went into the design other than industrial and economic concerns, lacking the beauty that Julian found in any of the buildings towards the center of the city. These monstrosities stood beside one another, nearly indistinguishable from each other besides from wounds from the war. Although Julian had no memory of the events, he remembered learning in school, hearing whispers from anyone old enough to remember the terror. Bombs dropped on civilians as people slaughtered each other in the streets for rations. The land was left uninhabitable by particular weaponry used, and the remaining unscathed earth was left in ruins.

"We have orders to have ninety percent of the population installed with this technology at least within the year, and from there we'll pick up the stragglers. Why don't we ask our intern here what he thinks we should do?" asked Agner disinterestedly.

Elex watched Julian with a pen in hand, ready to scribble down notes onto his tablet.

"I think the first issue is to prioritize who gets the I28-Vision. After all, this is aimed at a certain demographic, and to pretend like it's not isn't advantageous to us. Obviously, we don't present it that way to the general public, but we're aiming at the lower twenty percent first. We need to work backwards," finished Julian.

"Yes," agreed Agner, "But if the goal is to present this as a positive innovation, targeting the dregs of society doesn't send a great message. It makes it appear like some cure to a blight to society that should only be applied to criminals."

"We don't frame it in that way. Rather, we offer opportunities for debt relief, vouchers and healthcare as an incentive for getting the Vision. It's framed as a government initiative to help the less fortunate, and that's why it will be offered to the poor first. I mean, if we truly believe that these devices are meant to stop crime and help society, these ideas all align. The wealthy will follow suit in order to be seen as compliant citizens contributing to the greater good. We put out campaigns for them about how taking part is helping a neighbor and keeping their communities safe. They're going to want to see guinea pigs. They'd rather see the poor take the implant first, and once they realize it's safe, they'll get it of their own volition."

Elex looked up, halting his scribbling to speak, "We need

to recruit an array of people. The poor aren't going to trust us. We can hire them and train them to administer the implant. Not only are we providing jobs to the less fortunate, but they'll trust their own. And the upper class will continue to go to their clinics as always," said the older man.

"Mobile stations," piped in Julian. "We go to them."

The rest of the meeting consisted of Ina and Anna sparring back and forth with Agner over the best way to publicly unveil the product. Julian zoned out, staring down a knick in one of the gray walls. The way the light struck the divot, he was unsure how deep it went into the concrete. Letting his surroundings melt, he pictured himself in a sprawling apartment. He envisioned himself strolling through the place in boxers. He wouldn't need to bundle up in a sweater and heavy pants because he would turn up the heat. If so desired, he could amp up the heat, keeping the windows hanging open and letting the fog waft into his living room. Anytime he needed something or chores piled up, he would call on someone to take care of any concerns for him. Though he struggled to imagine a life where he didn't do dishes, he supposed he'd fill the time with something more fulfilling. If he hired someone to handle the menial tasks, he might take up a hobby such as tennis.

"...Reborn interference," said Agner coldly, snapping Julian back to the conversation at hand. "They are completely aware of the new implant, so far as even having specs of the device. Given the details, we think documents were leaked directly from someone on Martin Peterson's staff, and while there's currently an investigation, for the time being, we need to limit our communication with them as much as possible. Loget Tech knows about the existence of a team in order to implement their new technology, but they have no idea who is involved, or where we are."

Julian pictured that night in the Petersons' home. Perhaps that's another reason he was a candidate for this position. After all, he was already familiar with the project, and to not recruit him would be to leave a loose end. Shuttering, he refused to think about the alternative ways of eliminating the issue.

"I understand the hesitance to work with an organization with a known mole, but wouldn't it be beneficial to have someone on this team from Loget Tech?" suggested Julian.

Agner shook his head. "Once we find out who the mole is, but until then, it's just us."

"I know someone who would be a good fit for the team; related to Loget Tech, I mean," blurted Julian. "Desmond Peterson."

Agner gave a slight huff of amusement. "Nepotism at its finest."

"He already knows about the project, and he has absolutely no motivation to sabotage his own family's fortune. I've worked with him extensively at school. While sometimes he lacks work ethic, he's a very intelligent man, and I think he has the potential to be an asset to this team," argued Julian.

Agner considered this. "I'll pass the idea through Sands, but I personally don't think bringing in the entitled son of Martin Peterson is the solution you think it is. If you want to play house with him, you can do that on your own time."

Julian's face burned.

Ina stared at Agner with cold green eyes that seemingly never blinked. "I like it. I think it's a good idea. And if he steps out of line, we have his father on speed dial."

Julian's breath hitched in his throat at the insinuations. "I can talk to Des-Desmond about it directly, if you'd like. I think he'll be more likely to take the offer if it comes from a friend."

Agner shook his head. "Absolutely not. This needs to pass through Mr. Sands before we take any actions in modifying this specially selected team. There are checks to be done. This is an extremely high security operation."

Elex piped in, "Current theory is that word of the tech is what prompted the terrorist attack on the Lancut Tower. This is extremely serious. Every piece of information we have that they don't is an advantage. We need to stay one step ahead of them until any terrorist faction can be eliminated altogether."

"Are there teams doing that? I thought that we just found out that the Reborn were more than internet rumors?" questioned Julian.

Anna laughed, exchanging an identical look with her sister. "Oh, we've been hunting them for the past few years. And that attack just gave us the next lead. We need to squash them out of existence for good. Within the next six months, nobody will be muttering about terrorists ever again."

Julian hungered to barrage the team with questions- to pester away, but he resigned himself to one question. "How close, really, do you think we are to getting them?"

"What?" questioned Ina. "You want revenge for that scrape on your leg?"

"I—I just want to know if they have… I guess I want to know if they actually have a chance of causing actual damage."

Ina laughed. "No. There's not enough of them, and there never will be. We already know who at least a couple of the ringleaders are. Just a matter of time. But enough of that. This meeting has already gone overtime, and I need to be somewhere in twenty."

Agner stood, his chair squeaking against the concrete floor as he carelessly pushed it back. "Okay, well, I'll send out a message for our next meeting. In the meantime, I'm going to start working on the logistics of some of the strategies discussed today. You're all dismissed," he said, nodding at the door.

Before Julian rose, a light hand landed on his shoulder, hovering like a perched bird. Elex towered above him, bracing himself against the conference table. He sipped from his mug. It no longer steamed, and the liquid inside was dark and muddy at the bottom of the cup. Julian didn't stand, instead looking up at Elex.

When Elex finally spoke, Julian watched the man's lips move, but the words tumbled together no matter how he tried to focus. His ears rang, and his mind raced as Agner's words tumbled through his mind. .

"What?" asked Julian after a pause.

"I mean, this isn't particularly efficient. You'll have access to a car for as long as you're working on this assignment. It's all attached to your Lancut Account, so you can call on it anytime to make it to meeting or to use for leisure," said Elex, flipping around his tablet. On the screen was a sleek blue car. Julian wondered if the car had the same priority features as the one he took to the Lancut building. "We'll use your location to send a Lancut vehicle from one of our garages, so plan to call it at least five minutes before you need to leave so it can get there."

"Oh," was all that Julian managed.

"And the stipend," continued Elex. Julian's heart leaped, and he tensed his shoulders. "Sands is offering you 20,000 per month to cover rent and expenses."

Julian frantically mulled the number over in his mind. He didn't need to be perceived by Sands as ungrateful or greedy, but 20,000 was nothing, a slap in the face. It was throwing crumbs down to the needy from a throne and demanding their praise. Yes, it was enough to manage. Rent for the month was just over 15,000 civiks, and the rest could go towards groceries. He could afford a couple of new shirts and maybe a proper suit for required occasions, but he wouldn't be leaving the meager apartment he called his home. He anticipated no tangible end to his shameful living conditions beneath the stairs while those around him retreated to their penthouses, throwing their jackets into closets larger than his kitchen.

Julian quickly calculated his expenses. With the money, he would not need to engage in extra work to scrape together two meals a day, yet his looming debt still dangled above his head in the clawed hands of Edmund Sands. A bundle of cash swung out of his reach from one end of a silver thread, and the other end was tied neatly in a knot around Sands' little finger. As he considered the imposing figure in his thoughts, his place in the hierarchy was clear.

"Does that work for you?" the voice snapped him out of his daze.

"Um, yeah, that should be enough," said Julian quietly.

Elex gave him a puzzled look. "Are you sure?"

Julian scrambled for a response.

"Sands and I discussed my payment as an intern, and I told him I needed nothing. I'm just thankful for the opportunity, but he insisted he give me something. He's a generous man."

Elex opened his mouth, eyes darkening, but the expression faded into a smile. "Welcome to the team, Julian."

CHAPTER ELEVEN

He couldn't tell Syd.

Not that it was none of his business. Every other person in his life either heard the news over the speakers or in the wake of an emergency. Syd stood as the final ignorant frontier. It was pure luck that the other man had not yet stumbled upon the information, and Julian was not inclined to provide insight. With this slight maneuvering, his home remained a sanctuary. Despite the roaring chaos outside, his apartment reliably remained as drab and uninspired as ever: both qualities Julian increasingly appreciated.

Syd walked back into the living room, plopping himself onto the couch beside Julian. The tattered fabric strained where Julian had stitched it back together. Julian shifted as a spring dug into one of his butt cheeks. After a long drink of his beer, he placed the drink on a makeshift table made from an overturned cardboard box. The structure swayed slightly under the weight, but Julian paid it no mind.

Shoveling spaghetti into his mouth, Syd flipped through programs on the projector system. Each time he changed the channel, the audio cut out, replaced with new meaningless noise. Momentarily, he stopped on a dim screen with soft piano music. Syd stared intently as two birds danced, displaying brightly colored feathers, yet soon enough, another set of nameless actors replaced the birds.

"If you want any, there's plenty left," offered Syd, gesturing to his bowl of pasta.

"I'm alright," replied Julian. "I'm just tired. Too tired to be hungry."

Syd didn't finish chewing, just covering his mouth as he spoke.

"I get that. But, hey, soon enough you'll graduate, and you'll be living the good life."

Julian forced himself to respond with something other than bleak denial.

"You're right."

"You're always so busy. I'm surprised you're even renting the place anymore," Syd said.

Julian spoke to the other man while he halfheartedly watched the screen. "I mean, I've gotta crash somewhere, right? Last I checked, we weren't allowed to sleep in the study rooms."

"Have you thought about it all? I mean, finding somewhere else?"

"No, why?" Julian asked.

Syd was silent, the apartment perfectly quiet beside for the chewing of the man beside him and the muffled dialogue of the cartoon.

"I mean, I've been thinking about moving in with this girl. She's a friend; more than a friend, but we both think moving in together would be good," Syd said hesitantly.

"Oh," Julian managed.

"I mean, with the lease up and all, it would be good timing. I was thinking her and I might find a place together. I mean, we've already been looking around."

Julian nodded slowly with a straight face. "I mean, I'm sure I can find another roommate," he said. "Unless you wanted to move her into here, and I might start looking elsewhere. I mean,

I wouldn't mind moving out of my broom closet," he forced a strained laugh, nudging Syd.

Syd looked over.

"I mean, it doesn't really matter either way. I just didn't want it to come out of nowhere."

"I won't lie and say this isn't last minute," said Julian, suppressing a sour tone.

"I'm sorry, man. Things have just gotten serious suddenly, and I can't really bring her over here. We just don't have the space for a third person," Syd responded. "I really appreciate our arrangement, but with my internship about to end and you about to graduate, it's time to start our real lives." The other man's face was visibly tense with a forced smile. "This is exciting."

Julian hesitated to say anything at all, holding back anything unsavory that threatened to slip from his lips. "You're right. I'll figure something out."

Syd set down his bowl of spaghetti.

"I mean, you understand? I can't sign another lease here?"

"No, I get it," assured Julian. "I'm gonna make some calls," he said, standing up and leaving his sweating beer behind.

Shoving his hands into his pockets, he started up the stairs. He took the first few steps with an ignorable throbbing pain, but only halfway up, his leg was trembling. Each step demanded more than the last. His breath quickened and his shoulders grew tight as he hauled himself upward by the cracked railing. When he reached the top, he leaned against the wall, chest heaving. The ache in his thigh was sharp now, demanding his attention as he gritted his teeth. He should have brought his crutches. It was stubborn pride that told him not to, but as he looked back down the stairs, his face burned at the thought of turning back.

Stumbling out into the cold common space, he shivered.

The frigid air bit at his face. He stood there for a long moment, bracing himself. Then, with a small, defiant push, he opened the door and stepped out into the night.

The air was crisp, the usual unforgiving wind softening in moments of brief reprieve. He limped along the edge of the road. Since abandoning his crutches the morning before, he moved unsteadily, and his typical gait had transformed into a stubborn drag of one foot behind the other. Every time his weight shifted onto his injured leg, a jolt of pain shot through his thigh and up his spine. He hissed through his teeth, clutching at a nearby wall to hold himself upright. The rough brick bit into his palm, the cold sinking deep into his skin. He forced himself forward with a rebellious step away from the wall.

As he glanced over his shoulder, his apartment was still in sight, even in the evening's darkness. He knew he should not, and could not, wander far. Anyway, where was there to go? He continued his aimless trudge into the cold night as his mind raced.

There were ways to secure a housemate, some more savory than others. He juggled the thought of crawling to Sands, begging him for more help than he was already given. If granted his request, he would only launch himself deeper into the pit he was desperately clawing out of. The civiks Sands gave him were enough for rent and food, but nothing more, not considering the loss of a roommate with which he split half of the expenses.

Even with a greater stipend, once his role was complete, he thought about what position Edmund Sands might assign him to, towering above the city in a high-rise, or laying six feet beneath concrete. His mouth dried at the thought, and he struggled to swallow. His tongue lay like a beached whale in his mouth. Edmund Sands held complete control over his life as if he were an insect under a microscope whose legs a bored scientist might pluck off for entertainment.

Julian spoke aloud as if the city air would respond with reassurance.

"This is viable," he said meekly.

He needed someone on his side. With that thought hovering at the forefront of his mind, he quickly flipped through his watch, ordering a car to his location. As he leaned against the closest building, he took any pressure off his wounded leg. He hissed at the sensation of his pants grazing over broken skin as he sank down. He pulled his knees against his chest with his back pressed against an old building. With his head on a swivel, he cursed himself for going out in this state.

Julian stared up at a streetlamp that illuminated him as if he were beneath a spotlight in a tragic play. The shadow of his compacted figure mirrored a gargoyle, stretching out from where he sat.

"Why are you out here again?" asked a low voice.

With an upward gaze, a smug expression adorned a familiar face. The Enforcer wore the same uniform as any other, but Julian immediately recognized his tone.

"Get up," the man barked.

Julian struggled to maneuver his feet beneath him, gripping onto the wall behind him for support. Losing traction, he caught himself on his palms, the gravel of the road digging into the flesh of his calloused hands. With a set jaw, he lowered himself to his knees, gazing up at the grinning Enforcer. The man didn't offer a hand, instead crossing his arms over his chest in amusement.

"Stay there," the man ordered.

"What?" managed Julian.

"Don't play stupid, man," he snapped.

Julian prayed the car would arrive at any moment, whisking him away from the man. "I'm waiting for my car to arrive," he frantically sputtered. "It should be here any minute now. I work for Lancut."

"Yeah? And I'm the President," the Enforcer responded. "Give me everything you've got, or I'm taking you in for prostitution or possession. Doesn't make a difference to me."

Julian sputtered, "No, you can't do that. Please."

"It's probably not much, anyway. Just hand it over, and you can go on your way," said the Enforcer, a snide grin on his face.

"Please, it's my rent money. I just got paid," he said. "I'll do anything else you want. I can talk to my people and try to get you stationed somewhere better."

Julian's face snapped to the side as the Enforcer's hand collided with his cheek. He yelped in surprise, hands immediately going to his face.

"You'll do anything? Well, I want you to hand over the civiks. Your tricks aren't gonna work on me."

Tears welled in the corners of Julian's eyes. "I can't. I'll take the charge before I'll hand it over."

As a green car crept down the road towards him, he nearly cried. It stopped in front of him, and the Enforcer took a step back, an expression of shock flashing through his eyes.

Clambering towards the promising heat, he pulled himself into the car, slamming the door shut behind him. Quickly typing an address into his watch, he sighed in relief as the car pulled away. A click echoed, signaling the doors locking him safely inside, protected from whatever evil lurked outside, simply waiting to spring in a moment of vulnerability. The car beeped repetitively. In his tired haze, the constant droning lulled in the back of his mind. A signal flashed on the seatbelt lock.

Groaning, he pulled the seatbelt across the seat, stringing it behind his back before clicking it into the locking mechanism. The noise ceased. Julian laid back on the bench seat, staring up at the neatly upholstered gray ceiling. He let himself drift in and out of consciousness as the car took slow turns, driving so smoothly that it rocked Julian to sleep like a small child in his mother's arms. With one arm over his eyes, he blocked out the city lights, staring intently into the blackness of his own eyelids. As if wading into the cool darkness, he sank further into the calm void, allowing it to swallow him.

When the car came to a stop, Julian savored the moments of stillness he allowed himself. For seconds, he humored the illusion that the car stopped at a light or some other junction. His fingers tingled as if they did not belong to him, yet it was his entire body that was not his own, no sector of his skin remaining untouched by groping hands or the greed which commanded them.

Hesitantly, he opened the car door, shuffling towards the front entrance of the lobby. Surrounded with thick wrought iron designs caged over the windows, there were no benches or barren winter trees outside to welcome guests. Hostility dripped from the deep red canopy extending out over the short walkway towards a glass door. Peeking through the door, a woman perched desk with glasses dark enough to obscure her eyes. Julian was unsure if she saw him, but if she did, her indifference did not move her.

He stared at his watch, then hovered his finger over the device. Julian snapped his hand away from the screen as if it were made of molten metal. Beside the door, a panel bearing a blank screen reflected his harrowed expression. With two touches to the screen, it immediately brightened, illuminating his face in the dark. The panel spoke to him in a pleasant woman's voice, yet the slight robotic lull of her pace failed to mask the detached nature of the machine responsible.

"Who would you like to reach?" asked the monotone voice.

Julian struggled to form words in his dry mouth. He eventually spat out the name: "Desmond Peterson."

"Mr. Peterson has been alerted to your presence," the voice replied.

Julian struggled to keep both legs straightened beneath him. As he sat on the stone walkway, the cold easily seeped through the thin fabric of his pants. Exhaustion tugged at his eyelids, yet his pounding heart warned him against letting down his guard for a moment.

Julian nearly tumbled back when the door behind him opened inwards. A bald man who he did not recognize stood, dressed in black pants and a button-down white shirt.

"Julian, please follow me," he said with an emotionless expression.

The lobby of the building featured chairs upholstered with golden velvet and finished with dark wood. If it were not for the desk, Julian would have mistaken the place for an extravagant living room. He carefully trod on the carpeted ground, all too aware of the salt and grime clinging to his boots. The man led him towards an elevator, scanning his wrist for instant access. When the doors opened, the man gestured for Julian to enter first. When the man did not follow behind him, instead watching blankly as the doors shut, Julian's heart leaped.

The doors peeled up. As late as it was, seemingly every light in the apartment brightly illuminated the space. Julian slowly stepped out of the elevator, peering around in either direction for any sign of activity. A soft melody spread through the house.

Julian followed the song towards a wing of the apartment he rarely saw. With accommodations of such size, there was little reason for friends to come to Des' bedroom. Des only allowed his late-night companions to join him there.

He peered into a room painted a deep blue with crisp white molding decorating the edges of the walls. On his walls, Desmond framed maps, carefully organizing them around a collection of paintings mostly depicting the sky. Des laid on a king mattress with a simple deep brown comforter pulled partially over his effortlessly sprawled body. The man leaned against a headboard made of dark wood carved with intricate floral designs. On the table beside him, a clear bottle caught the light in its many crystal facets. The lid sat abandoned beside it. Surrounding Julian, the music bathed him from all angles of the room, the strumming of an acoustic guitar filling the air. With two touches on his watch, the music ceased, leaving the two mans in silence. Des looked up at Julian, his face void of emotion.

Neither man spoke as the air hung heavily between them. Julian leaned against the doorframe, hesitant to invite himself further into the forbidden space without explicit permission. He feared to accept the apple in the garden laid out before him. Des met Julian's eyes, his stare revealing nothing to the other man. His expression remained blank, as if gazing on a stranger for the first time. A chill ran through Julian, and he shuddered at the notion.

"I'm sorry for not appreciating your hospitality," said Julian.

He looked to Des for any response.

When the other man spoke, it was quiet.

"Okay."

Julian took a careful step into the room, repeating the hesitant act until he stood beside the bed. He dropped his gaze to the dark wood floors.

"I really am. I shouldn't have acted like that. I would like to apologize," said Julian, stuffing down the indignation rising in his chest.

"Are you sorry for lying to me and God knows who else?" asked Des.

Julian weighed the question. "I did what I thought was best."

"So, no."

"I'm sorry for treating you poorly. I'm sorry for a lot of things, but I'm not sorry for doing what I had to."

Des shook his head, an odd smile coming to his face.

"You're a liar, Julian."

"I've never lied about the things that mattered," he said. "It's not like I took some kind of perverted joy from it. Every time I was with you, I was myself. None of that is a lie. I'm not a lie."

"Are you sure?" asked Des coldly.

Julian stifled the urge to snap back.

"No secrets, Des. I'm sure."

"None?" asked Des.

"Everyone has some."

Des shook his head. "No. None. Not between us."

Julian bit his lip. "Okay."

"Okay," agreed Des. "What do you want from me?"

"What?"

Des repeated himself. "What do you really want from me?"

"What I've always wanted from you."

Des tilted his head slightly. "I don't know what that is."

"You're a good person, Des. I need to be around someone good."

"Then let me be good," said Des, a desperation in his voice.

Julian nodded. "Okay."

Neither one of them said anything in the dim lighting, as if speaking would shatter the fragile web holding them tightly together in the moment. A flicker from a shelf in the corner caught Julian's attention, and he noticed a candle burning. The flame danced, glinting in Des' soft gray eyes. Julian's feet tethered him to one his place at the foot of the bed, unable to move towards the other man or flee. Des' expression was no longer radiated cold indifference, but his stone-like blank face melted into a familiar smile.

"How's the leg?" Des asked.

Julian shrugged. "Not terrible. I ditched the crutches. They were more of a hassle than anything. Thankfully, I haven't had to walk too much."

"My dad said that they were going to give you a car," he replied. "Have you started with Lancut?"

"Yeah," said Julian. "Not that you're supposed to know that."

Des appeared as if he were about to ask him something before patting the edge of the bed, gesturing for Julian.

"Sit down. Why don't you have a drink?" he suggested.

From the side table, Des lifted the crystal bottle and drank deeply as if it were only water. Julian hesitantly sat opposite Des. The soft king bed dipped underneath his weight as if it would swallow him entirely. Once Des handed him the bottle, he took it by the neck, raising the rim to his lips. He sniffed it and instinctively moved the bottle.

"Potent stuff," Julian remarked.

"Only the best."

Julian allowed a few measured drops to fall onto his tongue before tipping the bottle all the way, taking a short sip. The liquor burned down his throat, heat immediately filling his chest. He took another meager sip before handing it back to Des. He fought the aftertaste, but Julian's face crinkled. For a moment, he considered laying down beside his Des. In the warmth of the apartment, he could crawl beneath the covers and fall asleep to the familiar scent of an old friend. Instead, he pushed himself further towards the edge of the bed, quickly glancing away.

"How's it been?" asked Des. "The internship, that is."

"I mean, it's a job," he admitted. "It's a means to an end. It doesn't have to be fantastic."

"Did they at least give you benefits?"

"Stipend and access to a car, but nothing like healthcare. Lancut wouldn't bother with something like that," said Julian, as the liquor dissolved his resolve. "Supposedly Sands will take care of that directly. My very health is right under his finger."

Des choked out a grim laugh, "And the stipend isn't enough to pay for healthcare, I'm sure."

"It's not even enough to pay for my apartment and food," he admitted. "And whatever you're going to say about that, please, Des, please don't. I'm going to ask for more."

Des shook his head. "Don't let them trick you into thinking this is generous. A hungry dog is an obedient dog."

"Good thing I'm not a dog," he said. "Pass me that bottle again."

Des gripped the crystal bottle by the neck, handing it back to Julian, who took another sip. He closed his eyes, letting the warmth wash over him. As the liquid trickled down, his empty stomach ached desperately. Julian cowered at the notion of voicing any need. He opted for another drink, hoping to quench the emptiness of his stomach or dull his mind until he no longer felt the hollowness threatening to envelop him from within.

"I'm so tired, Des," whispered Julian. "I'm so fucking tired."

He sank down onto the mattress beside his friend, uncoiling

his hunched shoulders to lean back. As his gaze locked with Des', he struggled to ascertain his own desires, unable to untangle dreams from reality. He grappled with the overwhelming urge to wrap his arms around the other man and pull him close. He told himself he only wanted warmth, then pulled a throw blanket over his shoulders. Julian pulled his arms in towards himself as if he were able to burrow into his own body.

"Say the word, and you don't have to work for them anymore," said Des quietly.

Julian smiled with bittersweet amusement. "No. There's no out. Once I walked in, the door shut behind me. Looking back is no use."

"There's always a way out," argued Des.

"For people like you, there is."

The other man was quiet for a moment. "I can get you out of this."

"How?" urged Julian.

"I just… can. Just give the word."

"They'll never let me just walk away. They can't have anyone walking around with knowledge of the project. They're busy enough tracking down one leak. They would eliminate me before it became a problem," muttered Julian.

"A leak?"

Julian replied with a sigh.

"Someone knows something who's not supposed to, and they're working with The Reborn. I don't give a fuck who it is so long as I get my debts paid and I'm finally free."

manDes didn't reply immediately, chewing on the word as though tasting it for the first time. When he finally spoke, his voice was quieter.

"Freedom's not something they can give you, Julian. You

have to take it."

Julian scoffed. "You make it sound simple."

"Maybe it is."

"Then you've never been where I am," Julian said sharply.

Des's expression softened. "You think I don't know what it's like to feel trapped?"

Julian rubbed his face, exhaling. "Not like this."

A silence settled, heavy and awkward. Julian itched to reach for the bottle between them, but he feared what would come out of his mouth if he let his carefully buried sentimentality bubble up in a drunken haze. Instead, he pulled the blanket tighter around his shoulders.

"I'm tired," he murmured.

Des nodded toward the bed. "Then lie down. You can stay here tonight."

"Here?"

"Yeah, here," Des repeated nonchalantly, though something flickered in his eyes.

"I'll take the floor," Julian said quickly.

"You don't have to."

Julian hesitated. "I don't want to be in your way. I roll in my sleep."

"It's a big bed."

"I'll be fine down there."

"What about your leg?" Des countered, leaning back.

Julian let out a humorless laugh. "What about it?"

Des shook his head.

"At least sleep in one of the spare rooms."

Julian's heart raced as he scrambled for an answer. Why didn't he sleep in a spare room?

"I'm fine here," he said.

They stared, neither yielding. Finally, Des sighed, leaning back further. "Fine. Sleep on the floor. But take a blanket, at least."

Julian hesitated, then nodded. He slid off the edge of the bed, holding his leg carefully as he maneuvered. The floorboards were cold beneath his palms as he carefully lowered himself to the ground. He settled near the wall, carving out a gap between them, but in the dim light, Des' shadow stretched over him.

Minutes passed. Julian's back ached against the hard floor, and his leg throbbed. Every instinct told him to stay put, to preserve the wall between them. Exhaustion and pain were quiet voices in the back of his mind, but it was the tug in his chest that pulled him up. He sat with the blanket gathered around his shoulders.

"Maybe not the floor," Julian muttered finally, voice low.

Des's eyes glimmered in the dim light. "Why don't you take my bed, and I'll sleep in the spare."

Julian froze, chest tight. "That's not fair." He swallowed, words catching. "I don't want to impose."

"Then just get up here. You stay on your side, and I'll stay on mine."

Something in Julian cracked. He shifted, dragging the blanket with him, and slid onto the bed, keeping a measured distance. His shoulders were stiff, and he turned so his back was to Des.

"You're sure you're okay with this?" he asked, voice tight.

"Of course," Des said, a hint of something more in his tone that made Julian's heart stumble.

Julian exhaled and closed his eyes, feeling the mattress dip slightly as Des adjusted beside him. He lay still, heart thudding, trying to ignore how close Des was-- how he imagined he felt the warmth radiating from the other man across the bare bed between them.

"Goodnight, Des," Julian murmured.

"Goodnight," Des replied softly.

The lamp clicked off. The light from the window bathed the room in pale blue light. Julian's pulse slowed but his face burned. He could hear Des shift and felt the tug on the sheets. Julian lay on his back, blanket pulled to his chin, listening to the faint sound of the other man's breathing until his muscles softened and his eyelids fell shut.

CHAPTER TWELVE

The car veered left where he anticipated a right turn, snapping Julian out of his thoughts. Days prior blended together in a monotonous routine, with one hour indistinguishable from the next. The morning he woke up in Des' bed, he excused himself before the other man woke for the day, slipping out of the apartment. Before he left, he scribbled down a brief note of gratitude on a paper napkin, setting it on the bedside table. While Des hadn't acknowledged the gesture, the other man messaged Julian about going to the bar sometime in the coming week. Julian replied with a dismissive few words, the images of their last bar romp souring the idea of returning.

As he sat in the car, he could not recall the individual events that led him to the current Thursday afternoon. During a droning lecture, Julian emailed Sands to request they meet in person. The quick response startled Julian, and when he climbed into the unmarked vehicle at the end of his classes, he assumed he was on his way to the Lancut Tower. Now that the car quickly headed in the opposite direction, Julian questioned whether he was being brought to Edmund Sands at all.

Granted, he supposed that given the attack that perhaps the powerful man laid low, camped elsewhere as a precaution until tensions resolved. Locked away in some safe house, Julian imagined the middle-aged man surrounded by faceless security standing in formation with weapons braced across their bodies. He sneered at the thought.

If the man chose to point his dagger, the allure of his briefly exposed flank was his fault alone.

After a day of classes, he struggled to hold his head up. Today was nothing out of the ordinary. Classes started as usual, and Julian forced himself through the lectures of the day. As his wound healed, he continued to take the car to the university. The thought sent a pang of guilt into his chest.

The car came to a steady halt, stopping directly in front of another one of the featureless structures. With a sense of unease at the looming menace, he stepped out of the car, limping slightly as he stumbled around the building. The message he received earlier instructed him that the entrance he needed was one next to cargo doors. Large purple graffiti letters stretched over the side of the building, far above the height of any man.

"Freedom through death," he read the words under his breath.

At the rear of the building, there were three trucks parked in front of a door. The center most truck bowed at the front on a deflated tire. Slowly circling them, he ducked beneath, running his hand over the cold rust. As Julian halted at the rear, he huffed, reading the long-expired date on the registration.

Slinking around decrepit buildings felt unwise in the winter climate. He hugged the wall of the building with his back until his fingers grazed the cold round handle of a door.

Carefully, he turned the knob, not daring to push to all the way open before slipping through the narrow opening. Once inside, he squinted his eye. Blinking profusely, the abrasive bulbs slowly became bearable. Still shielding his eyes, he shuffled his feet, turning around where he stood. Once again, gray walls surrounded him. He strode towards a metal door at the end of the hall, noting the familiar panel. He touched the device and waited for a response. As the machine gripped him, immobilizing his body, he braced himself, but a hiss still escaped his lips. Julian gritted his teeth. He couldn't fight even if he tried, his muscles betraying his mind. Without warning, the machine released, and Julian stumbled back. He caught himself on the far wall as the door opened without prompting.

Following the instructions from the message, he walked not even ten meters further into the building before stopping at a wooden door. He held up his fist to knock on the door before hesitating. Instead, he gripped the handle, slowly twisting the knob. Glancing in, he first spotted Elex's smiling face. The man offered him a nod of acknowledgement, waving at Julian until the man carefully chose his seat. The scuffed wooden table stood on thin metal rods. This time only Elex, Agner, and Julian occupied the small space. Agner, with a furrowed brow and down turned lips, scrolled through his watch.

"Mr. Harper, I was told we should wait for you until we started," said Agner bluntly. Julian considered explaining the hassle of getting into the building before silently taking a seat. "Don't bother getting comfortable here. We're taking a walk."

Julian glanced over at Elex, but the man's eyes glimmered as if enamored with his tablet, scribbling something down with an odd smirk on his face.

"Are we going to meet in a new building every time?" asked Julian.

Agner shook his head. "Do you know what this place is?"

Julian spoke quietly, "I do not."

"When you use your soap every day, you know how it says it wasn't tested on animals?" Agner huffed, continuing before Julian had a chance to formulate a response.

"What?" Julian asked.

Elex looked away from Julian. He exchanged glances with Agner, who gave the man a nod. Elex's tone was soft as he spoke.

"It's a last resort, really. They're going to train us on how to administer the I-28 Vision, and we're overseeing some of the initial instruction of nurses."

"Do they," Julian glanced at Agner anxiously, "do they need us to help with that? I thought it was our role to set a plan of action into place."

Julian pictured rows of dimly lit cages and the sounds of scratching claws against cold metal confinements. There weren't many rabbits around the city, but he'd seen pictures of the creatures with their wide eyes and large ears, and with no other reference, he heard the screams so much like a small child's as a needle punctured the surface of its eye. At the thought, Julian clenched his eyes shut. He wondered if it smelled like fear there, or if the odor of feces and blood would overpower anything else. A scalpel shone in his mind, catching the cold lighting in its blade and reflecting across the room.

A woman knocked twice before inviting herself in. The lanky figure in scrubs peeked her head through the door. She smiled widely, and her massive pupils sank like dark voids in her eyes, nearly covering the entirety of her irises. She moved swiftly across the room, shaking hands with Agner, leaning in for a brief embrace. When she pulled away, she surveyed the room, quickly glancing over at Elex before lingering on Julian. For a moment, he thought he caught a hunger in her eyes. Her glare was primal yet too calculated to be purely animalistic. She watched him like a predator stalking its trapped prey, teeth bared in a smile.

"Dr. Wood, it's been too long," said Agner, an unfamiliar cheerful lilt to his words.

"Same to you. Why don't I give you all a tour of the facility, and I'll explain where we are on the training process," she said cheerfully, the corners of her eyes creasing into crows' feet as if she were a benevolent nurse smiling down at her charges.

Julian limped slightly behind Elex and Agner as they followed the woman out of the room. The hallway soon widened, and at the end, a sturdy metal door blocked the way. The doctor typed something into a panel, allowing the machine to scan her before the locked clicked, allowing them inside. Immediately, Julian recognized the bleak scene.

The stench hit him first: ammonia, rot, and something sour beneath it. Then the sight.

Rows of cages—not cages, but cells, Julian noted, lined the walls, stacked nearly to the ceiling. Where three should have fit, six or seven bodies were crammed together, crawling over each other in filth. For a moment, Julian thought they were animals. But then one of them lifted its face toward him. Human eyes. Human hands, though misshapen, gripped the bars.

The creature pressed closer, its mouth forming words he couldn't make out. The doctor's wand cracked across its knuckles, igniting a small burst of light and the smell of charred flesh. Julian stumbled back a step, heart hammering against his ribs. He couldn't get enough air, and his sight blurred. The figure whimpered and withdrew, retreating into the dark corner of the cage. Two others lay motionless behind it. If not for the shallow rise and fall of their chests, he might have thought they were corpses. On what remained of their limbs, he saw only rounded scars where arms and legs should have been.

Bile surged up Julian's throat. He swallowed hard, forcing it back, but the taste clung to his tongue. The air felt heavier now, pressing down as he stared through the bars. He wanted to look away, but he couldn't. These weren't animals. They were people, and someone had decided they didn't need to be anymore.

"Who are they?" Julian quietly asked.

Elex shot him a look of caution, but the doctor appeared unphased.

"Lab rats. We keep the program fairly quiet for the privacy of our subjects. They didn't qualify for any work programs, so rather than liquidations, they chose to serve their country. If they make it through the allotted two years, they can be released back into society under a new name and debt free.

"These ones have been selected for the project. We've trained them not to speak to any staff unless expressly told so. It might seem cruel at first glance to use them for experimentation, but most of them come to feel purpose in being part of something so much larger than themselves. They truly understand they're earning their way out of debt. Some resist at first, but there are ways to combat that," said Wood.

Passing by a cell, there was a single subject inside. His hands were chained together, with metal cuffs strung up to a hook on the ceiling. His toes barely grazed the ground beneath him, and he struggled to maintain any traction. The young man's wide eyes locked with Julian's, and for a moment, Julian half expected him to say something. Rather than a voice, the echoes of rattling chains melded with the gurgles the man managed.

"There was so much anger surrounding animal testing. All of those organizations calling for us to stop eating meat, stop testing on animals, stop the abuse. After all, those poor lab rats are innocent. It's not fair to torture innocent animals," she said as coldly. "We've extensively tested the best ways to administer the device. The most efficient is directly through the eye, but this often leads to resistance and struggling, which then leads to complications with the procedure. Immobilizing the patient seems to be the most successful method, but sedation is unnecessary."

Julian felt himself unable to flee, forced against a wall in the city with a needle up to his eye. He wondered how excruciating the pain would be as the needle pierced the surface in his eye, implanting a small device. The notion brought bile to his throat. He would resist taking the device for as long as possible. After all, he wasn't part of the group they wanted to watch, or at least not anymore. The constant human eyes on him eliminated the need for that.

Julian collected himself, addressing the doctor, "I'm not sure how this is going to be translated to the public. The people won't want to be immobilized for this. A needle coming towards your eye- well, I'm sure we can all agree that's not something we want to see."

She pursed her lips.

"Isn't that your job? To make it appealing to the public?"

Julian breathed in sharply.

"Yes, it is. That's why you work for us."

Agner shot a look at Julian that he was certain was approval. The doctor gave a nearly inaudible huff, walking even faster now. Her clogs tapped against the ground, which mixed with the occasional sound of rattling chains or guttural moans. To his left, at least four sets of eyes stared at him out of near-total darkness, huddled against one another as if one tormented beast, fused together in the depths of some man-made hell. With a closer glance, he realized that where one body should have ended and another began, jagged white scars joined limbs. He glanced away.

The doctor guided them into a large room. Dark streaks stretched across the once white tile floor toward a drain in the center of the room. Gray walls surrounded the group. Two men in Enforcer uniforms stood motionless beside a middle-aged man with cuffs around his ankles. He lay on the cold tile floor, stripped of any clothing. The swollen, fresh stubs where his arms once were exposed. Julian imagined the subject would have shivered if it were not for his immobilization. The way he only moved his eyes when the doctor entered the room was enough to denote the terror he could not otherwise express.

"It's against protocol, but we can silence them, too. Freeze their faces so they can't mouth off," said the doctor as if reading Julian's questioning glance. "It's better than gagging them. Easier to turn it off so they can give us feedback, and then we can quickly get back to work."

Julian suppressed a string of questions, narrowly holding them back as he bit his tongue. As he looked at the shackled man, for a moment he swore he saw himself with eyes sunken in and ribs poking through his skin. Even as he stood fully clothed, he squirmed beneath the probing eyes of the scientist, picking over his body as if he were cattle.

Julian snapped back to attention as the man toppled forward, unable to catch himself. A smack rang out as his cheek met the tile, and he let out a cry of shock. With a baton pointed at the man, one enforcer jabbed the end into the man's shoulder, sending spasms through his body. Once the man in a crimson uniform pulled back the baton, the man slowly inched forward, pulling his knees up to push his chest forward across the ground, inching forward like an insect. Julian shamefully hoped the man's eyes would be emotionless or distant, but instead, his terror was clear in the wide pupils of his eyes, painted across his entire face.

"Stand up," ordered the Enforcer.

The man struggled to his feet, squirming on the ground.

As he stood, he lost his balance, tumbling back to the ground. One of the inflamed stubs collided with the ground, and he let out a shriek that bounced off of every surface in the tile room. The Enforcer angrily yanked the man up by the neck, dragging him across the room until he regained his footing. The Enforcer shoved the man up against a metal table, pinning him face down on the aluminum surface, his bare feet dangling. The skin on his soles sluffed away as if he had been forced to stand in dampness for days on end. The Enforcer turned to the doctor for further instruction.

"On the table," she said, walking to the far side of the room from which she retrieved a cart that rolled forward with a squeal of one of its rusted wheels.

The Enforcer hauled the man onto the table without grace, and the man's sounds of protest were quickly cut off as his body rigidly froze in position. As the doctor hovered gloved hands over the cart, she smiled down lovingly at her instruments, including two long needles. Gently, she stroked the finger against one of the vials.

"See, if I were to let the Enforcers release him, he'd thrash around and not only ruin the procedure, but his own vision in the process. It's best to have the subject entirely still so, even if they are willingly taking the procedure, they can't accidentally flinch." She picked up the needle, carefully positioning over her subject's left eye. "It's not a difficult procedure at all with a little training, and we've already begun training staff on our subjects."

Julian steadied his breathing as he moved closer. His pulse still hadn't slowed from what he'd seen in the cages, but he forced his lips into a stiff line and grit his teeth. The doctor didn't look like the kind who forgave weakness.

"Is this something an ordinary civilian could be trained to

do?" he asked, careful to keep his tone steady as he trembled.

"Maybe with quite a bit of practice," she replied, eyes narrowing as if weighing his motives. "They'd have to train, and that would mean granting them access to this facility, which, even with your special connections, will never happen. You should leave it to doctors and nurses, at least for the ones where the damages matter."

His jaw tightened. *Damages.* Is that what they were?

"That's fine," he said. "We can have them learn on actual lab rats or other small animals. We had no intention of asking you for your nurses and assistants. And there's really no way to do this without immobilization?"

She shook her head, lips curling faintly. "Watch, and then tell me your expert opinion."

He nodded, feigning interest, but his stomach churned. He fought the urge to clench his fists, to dig his nails into his palms until they bled, to reach for something, to stop her. But instead he clasped his hands behind his back. The skin at the base of his neck prickled as he fought to keep his mask in place.

Peeling back the man's eyelid, she tilted his head slightly, positioning the needle directly above the surface. Satisfied, she carefully lowered the needle until it disappeared into the tissue. Pressing down on the plunger, she carefully extracted the needle, pulling it out in a slow yet smooth motion. Once the doctor was clear, the Enforcer pressed a button on a tablet. The man immediately shot up, blinking profusely as he wailed.

"It doesn't actually hurt," she said. "It's just the fear. It would be advisable to observe patients for thirty minutes after to ensure they don't do anything irrational. We had one claw out his own eye. The damage was so extensive that his only use was to scrap him for parts."

Julian's head swirled, his stomach queasy. The urge to bolt out of the lab and into the open air overwhelmingly tugged at his legs, yet he kept himself in place.

Agner spoke up, "Yes, yes, but we can't deal with panicked people going around telling their family and friends what a traumatic experience it is. I'm not saying they should be fully put under, per se, but perhaps some kind of sedative? Something to calm them down."

"Do you have something that would inhibit memory?" asked Julian. The doctor turned to him, a genuine look of interest on her face.

"There are some drugs that don't render someone unconscious, but the person is so mentally inhibited that they usually don't remember the hour or so after a procedure. Often, they're left with a sensation of euphoria even. It's expensive though. Not something you want to waste on the masses," she remarked.

"Maybe we don't use it on everyone. Just the ones who might cause trouble. We get them to trust us, and then we ditch the use altogether," Julian said.

Elex was quickly scribbling down these notes onto his tablet.

"What's the budget?" the doctor asked.

Julian looked to Agner, who responded, "Doesn't matter because you're going to get those drugs produced as inexpensively as possible. And train your nurses in administration of the drug. Unless you can come up with something better, Mr. Harper is correct. We cannot have traumatized people running their mouths after the procedure and scaring others."

"I'll make it happen, but with the addition of this new drug, it might add a few weeks to the operation," she remarked.

"A few weeks isn't an issue. Just don't let it be any more than that," Agner replied curtly.

"Not an issue," she agreed. Centering her stare on Julian, she sneered. "Would any of you like to try administering it yourselves? Maybe we could find out if a civilian could do it while you're here. Very few people have the clearance to visit."

Agner shook his head. "That should be sufficient. Mr. Harper, does anything strike you as noteworthy of asking?"

Julian was unable to peel his eyes away from the man. An Enforcer hauled him back to the wall, leaving him immobilized once more in a kneeling position, unable to so much as blink. Every time Julian snuck a glance back at the doctor, another pang of guilt pressed into his gut, forcing bile into his mouth. He swallowed it back down, thankful for the deserving burning sensation as his penance.

"Mr. Harper," Agner repeated. "Is there anything else?"

Julian shook his head.

"This meeting is dismissed," said Agner. "If you could guide Mr. Harper back to the exit, I have other business to attend to here. I'll hang back."

"Of course," said the doctor. "I'd just like to talk to Mr. Harper about a few more ideas outside of this project, if that's alright with you?"

"He's a free man," replied Agner, giving Julian a nod as he departed the room. Agner marched through the doorway with the same militaristic form he strode everywhere with.

Once he no longer heard the slapping of soles against the floor, Julian turned to the doctor.

She smiled, her white teeth perfectly straight and nearly blinding in the already abrasively lit room. "Who are you?" she asked. "How did you get here?"

"What?" he managed.

"If anyone knows the terror of having their eyes operated on while you're forced to sit there, perfectly still, it would be you," she said.

"I'm sorry, but I don't follow."

"I've done plenty of that procedure myself," she said, stepping towards him and leaning in until he felt her warm breath on his face. She gripped his chin in one hand, pulling it forward. "Or did they sedate you? I never put mine under. Seems unnecessary."

Julian held his ground, meeting the doctor's eyes, their noses nearly touching.

"I'm not sure what you're implying, but I have other meetings to attend to today. If there's anything relevant to the project, I'd be happy to discuss further."

He pulled away, forcing a stiff smile.

She met his smile with an equally empty grin.

"I can give you your vision back. It's all yours if you just admit it. Don't even worry about a donor. I've been growing spare parts, you know. You ever see a man grow an ear out his back, or patches of luscious hair on their stomachs to be harvested? Eyes are delicate, but it's very possible."

"You're just as delusional as I thought you were," he said, turning away. As he walked out of the room, he stopped, turning around in the doorway. "I don't need anything from you other than your compliance with this project. If you have any other business, please reach out to my team."

She cocked her head.

"You know, if this doesn't work out for you, I can help arrange a kidney extraction. And when I'm in there, I can take part of your liver, and, well, if you're in too deep, I can take your beating heart out of your chest. Can you even imagine the exhilaration of cradling a pulsating organ in your hands? It's the closest man will ever get to becoming a God. Is that what you want, Julian? To be God?"

"Have a pleasant day," Julian said calmly, turning back around and disappearing down the hall.

CHAPTER THIRTEEN

"He will see you," the man said.

A crimson sofa, pushed against the wall with a small table beside it, stood in the hall. Though no dust gathered, the carefully procured magazines sat atop another as if nobody dared disturb the order. The space was far more compartmentalized than the mansions or penthouses Julian associated with the wealthy. Rooms stemmed off of hallways to create a maze high above the city, most without windows. Dim lighting did little to illuminate the emerald green wallpaper. The slightest fondness for the decor sent shame through Julian.

When Julian slowly walked into the room, Edmund Sands sat hunched, almost comically so, behind his large black desk beneath the high ceilings. The windows in the office remained obscured by thick velvet curtains that blocked out any lights of the city. Julian couldn't say what floor he was on.

Julian carefully tucked his hands behind his back, holding his shoulder up before walking to meet the distracted man. Only when Julian nearly stood atop him did Sands look up from his tablet, his expression unchanging. The man said nothing, leaving Julian standing.

"May I have a seat?" Julian asked, glancing down at a cream-colored armchair.

"Yes, yes, have a seat," Sands muttered.

Julian pulled the chair out, careful not to scuff the hardwood floors. Paintings with bold golden frames, flourishing into leaves and spirals around the artwork, were arranged around the room. Beside Julian, an image of a cardinal perched on a snow-covered branch hung at his eyes level. The strokes of a paintbrush created feathers that rose from the canvas. As he peered around, he spotted a sparrow, a woodpecker and a family of finches.

When Julian returned his attention, Sands was smiling.

"Do you like the birds?"

"Um, yeah," replied Julian. "Just don't see many besides the crows and pigeons around here."

"I painted these myself, you see," he said. "I like to paint them from real life. I've had them captured and caged for me. Some of them imported from savage places."

"You're very talented."

As if he didn't hear the man at all, Sands rambled on, "When I grew up, you could walk outside and just see them flying free. I'd walk through the forest, and they would dip to snatch insects right out of the air in front of your face."

"You didn't grow up in the city?" he asked.

The smile slowly faded from his face. "No, I didn't. My parents sent me away to a boarding school for most of my life. It was a different time. Then it all disappeared in a blaze, and all I have left are my birds," he said somberly. "So many different types, all with their own unique calls and dances. For all of their pretty colors, they'll eat their young and tear one another to shreds. Small creatures, but not innocent. Fragile, but not helpless."

"Why hide them away here?" Julian asked.

"Truthfully, because I don't wish to share them, so I keep them here. This is my home, after all," he said.

Julian gazed around, taking in the sprawling office. "You have a beautiful home."

"Thank you," he said plainly. "I assume as our business

relationship grows that you'll be spending more time here. I, of all people, am not immune to a dinner party," he laughed, standing up. "Have they told you about the parties I throw?"

Julian shook his head.

Sands laughed, "Well, I'll make sure you get invited to the next one. Anything you want is yours when you're there. It's an escape like no other- an exercise in indulgence we must pretend to resent as humble servants of the state."

"Thank you," he said. "I look forward to attending."

Julian crossed his legs, uncrossing them, then repeating the motion.

The older man made his way over to a cabinet at the corner of the room, removing a bottle of amber liquid and two glasses. Carefully, he poured the first glass halfway to the top. After pouring a second identical glass, he sat back down at his desk. He slid one across the polished surface towards Julian.

"Tell me, how have you been finding your assignment?" Sands asked.

Julian set the glass down, careful not to place it on any of the documents strewn across the desk.

"It's fulfilling to be a part of something bigger than myself," Julian remarked. "All of this time in school has been great, but sometimes it gets monotonous sitting in a classroom completing meaningless assignments. It's nice to get hands-on experience."

"You understand," agreed Sands. "Sometimes it's not pretty, and we have to deal with the unsavory, but we do what we must to keep order. Some people claim that it's cruel. They morally could never partake in such a thing, so they pawn of the responsibility onto those of us who can, and they benefit. We carry them on our backs."

Julian cautiously nursed his drink. "It must be done in the

name of a functional society. I took no joy in visiting that testing facility, but how would we progress without such programs? I only fear that there are people with the same mentality directing their energy towards other causes."

"Ah, yes," said Sands. "They can set off bombs and send threats, but it's nothing we can't handle."

"Sir," Julian started, "I don't even know who our enemy is, and I feel like that's unwise. I know my personal responsibilities don't directly involve counterterrorism, but I was told there was a mole within the project somewhere- a mole for The Reborn. And I suppose I'm not even sure what they stand for."

Sands set down his glass, "It's nothing you need to worry about, Mr. Harper. We have a task force handling the situation. The Reborn would see the destruction of life as we know it in exchange for a government based on nothing but violence. You saw what they did. Every time you take a step, you're reminded of who they are."

"Are they a threat?" Julian asked plainly. "In reality, how dangerous are they?"

"This project comes at a necessary time. It prefaces much larger reforms; plans, but that's still in the works," replied Sands with a slight strain to his voice. "We've let too many things slip between the cracks, and it's time to put a stop to any radical behavior before it *becomes* a threat. But no, they are not a genuine threat. They never have been. I can assure you of that."

"I heard Lancut has identified at least one of the terrorists," said Julian. "Why don't you make an example out of them?"

Sands gave Julian a warning glance.

"Some things are far more complicated than you realize. We've killed plenty of them, and we'll continue to pick them off one by one. "Anyway," he said, and Julian wondered if he sensed nervousness behind the glistening mask. "How are you finding things so far? Settling in?"

Julian hesitated, shifting. "It's been fine, sir. I'm keeping up with the workload."

"I should hope so," Sands replied lightly, though there was weight behind his words. "You've done well for yourself. But I know the adjustment can be difficult. So many new expectations, and a new life to adjust to. There are so many things to learn that nobody ever says out loud. Have you found somewhere better to rent?"

"Not yet, sir," he replied with hesitation.

Sands nodded slowly, as if making a note to himself. "You're still paying rent on that tiny thing?"

Julian nodded.

"It hardly seems right for you to be worrying about things like rent when your focus should be on the work ahead. Lancut looks after its people, Julian."

"I'm not sure what you mean."

"If rent and food are your greatest expenses, you can keep the stipend, and I could set you up in Lancut housing. You wouldn't have to worry about anything. Meals would be prepared for you three times a day. You'd never want for anything."

Julian hesitated. The offer sounded generous, but generosity with a price was a transaction, and what did he have to give away? Control? Privacy? It meant submitting to walls that belonged to Sands and locks he didn't hold the keys to.

He forced himself to smile. "That's very generous, sir, but I have obligations to my roommate," he said, the pause barely long enough to notice. "I couldn't consider moving out until he's settled somewhere else."

He hoped his tone didn't sound as weak as he felt. His roommate wasn't settling anywhere. Syd was packing up for good, and Julian had no idea how he'd cover rent once the door shut behind him. Still, he couldn't walk into Sands' jowls so easily.

Sands nodded.

"I respect your loyalty, but I trust you understand that the offer stands. I think it would be very beneficial for you in the long run."

"I hate to ask more for more, sir, but I have someone who I think would be a fantastic asset to the team."

"And who would that be?" asked Sands.

"Desmond Peterson. I've been going to school with him for a long time. He's very intelligent, and we work together well. I think he would be a great fit. He has motivation to succeed for his father's sake," said Julian.

"I'll consider it, but I do not think it would be wise," said Sands after a moment. "We're keeping this team small for a reason, and I'm afraid offering him a position may be interpreted as nepotism, as well. This is a merit-based society, and we intend to uphold that value."

"I appreciate your consideration, and I'm thankful for the increased stipend," he said.

"I hope you'll consider a housing accommodation with us," added Sands. "You know, if you stayed with Lancut, you would have people to take care of your needs. People to distract you from the Peterson man."

"What do you mean?" asked Julian.

"Desperation is weakness. You need to cut connections with him. It's not a good luck."

"He's my friend," replied Julian.

Edmund Sands shook his head.
"Just think about my offer. That's all I'm asking."
Julian looked down at his empty glass.
"I'll definitely consider it."

CHAPTER FOURTEEN

When Julian opened the door to the small apartment, he breathed a sigh of relief.

Alone.

In the many days since their discussion, he only saw his roommate twice, both times in the morning when the two prepared for the day. After the evening of their discussion, Julian figured the other man was spending more time with this girl he mentioned. He considered whether Syd avoided the apartment, or whether it was Julian he steered clear of.

With his stipend secured, he could inform Syd that he had his finances settled. The sudden changes were no detriment to his life, and the other man was free to leave next month without guilt.

Forty-thousand was not enough to eat out or go on take a vacation, but he freely poured the entire box of penne into a boiling pot of water without a pang of guilt. He gently stirred them with an old plastic spatula. He rummages through the cupboards, producing a can of sauce. Carefully turning it over in his hands, he admired the ripe red tomatoes plumply displayed on the packaging. He pried open the lid and dumped the contents into a separate pot.

In the background, the television quietly played an old sitcom. A laugh track flooded the room with a myriad of voices. As the pasta continued to roll over the boiling liquid, Julian slumped down on the couch, sinking in until his knees rose above his hips.

As he looked around the small apartment, he considered how he would rule a space entirely on his own. Perhaps he would move his mattress into Syd's old room.

He might tack up artwork over the cracks in the walls like colorful patches on old jeans. Although he couldn't repaint the place without permission, he considered a space so overwhelmed with posters and papers that the walls were no longer a visible factor. With a proper salary, he would buy the entire building. The place could be his. He smiled at the prospect of evicting his neighbor.

A knock on the door snapped him from his thoughts. His heart leaped, and he took the stairs two at a time. He braced himself as he turned the knob, hesitating before pulling the door open. The darkness did not do justice to the man's gray eyes, nor his bright smile and sandy blond hair. Des stood in the upstairs entryway, a bag slung over his shoulder. He wore heather sweatpants that hugged thighs, and his black hoodie was adorned with a light coating of snow. Noticing Julian staring at his shoulders, Des brushed the snow away, running his hands through his hair to clear away any gathered flakes. Julian's breath hitched in his throat. Des stepped on the backs of his heels, pulling off his sneakers to set them at the top of the stairs. Julian was unable to stifle a small laugh.

"You don't have to do that. The dirt is literally embedded into the floor."

"Nah," dismissed Des. "Looks clean enough to me."

Des glanced around the room, slinging off his backpack. Setting it down on the couch, he unzipped the bag, pulling out a tall glass bottle. Julian was too busy studying the other man's face to notice until Des lifted it up, gesturing at the label.

"Wine?" questioned Julian.

"It's a housewarming gift. I was always told that's what you're supposed to do when you go over to someone's house for the first time. Stuffy tradition, I guess."

Des switched his weight from one foot to the other, eyes darting back to his host.

Julian laughed.

"Then I owe quite a few people wine."

Des carefully leaned against the wall, and Julian followed the man with his eyes, scanning for any signs of disgust or repulsion. To Julian, the other man's expression appeared unchanged. Julian gestured at the couch.

"Feel free to have a seat. I have dinner on the stove right now…if you haven't eaten, I mean. I won't force you to eat pasta"

Des took the invitation, collapsing down onto the couch.

"I could eat. I'm starving."

"But first," said Julian, taking the bottle of wine from Des, "we drink."

He came from the kitchen with a corkscrew and plunged the sharp point into the cork, working the spiral into the soft wood. He pulled off the cork with a pop, nearly stumbling back. Des took the bottle from him, raising the rim to his lips, tongue darting out to catch a drop. He stared into Julian's dark eyes, his eyebrows arched, as he downed the wine.

"Shit," muttered Julian, rushing back over to the stove.

The rolling water cascaded over the edges of the pot, overflowing the pasta with it. As it hit the stovetop, it sizzled, sending up steam. Quickly, he brushed away the charred spaghetti with his spoon. Glancing down, there was still a decent portion of pasta left. His face burned red as he turned back to his guest.

"I'm really sorry. I wasn't paying attention. I can throw some more in."

Des shrugged, "I'm sure there's still plenty."

Julian bit the inside of his cheek, staring down at the meager amount. Prodding at one piece, he concluded it bounced back easily. Carefully, he drained the pasta over the sink; the steam enveloping his face in a warm cloud. Without a strainer, he was used to an inch of water left in the pot's bottom. If he were alone, he wouldn't think twice about dumping in the sauce. That made the sauce stretch for longer, anyway. With his spoon, he scooped the water out slowly as if he were bailing out a lifeboat. He dumped in a small jar of sauce.

Stirring mindlessly, he only half-watched the pot. Rather, he stared at the man on his couch, who pressed his hand against the cushions, brushing his fingers against the fabric. He made an odd expression as if shocked by the texture. Before Des could catch him watching, he returned to his task. Julian pulled two bowls from the cupboard, both made of ceramic with small floral designs around the rim. One bowl had a chip, its edge sharp to the touch. Carefully, he dished an even amount into each bowl, carefully distributing the remaining sauce at the bottom of the pot. He stuck a fork into each, carefully taking one in each hand.

"Well, it's nothing special, but it's filling," Julian said, skewering a few pieces of pasta on his fork before taking a hefty first bite. He covered his mouth with his hand as he spoke again. "Syd really hasn't been around lately, so we probably have the place to ourselves."

Des handed Julian the bottle of wine, which was now at least a quarter of the way emptied. He placed his bowl on the short table beside him, then he took the wine in both hands, measuring the heft of the bottle. Julian took a short sip first before giving in. Gulping down enough to bring the bottle to the halfway point, he sat back, hand wrapped around the neck of the bottle.

"Tastes expensive," said Julian. "More expensive than vodka at least."

"If you'd prefer cheap vodka, it's still early," replied Des. Julian noticed how he carefully picked at the pasta. "We could get a handle, and then we can pass out watching something. Now that's what I need."

"You're right about that. If Loget Tech comes up with some device to wipe memories, I'd take that, but until then," Julian raised the bottle, taking another long gulp.

Julian stared down at his empty bowl, glaring at Des' substantial pile of pasta, his fork stuck into the mound like an abandoned flag. He leaned back, resting his head against the couch, staring up at the discolored ceiling. Swishing around the contents of the bottle, he took a final sip before handing it back to Des.

Des fumbled with his hoodie pocket before producing a tin. He popped it open and gestured at the contents within. Des pushed three ovular yellow pills to one side. He plucked one out, cradling it in the palm of his hand. Without hesitation, he brought his hand up to his mouth, swallowing the pill with a gulp. Washing it down with the wine, Des gave a heavy sigh.

"This'll make everything but the present really fuzzy," said Des, gesturing to one of the small pills. "They're a pretty new product."

"Yeah? Make me forget my day?"

"Isn't that what you want?" asked Des.

Julian bowed his head, taking his face in his hands.

"No, no, there's so much more. Things I wish I had never seen."

Des' smile faded into a concerned look. "From the attack in

the Lancut building?"

"Yes," Julian said instinctively. "I mean, no, There's more. Every day there's something new. Something horrifying."

"What could be worse than being shot?"

Julian hesitated. "You won't remember this in the morning anyway," said Julian, gesturing at the bottle and then the tin.

"Then what's the harm in telling me?" Des asked.

Julian quietly sighed, "I wanted to ask you to come work with me. I even asked my team to get you approved to work with us, but now," Julian shook his head, "I don't want to be near it. You don't want to be anywhere near it. I take it all back. I'd never drag you into this. I understand why you don't want to work for him- for your father's company, either."

Des' eyes widened, and he up straight, "You asked them to screen and approve me?"

Julian replied, "Yeah, I told them you'd be a good fit. I figured they'd do a quick check, but that you'd be a shoe in. I take it all back, though. If they reach out to you, I'm begging you to reject the offer." Julian pushed down the boiling anger in his chest, letting his face fall into his hands. "It's evil. It's so evil, but there's nothing I can do but go forwards. There's no way out but through."

Des sat up straight as if sobering up for just a moment.

"What did you say about me?"

"Oh," Julian said, "Just that you're a hard worker, and it wouldn't be a security concern because you're already involved by default through your family. What motivation would you have to betray the project and damage your own future?"

"You're right," he said. "But it's evil, and I want no part of it. You don't have to be a part of it either, you know. Just say the word."

"We're not talking about this again. All I'm saying is that I'm already fucked, and you don't have to ruin your life, too. I need this stipend. I quit my other job. This is my last chance."

"Do you really think they're going to let you go at the end of this all? They're going to forgive your debt and invite you with open arms into their elitist society?" asked Des.

"I have to believe them. I need something to hold on to. I have to believe it. Some people have a god who reigns terror down on his people, but they still fall down and kiss his feet. I have Lancut."

"Do you?" Des replied. "You have no social capital. It would be easier to dispose of you once they're finished playing with you. They wouldn't have to waste their civiks or worry about their secrets."

"What would you have me do instead? Run away? Get myself killed trying to cross the border? Join a terrorist organization?"

Des anxiously laughed. He opened back up the small tin container, gesturing at the pills inside. "Let's just forget this all. One night of peace for us both."

Julian's mind, already foggy, churned over the words in his mind, to no avail. Shaking his head, he declined, and Des put them away. He took another long swig of wine, closing his eyes as his limbs became light.

Smiling sadly at Des, a warmth bloomed in his chest that he couldn't attribute to a pill he hadn't taken. As he swayed where he sat, he sunk down against Des' shoulder, pressing his face into the other man's hoodie. He closed his eyes, pulling in a long breath through his nose, sucking it in like a drug. Even as his heart rate slowed and his vision softened, a thought drifted to the forefront of his mind. He shook the sour notions out of his head. Instead, he pulled himself further towards the other man, clinging to his warmth in the cold basement apartment. He couldn't smell the mildew over Des' sweet scent.

"I don't know what's going to happen next," admitted Julian. "The more I see, the less I trust Sands…trust any of them."

Des wrapped thick arms around his Julian. "What if we just left?"

"What?"

"We could get a car and just get out of here. Or a boat," Des replied. "Fuck all of it," said Des, rubbing his eyes. "I know we can't, but I wish we could; leave all of this bullshit behind."

"You can't get us a boat out of here?" asked Julian with a grin.

Des sighed.

"Even if we wouldn't automatically be killed, we can't run away while there's still so much to do. Isn't that what you're always saying?" asked Des.

"And I'm going to do it. Do it all. I'm just not sure how anymore. But I want to forget for a minute," said Julian, staring up at Des with wide brown eyes.

Des stroked Julian's back in a firm yet gentle motion. "What do you need?"

Julian struggled to speak, floundering for words. He opened his mouth, choking on the air until he finally managed a hushed tone.

"I don't want to think," Julian said.

"Okay," said Des, cupping Julian's cheeks with two hands, framing his face within his warm grasp. He slid his hand down, lightly gripping the back of Julian's neck. "Just tell me you want this."

"I want this," Julian whispered, leaning into the touch. "I want this. I want this…" he repeated as Des brushed his lips against Julian's cheek, running fingers through his long dark hair.

Julian let out a choked moan at the touch, heat running through his body. Des pushed him onto his back, straddling the other man. Julian felt the hard bulge in Des' pants pressing against his abdomen. Running warm hands over Julian's clothed chest, he worked his way up, nipping at the tender skin of his neck.

"Are you sure you want to do this?" asked Julian. "Where is this coming from?"

Des' words were breathy in his ear, "You're oblivious, Julian."

He pressed down a gentle kiss on Julian's lips.

Julian moaned as Des crawled over him, pinning his chest down with one large hand. The constriction of Julian's pants was suddenly at the forefront of his mind, enveloping him in aching need. He jutted his hips up, unable to move more than millimeters with Des' weight atop him.

"Please," murmured Julian. "I don't want to think."

Des hooked his finger on Julian's shirt collar, pulling him up until he felt Des' warm breath against his face. Julian keened, bucking his hips up in search of friction but finding none. Sliding a hand beneath Julian's shirt, Des explored the other man's stomach, following a trail of dark hair up to his chest. Julian yelped as Des pinched his nipple, pleasure blooming from the pain.

"You like that?" Des asked.

Julian nodded, running his hands over the man above him, staring up in unbridled awe. Julian watched breathlessly while his friend sat back, pulling off his shirt in one smooth motion, tossing it to the ground. Des had freckles peppered across his shoulders and chest, and his blond hair was neatly managed. Julian ran his hand down Des' chest, trailing one finger down to the other man's waistband. Through the fabric, Julian groped downward until he found what he wanted.

"Not yet," hushed Des, pulling at Julian's shirt.

Julian raised his arms up as Des pulled his shirt off, momentarily blinded by the fabric. He glanced down at his own lithe body, the indentations between his ribs suddenly vulnerable; he looked away as Des ran his fingers over the hills and valleys. Warm breath brushed his skin before Des gently laid his lips on Julian's stomach, working his way up. Des licked a trail up to Julian's left nipple, taking the nub in his mouth. Moaning, Julian arched his back, pressing into the sensation.

"Please," Julian managed, the words barely audible.

"Please what?" Des stopped, locking eyes with the man beneath him.

"Please keep going-"

Julian gasped as Des bit down on his nipple before letting it go. Des sucked on the skin beside it, leaving a small purple mark behind. He pushed his hips up, rutting against Des' leg, which was now planted between his. Des nipped at Julian's neck, then chin until taking the other man's lip in his teeth, gently biting down. Julian reached up, running his hands through Des' short blond hair as Des pressed a kiss down on his lips. Groaning into his mouth, Des continued to push his lips against Julian's, pulling away for just a moment.

"You've never been subtle, especially not lately," he whispered before taking Julian's mouth once more.

Julian threw his head back, and Des brushed his lips against the sensitive skin of his exposed neck, kissing down until he reached Julian's collarbone. With a meticulous hand, he rubbed against the hardening bulge in Julian's pants, massaging over the area as the other man keened. Julian felt the dampness of pre-cum leaving a wet patch on his boxers. As he planted his hands behind him, Julian pushed himself up until they were nose to nose. Julian took in the sight, panting with wide eyes before resting a hand against Des' chest. He eased the other man back until Des' head was resting on the arm of the couch.

With one hand on either side of Des' shoulders, Julian admired the man below him, hands roaming across his chest. Slowly dragging his hands down, he worked his way across the couch until he was staring down at the distinct strain in Des' sweatpants. Clutching the waistband, he glanced up at Des, who nodded. As he pulled down the elastic, Julian's hands shook with anticipation and need. Julian stared into warm gray eyes as he wrapped a calloused hand around Des' cock, slowly licking up the underside of his before swallowing it down. As he took Des in his mouth, he relaxed his throat to push himself down further. Tears welled up in his eyes as he resisted his reflexes. He moved back slightly, watching Des recoil with a sharp gasp. He worked Des in his mouth, taking him with a smooth rhythm.

"Yes, yes, yes," repeated Des.

Pulling his lip from Des' cock with a pop, Julian took Des in his hand, stoking him, gently running a finger over his tip. Lapping at the weeping pre-cum, he swirled his tongue around the sensitive area, earning him a moan, before swallowing him back down to the stem. He sank down until he nestled his angular nose in Des' light curly hair. Julian set a steady pace, moaning around the intrusion as he drank in the noises he pulled from Des.

Des gripped his hair by the root, holding his head in place as Des' spilled into his mouth and down his throat, letting out a cry. Julian swallowed around the other man, a few drops escaping his lips and dripping down his chin. Panting, he gazed up at Des through dark, thick eyelashes. The other man smiled with dazed eyes. Des ran his fingers through Julian's hair, brushing it away from his face. Julian dragged the back of his hand across his face, wiping away any evidence of what had occurred.

"Thank you," choked out Julian with a hoarse voice, palming himself over his own pants. "Thank you, thank you…" he repeated, pushing into his own hand. It didn't take over thirty seconds before he gasped with release. He clamped his other hand over his mouth as he moaned, stifling the loud cry. The wet splotch grew in his pants until it began to seep through the fabric, expanding out from what was once just a pinprick of darkness. His face reddened as he made eye contact with Des once more.

"Thank you," he panted.

Des laid back, grinning. "That was fantastic."

"I'm gonna clean myself up," said Julian, climbing on wobbly legs off the couch and scurrying to his room.

He pulled the door to his nook shut behind him, glaring down at the mess. Once he his pants, the evidence was more obvious than before. He peeled his underwear back, using it as a rag to wipe away the rest of his release. For a moment, he stood frozen in place, unable to move. His heart pounded in his chest as he pictured Des sprawled out on the sofa.

Resting his face in his hands, he took in a deep breath.

"You alright?" called Des from outside of the door.

Julian quickly tucked the soiled underwear into the dirty clothing bin, pulling on a clean pair. He forced a smile as he stood alone.

"Just a second," he replied.

Des gave a tired laugh before lounging back down onto the couch. Julian approached hesitantly, noticing suddenly that the television was still playing.

"I guess we never turned that off," mused Des.

"Guess not," agreed Julian, hesitantly sitting on the other side of the couch. "Want to watch a movie? Like, for real?"

"Sure," agreed Des, lazily leaning back against the arm of the couch.

Julian pictured himself climbing back atop the man their legs tangled together as they drifted off. He shook the image from his mind as he began to flip through options.

"We don't have to ever talk about this again, if you don't want," Julian blurted.

Des suddenly sat up, eyes no longer distant. Julian struggled to read the other man's expression even as he stared deeply. "I mean, if you want."

"We're both drunk," said Julian. "We weren't really thinking. I don't want you to worry about a silly mistake. "

"Do you think it was a mistake?" asked Des.

"I— Julian stopped himself. "It doesn't matter what I think so long as is doesn't destroy what we had. A friendship, I mean."

Des tugged on Julian's shirt, pulling him in until his lips brushed against the other man's ear, "Nothing wrong with a fuck between good friends, is there?"

Julian's heart leaped. "I guess not."

CHAPTER FIFTEEN

Julian blinked awake to Anna's glare beside him in the crowded lecture hall.

"What's going on with you?" she asked, her tone sharp.

"Nothing," he muttered, standing and shaking off the stiffness in his leg.

"Either something's seriously wrong, or you've just given up," she said, arms crossed. "You've been slipping for weeks."

Julian had no chance to answer before she spun on her glossy heels and melted into the crowd.

He trudged through the halls, his head heavy, thoughts spiraling back to Syd. He hadn't seen his roommate in two days. No texts, no sign of him—just silence. Guilt bit into him as he thought of their last conversation which hung over him like a cloud hovering just above messy hair.

He squeezed into the crowded elevator, the heat of too many bodies pressing in. When the doors opened on the fourth floor, he slipped out with the weight of isolation descending upon him. Syd had never been the most reliable, but this was different.

Julian sank into a corner of the library, trying to push the thoughts away. His watch buzzed—a message from an unknown number—but he ignored it. There was nothing from Sands, nothing from Syd.

His mind drifted to the thought of living in the luxury apartments under Sands' watch. He'd rather stay in the dingy basement and keep his independence than give up the last shred of dignity for a shiny place under surveillance.

Sighing, he rubbed his neck and stood up, heading back to the elevator. The halls were unusually quiet. Faces were still, eyes downcast. He frowned but stepped inside, the elevator ride to the ground floor seeming longer than usual.

When the doors slid open, the noise hit him like a wall. A mob of students had gathered in the atrium, jeering and shouting. Julian hesitated, weaving through the chaos toward the center. He searched for familiar faces and found Anna, standing with a trio of girls, whispering urgently.

"What's going on?" Julian asked, leaning in.

"Have you seen the video?" Anna shot him a quick glance. "It went out to everyone- same number."

Julian frowned. "Why's everyone swarming?"

Suddenly, a scream echoed from the center of the crowd. "Get the fuck off of me!" A girl shrieked, her voice cracking. "Get away!"

"Clear the area," a deep voice commanded. "Clear the area, or we'll use force."

The crowd parted like a wave, and Julian struggled to keep his balance, nearly shoved to the ground. As the space cleared, he caught sight of the girl. She was thrashing, her arms pinned behind her by an Enforcer. Her face, pale and twisted with defiance, was just visible beneath her wild hair.

"Who is she?" Julian asked, his voice tight.

"I don't know," Anna said quietly, her gaze fixed on the scene. "They think she dropped the video."

"Has she always gone here?" Julian asked, his voice uncertain.

"Not anymore, at least," Anna replied, her voice trembling. "Not now. Did you see it?"

"No," Julian said quickly. "What was it?"

"You don't want to see it," Anna said.

"But what was it?"

"Just be thankful you didn't."

He didn't respond, slowly walking forward as the Enforcer twisted the thrashing woman's arm, her feet coming out from under her. Not waiting for her to get up, he dragged her through the doors and down the stairs. Julian stole a last glance at the back of her head as the Enforcer yanked her towards a parked car. Standing in place, people circulated around him as the day resumed. Eventually, he wandered towards the door, staring up at the gray sky.

He lowered himself to sit on the steps to the university doors, wrapping his arms around one knee. Pulling up his tablet, he quickly found the video sent to everyone.

At first, the file opened an entirely black image. The shot peeled open as if lids raising up, and the lens pointed at a generic gray building. Darkness enveloped his screen again for a split second before the surroundings became clear again. Julian pushed back the progress bar, watching the first few seconds again. Both times, it was as if the camera itself were a blinking, rising and falling as if with an expanding and contracting chest. With the height of the lens, a sense of unease set over Julian as if he were looking through a set of foreign eyes.

The lens turned to the left and then the right before panning down to a pair of worn boots. A knot grew in Julian's stomach. From his device came heavy, panting breaths. The video documented another thirty seconds as the video explored an old alleyway, picking through trash.

"They're coming for you all," a low voice muttered in a steady tone. "They want to watch everything you do so you don't dare step out of line," said the voice, catching on the last word. "Let them see exactly what they're doing."

A lighter clicked, and a trembling hand braced the small flame in front of the lens. The lighter clattered to the ground with a thud, rivaled by the loud breathing. Fire roared up from the ground into a wall of bright flame. It licked upwards at the lens. Deafening screams echoed off the concrete buildings. The camera cut out time and time again as the man closed his eyes, thrashing in pain. Smoke enveloped the scene, and the hands clawed at the lens. In a hoarse voice, the man let out a final proclamation.

"Kill us, and we will be Reborn."

He tumbled to the ground, eyes rolling back in his head, and the video cut off, but the video continued in darkness until the shrieking died as well Bright flames danced on the insides of Julian's eyelids as he clenched them shut. Questions washed over him, flooding in too quickly to address any of them. He shook his head.

He leaned back against the stairs, staring up at the dark sky. A single snowflake settled on his cheek, floating down from beneath the thick clouds and smog. Dark clouds billowed like smoke above him, and for a moment, the image of the licking flames flashed in his mind. Fishing through his backpack, he pulled out a lighter, holding it out before him. As he flicked the lighter, a small flame brightly sprung to life. He threw the lighter to the ground, shattering the fragile plastic. Wires and screws scattered on the concrete.

He stared at the pieces, all useless alone, until a black car pulled up to the curb, slowing down to stop directly in front of the steps. Slowly pushing himself to his feet, Julian limped down the stairs, climbing into the backseat of the car.

The ride was silent and suffocating. No questions. No

explanations. Just the hum of the engine and the weight of whatever waited for him.

He knew to walk around to the back of the building, finding a door with a small light above it cocooned in spiderwebs. He leaned in, squinting in at the frozen corpses of unfortunate insects stuck in the trap. A spider crawled across its creation, glaring up at Julian with many tiny black eyes. He leaned over it, tilting his head as he studied the black voids that stared back at him. The creature's hairy legs moved slowly as the spider climbed further into the safety of its web.

Julian stumbled back as the door flung open, barely missing his face. The elder Peterson stormed out without noticing Julian, slamming an open palm against the concrete wall. With shaky hands, the man rummaged through the pockets of his overcoat, pulling out a small box lined in gold. He produced a cigarette, pinching it between his lips while he fished out a lighter. Julian shielded the flame from the slight breeze. He lit the end, taking a long drag. As he packed away the lighter and box, he froze, catching Julian's wide eyes.

"Sorry," Julian blurted.

Peterson let out a thick cloud that soon dissipated into the air.

"No, I'm sorry, Mr. Harper."

Julian remained quiet, standing by the door and unsure where to put his hands. Eventually, he crossed his arms over his chest, shivering in the cold.

"Progress comes at a price," said Julian eventually.

"I see why Edmund chose you," Peterson muttered. "We need to get a handle on this before outrage spreads. They beat us to the chase, and now we're going to be fighting against their stunt for traction. It's a nightmare," he spat. "We're gonna find them and crush them beneath tons of concrete before we set the whole thing on fire."

"Sir," started Julian, "the sooner we can roll out these surveillance implants, the less likely they'll be able to operate. There's no hiding when every living being is inadvertently feeding us the information we need."

Peterson replied, "As long as you don't pitch that to the people. As far as they're gonna know, we'll need a warrant to access any of the footage, and they'll have the power to delete their own."

"Of course not," Julian said through a forced smile. "After all, it's for the safety of the people in the long run, and that's not a lie."

Peterson approached slowly, with a lumbering gait. He placed a hand on Julian's shoulder, gripping it tightly. With the man so close, he caught the slight odor of alcohol on the man's breath. Julian ducked slightly as if he might slink away, looking up at the taller man. In the back of his mind, he saw Des in the man's gray eyes, and he squirmed.

"You're a good kid. You understand that?

"I—uh, thank you, Mr. Peterson."

The man pulled him into an embrace, pinning Julian's arms to his side so he could not reciprocate had he wanted to.

"You've been like a son to me. Like a big brother the way you take care of my Desmond. And now you're a part of the family business. I have half a mind to pass the dynasty onto you. Blood isn't all that matters. It's loyalty and drive. My man, you're going to do great things," he said.

Julian remained quiet, the air pushed from his lungs as Peterson held him in place, rocking him slightly from one side to the other on the cold pavement. He almost jumped at the sound of a click, and the door to the building swung open. Agner stood inside, arms crossing over his chest and a look of distaste on his face. Waiting for Peterson to remove himself, Agner gave a slight cough, as if clearing his throat. At this, Peterson looked up, loosening the grip on Julian as he did. Julian gently pulled away, taking the chance to turn his attention to the disgruntled man in the doorway. This time, he wore black joggers and a white tee-shirt, the back soaked through as if he'd been interrupted in the middle of a workout. His damp hair crispened at the ends in the cold.

Peterson spoke again.

"We're fighting an uphill battle. Once we roll out the Vision, there's so much left to do. It never ends. The technology is there, but the people just aren't ready."

"Dan, we have too much shit to get done for cigarette breaks and complaining. Smoke inside if you have to, and get a therapist," muttered Agner. "You too, Harper, get in here. You can chit-chat later."

Julian followed Agner in through the doorway, trailing closely behind him through the unfamiliar yet eerily predictable building. It was designed like any other in this sector of the city, with its long hallways and separate rooms blocked off by heavy doors. As he glanced back, he realized PetersonMartin Peterson had not followed the group in, and Agner slammed the door behind Julian, pacing to the front of the room.

Julian noted Elex jotting something down while the Martinez twins both leaned back in their chairs as if indifferent to the entire situation. Peterson did not join them, but out of the three new faces, he wondered if one of them was a Loget Tech representative. Two men in decorated military uniforms sat at the far end of the long table on either side of Agner, who stood at the head. Julian fidgeted in his seat, tapping his foot against the ground. Another character sat beside Elex with thick glasses and a bright purple eyeshadow.

"Has everyone seen the video?" asked Agner.

Julian grunted acknowledgement. Agner smiled, eyes shining.

"Well, just in case you've forgotten it, I'm going to play it again so we all grasp the gravity of the situation," Agner said, pulling up a projection on the wall in front of the group.

Julian's stomach twisted in knots as the footage rolled. He wanted to look away or at the very least close his eyes, but Agner straddled his chair to watch the group, studying each face in the room.

"We've all seen it," interrupted one man in uniform, turning off the footage. "The seriousness of the situation is clear to us all. If you want to watch that over and over again later and jack yourself off, that's on you, but we have work to get done."

"Colonel Philips," Agner addressed coldly, "I thought everyone should remember that we're fighting animals who light themselves on fire for a spectacle. They want attention. We need to react accordingly."

Colonel Philips planted his hands on the table in front of him, staring down Agner, "Yes, yes, we are all aware of that. But you seem to have a fondness for theatrics too. Maybe you should go join them."

"I know you aren't suggesting treason, Colonel. We have an issue to attend to, and we have no time to waste."

"I'm glad you agree we shouldn't waste time," said Philips. The man had dark skin and a beard that wrapped around his face and onto his upper lip, peppered with emerging gray. Beneath his cap, Julian could tell he had a shaved head, and thick eyebrows lowered like storm clouds above his eyes.

Philips declared authority with a deep commanding tone, "We know they're operating in the same district as us. I'm ready to deploy full forces to sweep every building until we find those fuckers and put a bullet through each of their skulls."

One of the twins, Julian had difficulty remembering which was which, chimed in, "That would be shortsighted."

"And why is that?" asked the Colonel.

"They'll record it again," she said. "They'll become martyrs. We need eyes on them immediately. Find them and watch them."

"They just arrested some girl," Julian piped up. "We get the information out of her."

The Colonel looked at Julian as if noticing him for the first time. "You're right. If we just ask her nicely, I'm sure she'll let us know."

"I'm not talking about asking nicely," Julian said coldly.

Agner shrugged, as if amused by the proposition.

"Maybe they saw something in you after all."

The Colonel shook his head. "This all takes too long. If it weren't for our operations here, I'd say we level this entire sector of the city."

"But we have operations here, and we're not some primal dictatorship. I say we let the girl go and let her lead us right back into the nest," suggested Agner.

The Colonel shook his head.

"Do you not understand? Is there nothing going on in that thick skull of yours?" his raised voice boomed off of the walls. "She's a sacrificial pawn. She knows she can't go back, and on the off chance that she does, I'm sure she'll be killed before she can lead us anywhere. You think all eyes aren't on her right now? If you don't want me to take matters into my own hands, you'd best get some answers out of that girl and now."

"She's my classmate," said Julian quietly.

"You know the terrorist?" the Colonel barked.

"No. I mean, I don't know her, but we go to the same university. Let me talk to her."

Agner waved his hand.

"No, this requires a proper interrogation. You need to go track down her little friends. That university is a breeding ground for treasonous ideology. We need to flush the whole institution for professors pushing these radical narratives, and any students who are expressing such sentiments need to learn their place or be immediately expelled. I expect you to come up with a list to start with. Once we have a few, they'll rat each other out."

"What kind of radical ideas are we talking about?" asked Julian.

"Anything against the economic system, leadership, the state. Anyone who gives even a sliver of humanity to these terrorists. We don't need that poisoning Lancut's pool of future civil servants. I want the worst of them at the top of the list, but anyone with sympathies towards these people should be noted and taken care of in a less severe capacity," ordered Agner.

"This will take time. A few weeks—"

The Colonel cut him off.

"No, it won't. You have one week to get us a list of names to start with, and as you finish your semester, you'll continue to feed us more."

Julian's heart thudded in his chest, a list of names already accumulating in his mind. The writing was in crimson red. He smudged away the names until they were illegible, but his throat felt as if it were constricting in on itself and he would soon begin to choke on the stuffy air in the cramped room. With the walls closing in on him, he nodded.

"Yes, sir," he said. "I'll do everything I can to help take down The Reborn."

"We're going to snuff that light out," said the Colonel gruffly.

"Are we?" asked Agner. "Because I heard you still haven't found our mole. Isn't that your job?"

The Colonel glowered at Agner. "We're looking into the possibility that there isn't a mole at all. Though, so far, we have found no data to have been stolen during the attack despite the initial presidential report," he said sourly.

"You can't accept that someone slipped past you?" taunted Agner. "I bet it's someone you've met half a million times and never looked at twice. I'm going to get myself put on the task force and do your job for you."

The colonel slammed a hand down on the table.

"Oh, I have my suspects. This will be dealt with, and I suggest you stop speaking otherwise. All in due time, Agner," he spat.

Julian broke the heavy silence, "Do you have any idea what department the breach came from? I mean, do we think that's how The Reborn got access to the technology before it's been released to the public?"

Snapping his attention to Julian, the colonel sneered, "Of course they did. How else would they have gotten it?"

"I'm not sure, sir," he admitted.

"If I had to guess, it's either someone in this room with us, or someone high up in Loget Tech, and whoever they are," the man slowly scanned across the faces in the room, "will be dealt with in a fitting manner to the damage they have caused."

CHAPTER SIXTEEN

The letter arrived in a cream-colored envelope with Julian's name carefully printed in black ink. As he held it, he resisted the instinct to crumple the fragile paper in his hand. Standing outside of Lancut Tower, he let his head fall back to absorb the looming building in its entirety. Lights stretched to the top, glowing above any other building in the city. He shuddered, the suit jacket shifting awkwardly on his shoulders.

A man and a woman sauntered past him. The man stared at him, looking him up and down before muttering something to his date. Dressed in a long green gown, the woman wore gold hoops that dangled from her ears. Her carefully manicured nails caught the city light as her hands brushed against her sides with her long strides. She placed her hand in his, and together they walked through the front doors and vanished inside.

Julian swallowed a growing wad of spit, yet his mouth was too dry to speak had he wanted to. His feet slid in the shoes despite the two layers of socks he wore. The slick pavement did not aid him. Like an unsteady foal, he hesitantly walked inside. As the door drifted shut behind him, he stood in awe, staring up at the cracked ceiling. He fell back on his good leg as he examined the golden veins traveling through the webbed fingers, where the cracked stone was fused back together. With the rubble cleared away, the open space shone brightly with polished stone, catching the light bouncing from a new chandelier. Crystal dripped elegantly down into four extravagant layers.

"Sir, may I guide you to the party?" a voice broke him from his enamored trance.

With a glance to his left and then his right towards the man in a tuxedo, Julian smiled coolly.

"Yes, please," he replied.

"Can I ask for your phone, watch, tablet or any other devices capable of recording?" the man requested.

"Uh," Julian started, heart throbbing. "I, um, I'm waiting for an important message from my mother. She's ill, and I can't risk missing any calls."

"I'm sorry to hear. We can monitor your watch for you, and we will alert you if any messages of such a nature come in," said the man nonchalantly.

Julian scrambled, "I would prefer to monitor it myself. This is a private family matter."

"I'm afraid I must confiscate all devices capable of recording. We will carefully store these for you to retrieve upon departure," the man said, an air of annoyance in his tone.

Unbuckling his watch, Julian cautiously handed place it into a velvet bag the man produced. He moved his hand across his back pocket, tracing the device's shape before pausing. The man continued to study him, holding the bag open in front of him.

"Your phone, sir," requested the man.

"I'm afraid I don't have any other devices to give you. I rely on my watch," said Julian with a smile.

The man nodded, gesturing for the man to follow him. Beside the elevator, two carved posts stood proudly on either side of the door.

"Can I see your invitation?" the man prompted.

Julian pulled out the paper, now damp with sweat. The man unlocked a tablet, scanning over the letter with his device.

Nodding, he gestured to the elevator. Julian considered asking what floor to get off on, but he struggled to form words. As he headed towards the doors, he walked between the two posts. An alarm buzzed.

"Walk back between the posts in the opposite direction," commanded the man.

Julian forced a laugh, "Huh, I wonder if my chains set it off."

When he walked backward through the posts, the alarms buzzed sharply.

"Arms up," said the man sternly.

"I—I, um," started Julian.

Before he managed to choke out a sentence, the man started at Julian's shoulders, patting down the collar of his shirt. Julian's heart pounded in his chest, and he realized his raised hands trembled. As the man worked his way down, Julian closed his eyes. Hands prodded at his abdomen, grazing over the curve of his lower back until the man stopped over his back pocket. Reaching in, the man pulled Julian's phone out, holding it directly in front of Julian's nose before dropping it into the velvet bag. Julian slowly lowered his arms, managing a weak laugh.

The man said nothing, but his heavy glare paralyzed Julian even as the elevator doors opened. Stumbling inside, he faced the wall, refusing to turn to meet the man's judgmental eyes. Shortly after he stepped in, the doors opened to a swarm of people mingling about. Any impression from the ground floor cowed compared to the arrogant display of wealth before him. Clinging to ears, wrists and necks alone, Julian guessed the room held thousands of precious stones. Stacks of brightly colored fruits adorned tables covered in silk cloths throughout the sprawling room. People dressed in sleek tuxedos carried drinks with slim stems on black trays.

Julian plucked one from a passing woman. The peach liquid inside rippled. Holding it up to his nose, he quickly sniffed the glass. Julian stood with one hand shoved into his pocket, staring down at his feet. Bracing himself with a smile, he forced himself into the crowd. People circulated around, speaking to one another, voices melding together.

A man lingered at the edge of the cluster, slowly sipping on a martini. Julian approached, raising up a fresh drink in greeting. The man nodded at him.

"Hi, I'm Julian Harper. I received the Presidential Internship, so I've only been working for Lancut for a couple months," Julian said. "I've never been to one of these events before."

The man grunted. "They're something."

"I suppose we just mingle? It's always good to make connections. What's your name?" Julian asked.

"Bill," the man replied.

Julian stood, shifting weight from one leg to the other.

"Well, I'm going to keep doing my rounds, but it was great to meet you. Hopefully, we'll work together someday."

"Hopefully," said the man.

Julian quickly walked away. He noted a familiar man in a rusted orange suit. Out of his uniform, his broad shoulders were more prominent, straining against the tailored fabric. The man's face twisted in a way Julian didn't consider possible. With a bright white smile, Colonel Philips laughed, resting his hand around the waist of a woman dressed in a black gown. Ornate beading covered the bodice, becoming increasingly scattered as the fabric neared the ground.

Once he found an opening in the small circle, Julian slipped into the arrangement, studying the other members. When Colonel Philips glimpsed him, the man stumbled over on unsteady feet, glass sloshing. Philips offered a hand to Julian. The man crushed Julian's fragile fingers before suddenly letting go.

"Colonel, it's wonderful to meet you in a less tumultuous environment," said Julian.

The colonel patted him on the back firmly.

"It's good to see you here. See, Lancut knows how to take care of their people, boost morale. This is my wife, Fiona. Fiona, this is the young intern Sands hired," he addressed his wife. He redirected his attention to Julian, speaking in what Philips considered a hushed tone, yet his voice still traveled.

"Don't take Agner too seriously. He has a stick up his ass."

The man exploded into laughter.

"You're doing good, man."

"Hey, I, uh—I appreciate that," said Julian. "This is some serious stuff we're dealing with."

"Oh, none of that bullshit here," said Philips. "Relax, have a drink, and let yourself have a good time."

Julian smiled. "I know, but I'm sure you never completely can turn it off."

The man sighed. "You're right. But I'm wise enough to know that when I'm a few drinks in that I can't work. That's the blessing of it."

Julian hesitated.

"But now feels like the perfect time. So many important people who might let something slip when they otherwise wouldn't."

"If you want to interrogate strangers, but I'm going to enjoy myself," said the man.

The man led his wife through the crowd. Julian stood, unsure where to turn. Another hand fell on his shoulder, and he flinched. Turning around, a man dressed in an identical fashion to the other servers stood at his side, but he did not hold a tray.

"Follow me," said the man.

Julian didn't have the chance to ask the man anything before he was chasing him through the crowd. He moved swiftly, weaving through the throng of partygoers. The man led him to a door Julian initially glanced over. Plain and white, Julian assumed it to be a storage closet. When the man pulled out a physical key, Julian stepped back, scanning the room behind him. As he opened the door, Julian recognized the interior as an elevator car. The man forced Julian into the elevator, placing a guiding hand on his shoulder. His heart leaped as the man shut the door behind them, pressing the only button.

During the ride, Julian clasped his hands behind his back. The dim red lighting cast the other man in a warm hue. When the elevator halted, the door opened automatically. Deep blue lights made the landscape difficult to decipher. The room, while small, showcased a bar with an unlimited number of bottles lined up on shelves. The bartender worked behind the counter, turning around briefly. Her bare chest glowed in the light. Long blonde hair swished at her back. When she turned around once more, she leaned down, and Julian glanced away quickly.

At the corner of the room, a group of men circled a pool table. They took their turns lining up their cues to take a shot. The man guided Julian towards another edge of the room in a curved booth. A woman straddled him, facing away from Julian.

"Sir," said Julian's guide.

Sands snapped twice, and the woman climbed off of him, disappearing into the dim room. The man smiled, waving for Julian. The guide quietly departed, leaving the two men alone. Julian approached the booth, standing until Sands patted the seat beside him. His eyes darted throughout the room, taking stock of the faces.

"I'm glad you made it," said Sands.

"I am too," said Julian.

His leg bounced on the ground as he glanced around.

The bartender approached. The light caught her long legs as she elegantly strolled towards the men with a drink in each hand. She towered over the sitting men in shimmering red heels. When she down the drinks, Julian offered a smile of gratitude. Studying the bubbles rising to the top of the drink, he hoped he imagined something settling at the bottom. His stomach dropped.

"Oh, I've had far too much to drink," said Julian. "You're so generous."

"That's alright," Sands replied. "I just wanted your company. This is somewhere I bring people I'm fully confident I can trust. It's an escape from reality. You can be anyone you want while you're here. I understand you weren't too keen on the personal device policy, but that makes all of this possible.

"I want you to have a good time without worrying about silly messages, or god-forbid someone takes an uncompromising photo. The only cameras allowed here are Lancut security devices for safety purposes. In seven days, all footage is wiped automatically. Nobody handles the footage."

"I appreciate the precaution."

"Kick back," offered Sands. "This is the highest quality you can find."

"That's alright, sir," Julian said.

"You need to learn to accept what's given to you," said Sands, planting a hand on the back of Julian's neck, pushing him down lightly.

Julian did not resist, closing his eyes. Mind racing, he inhaled through his nose quickly. Sputtering, he sat up, tears welling up in his eyes. He sneezed twice in rapid succession. Sands laughed, gesturing at the mess of spread about the table. Julian's face burned.

"First time?"

"Yeah," he admitted, his pulse racing. Suddenly, he felt the way his skin fell on his body, yet his mind cleared. The cloud of exhaustion lifted. "Woah."

"It's startling the first time," said Sands. "How do you feel?"

"Alive," Julian replied without a thought.

Sands leaned in close, a grin on his face.

"Let me find you someone nice for the evening."

"Oh, um, that's alright," stuttered Julian.

"Why? Is there someone else already?" asked Sands.

He stuttered, "No. I have classes early tomorrow, is all."

"None of that matters anymore," replied Sands. "How does it feel to be on the other side? You've finally made it. You don't need to worry about school because Lancut will take care of you. We take care of our people. Come stay in Lancut housing, and this can be your life."

Julian's mind raced, thoughts passing by too quickly to focus on any one idea. His jaw tightened, and he tried to relax his muscles. Tears rose to Julian's eyes, catching the blue lights and casting his face in gaunt shadows. Quickly turning away, he stood up.

"I appreciate the offer," said Julian, "but I can't take you up on it."

Sands shook his head. "That's alright. I'm sure you'll find your way. My people always do."

CHAPTER SEVENTEEN

Julian savored the walk home from the university. Dressed in corduroy pants and a sweater, he sweat soaked through his undershirt as the sun emerged from behind the sprawling clouds that hung low in the sky. The damp smell of spring was no rival to the odor of the city, but it was a welcomed addition. Julian walked down the side of the road, eventually crossing the street to his apartment.

Once he stumbled inside, he kicked off his shoes, and he let his head fall back for a moment, staring up at the strange splotches of rotting ceiling tiles. He sneered at a document blank save for a singular line: names. Past that, he couldn't bring himself to write anything more. In class, he could simply look around and jot down the names of anyone not reciting the pledge to the nation. Even easier, he was all too familiar with a professor whose name should be at the very top of the list, yet every time he set his pen down to his screen, he did not manage to scrawl down more than "Dr." before stopping, quickly erasing as if that were betrayal in itself. Dr. Cruz was an enemy of the state, he told himself. There were plenty more to be found if he just thought. Yet, at the top of his mind, one individual stood out in front of the others for crimes greater than any others combined. So long as he kept that to himself, he might as well write his own name instead.

In the dingy apartment, the brutal silence swallowed him. In a decaying shoebox of an apartment, Julian was entirely alone beside for a plate his roommate left out on the counter days ago.

A slight stench from Syd's room ruminated through the small apartment. Julian silently swore. He ignored the growing odor for the past two days, leaving it for his roommate to return to as petty punishment for abandonment. Yet, Julian concluded it was only himself who was being punished.

Trotting over to the room, he gave a knock. When he heard no response, he fiddled with the handle, shaking it, yet the knob failed to budge. He rummaged through the junk drawer in the kitchen until pulled out one of the extra keys. He inserted it into the mechanism, then turned the key until the door drifted open. The hinges moaned.

The odor slammed into Julian like a wall as he stood in the doorway. Immediately, he clamped a hand over his mouth and nose, venturing into the room. Two sweatshirts lay carelessly in lumps on the ground. A pile of pillows and blankets formed lumps on top of Syd's bed, which was pushed against the wall in the corner. Nearing, Julian traced the distinct form of a human tucked beneath a deep red fleece blanket. As he slowly crept closer, he gagged on the air, heart throbbing in his chest. He hovered a hand above the covered form, hesitantly grabbing the edge of the blanket, turning away as he pulled it back.

He stole a look before dropping the blanket, stumbling back. He gasped, only to gag on the rancid odor. Syd's face, drained of color, stared back at him with dull pale eyes. Dried vomit pooled on the sheet beside his face, remnants clinging dried to his cheek and chin. Dark bruises circled his neck with splotches the size and shape of grapes. Hesitantly, Julian pulled the blanket back the rest of the way to unveil the body, statuesque with rigor mortis. In his hand, Syd clutched his watch, fingers enclosed like a vise. Julian stood, unable to so much as cry. He stared at the cold corpse, taking in ragged breaths. Julian clasped his hands behind his head, closing his eyes as he ran through the scenario.

He broke free from his trance long enough to dial the emergency number on his watch, and waited for the dial tone.

"Public emergency services," answered a voice. "Can I get your location?"

"My roommate is dead. I think he was strangled, but I'm not sure," he stammered.

"Where are you located?" the woman asked again calmly.

"Oh, uh, ninety-four Wiles Street apartment D. He's not breathing."

The voice on the other end responded, "Do you know how to perform CPR?"

"He's dead. Like, I think he's been dead. He's really stiff."

"Are you in a safe environment?" asked the operator.

"Yes," Julian said. "I mean, I think. I don't know. Please, just send someone."

"We're extremely busy at this time, so since you are not in immediate danger, you can expect someone in the next two to three hours," said the woman coldly. "Please call back if this situation becomes urgent."

Frantically, he swiped through his contacts, landing on Des' name. He impatiently paced into the small kitchen, slamming the door behind him. When Des responded, he sounded winded.

"Hey, what's up?" Des asked, panting into the microphone.

"Des," started Julian, "Syd's dead. I don't know for how long, but he's dead in the apartment, and they're not gonna be here for a few hours."

"Did you contact public emergency?" he asked.

"Yeah," replied Julian, running his fingers through his curly hair. "I think he was strangled. I don't know what's going on. He was clutching onto his watch like he didn't fight back, or couldn't fight back. I don't know what happened."

Des spoke calmly on the other end of the phone, "Okay, I'll be right over. Are you sure he's dead?"

Julian wanted to scream that, of course, he was dead. His corpse lay in his bed, pale and stiff, radiating an undeniable stench.

"He's dead. I know he's dead."

"I'm coming over," he repeated.

"You don't have to," Julian urged. "Really, I just—he's dead. He's dead in the apartment. I don't even know for how long."

"I'll be over in ten minutes," insisted Des, hanging up the phone before Julian could protest.

He planted his face in his hands, forcing a deep breath in through his nose. Julian sank down against the bedroom wall, wrapping his arms around his knees.

He never met Syd's family. There was never enough space to bring over more than one guest for dinner, but Syd mentioned stories of his mother and father growing up. Julian was certain Syd mentioned at least one sibling. They had the right to know, but they didn't need to see him in this state.

The emergency team would take care of the situation. Once they launched an investigation, they would uncover the truth of his fate. A dull thudding on the door grabbed Julian's attention. As he walked up the stairs, he opened the door, prepared to meet the emergency squad. Instead, Des stood in the doorway, his shoulders damp with snow. Julian stepped aside as Des walked down the stairs, and Julian pulled the door shut.

"You made it here before the emergency team," remarked Julian.

"Are you okay?" he asked, pulling Julian into a tight embrace.

Julian pushed his face into the other man's warmth, clenching his eyes shut.

"I'm okay. I don't know what happened," he mumbled through the fabric in his face. "He's dead. I don't know what's going on. I think he was strangled. Someone was in the apartment. I don't know how long-"

"We should get out of here until the emergency squad comes," Des cut him off.

"I can't leave him," argued Julian. "I need to stay here. All he wanted to do was move out, and all I cared about was his share of the rent. And now he's dead. He'll never move anywhere."

"You had nothing to do with that," said Des, loosening his grip on Julian. "And you don't need to worry about rent money. Please, I'm begging you to just take care of yourself."

"Des, there are things more evil than death," he sobbed, burrowing his face back into Des' chest. "I don't want to die, but I can't live like this."

Des held Julian, rocking him through his stifled sobs. Julian felt his tears leaving behind damp spots on Des' shirt. His body convulsed as the distress surged through him. He was unable to decipher if it was anger, despair or desperation, but it dragged cries from his shivering body.

"Once you speak with the emergency team, you can stay with me. Please, you don't need to stay here," Des pleaded. "It's clearly not safe."

Julian shook his head, "I won't. But I can't stay with Sands. I know what this is. I know who's responsible for this… I'll stay here. I don't want anything from you other than you, and I don't want you to think that—" he sobbed, unable to push out the words. Instead, the tears continued to flow. "I can't betray you. I can't betray you. They want me to betray you and Cruz and everyone. I can't do it."

"What?" asked Des, pulling away for a moment.

"Anyone who has any sympathy for change, for The Reborn. I'm supposed to make a list. I can't, Des. What am I supposed to do?" he managed.

Des gripped Julian by the shoulders, "You don't have to do any of that."

"Yes, I do," Julian slurred. "They'll burn this apartment down until I move into their housing. They'll kill me before they let me go. There's no choice."

"You have a choice, Julian," said Des. "We all have a choice to make. Do you stand by any of what you're doing? Do you even know the extent of what they're doing?"

"They want me to betray everyone," repeated Julian. "They want me to betray Dr. Cruz. Anyone who opposes any of it. They want me to betray anyone with sympathy for the rebels. And I can't pretend to not know forever."

Des drew back, face pale, "Not to know what?"

"Not to know who they are. They want a list," said Julian, avoiding Des' gaze. "They gave me a week. And I know. I know more than they think I do. More than you think I do."

Des gripped his chin, forcing his eyes to lock with the other man's.

"Julian—"

"No," Julian cried. "I don't know anything. Unless I'm told, I have no proof. I don't know."

"Julian, I know you know. And I'm okay with that."

Julian violently shook his head.

"Philips doesn't know. Agner doesn't know. Sands doesn't know. I don't know anything."

Des gripped Julian harshly by the shoulders, leaning in. His warm breath brushed Julian's face, gentle in contrast to rough hands. "Tell me."

"I know you're who they're looking for," Julian blurted, "and you have access to all of your father's work. Nobody would ever suspect you. I know you're one," spat Julian. "I know you're one of them, and..."

"And?" asked Des quietly. "And what?"

"I can't betray you," he said. "And I can't betray myself," he spat. "I can't be a part of this anymore. And now Syd is dead too, and his blood is on my hands."

"That's not your fault—"

"He's dead because of me. Fate doesn't favor the rich unless they tamper with it," said Julian.

A sudden calm settled over him as the words left his mouth. As he pulled back from Des, he saw the knot with clarity, but he also found the end strand that would unwind it all. The world around him crispened. The constant buzzing in the back of his mind momentarily silenced- snuffed out like a flame.

"I'm not going to kill anyone else. I have too much blood on my hands already, and I've just begun. The only reason he ever took me on was as a pawn to control. He holds my life in his hands like a god in his glass tower. Well, he's not a god. Not mine at least."

The apartment fell into complete silence. Des looked into Julian's eyes, holding him up by the shoulders. Julian dipped his head in submission.

"So, is it true?" asked Julian in a hushed tone.

Des didn't hesitate. "Yes."

"Okay," he said. "I won't betray you."

"I know you won't. Does anyone else know?" asked Des.

"I'm not sure, but I don't think so. They think it's someone working for your father, but the man in charge didn't bring up family. Nobody will ever know," he said. "And I don't plan on changing that."

"Thank you," said Des. The two stood in silence for a few moments. "What are you going to do?"

Julian smiled weakly. "I'm not sure. If I don't work for Lancut, they'll have me killed in April. If you pay off my debts, it'll draw attention to you. We're in far too deep. The walls are closing in. You and I can't live in this world."

"I'll take you to them," blurted Des. "But if I do, you can't come back."

"What?" Julian managed.

"If you join them, if you're Reborn, I mean, there's no going back," said Des. "But it's a way."

Julian sat silently, mulling the words over in his mind, "How free am I if I lose everything?"

"Not everything. Not forever. They can deactivate your Disc. You'll be a ghost."

"But how?" asked Julian. "How is that even possible?"

Des shook his head, "That's a secret. Far beyond my place. They recruited me for the occasional project, but they don't dare bring someone like me in. Let me bring them to you. You have inside knowledge. You have relationships with these higher ups, but you're more trustworthy than me. You have debts. Change is coming. Can't you feel it in the air?" asked Des.

"If I do this, there's no return," said Julian.

"Yes," agreed Des.

"This isn't right," he said. "It was never supposed to be like this. Climb the ladder with hard work. But there is no ladder, is there?"

"Not for you," admitted Des, "not there. But you've scaled the building yourself, and you're dangling from the ledge while someone offers you a hand. You just have to reach out and take it."

Before he responded, a knock on the door cut through the building energy in the room, and Julian nearly leaped out of his seat. "I'll talk to the emergency squad," said Julian. "You should get out of here. Who knows if this place is bugged?"

Des stood up, pulling Julian into an embrace. "Please, come with me tonight."

"Lancut is my only way out. Edmund Sands is an evil man, but it's the only choice."

"It's not. History is being made, and we're going to be a part of it," urged Des. "Please, I'll meet you tonight at the bar. Eleven. I can take you to them, or we can drink until we forget."

"I work for Edmund Sands; for Lancut. Why do you trust me?"

"Because I know you, Julian. And I have no doubt you'll do what's right, even if it's not for yourself," he said, planting a kiss on his lips before fleeing up the stairs and slipping through the door.

CHAPTER EIGHTEEN

They hauled the body out in a black plastic bag. If it weren't for the formal way in which they carried it, careful not to tip it over or jostle it, Julian would have assumed it was trash being brought out to the street. He asked the Enforcers if he could get the information to contact Syd's next of kin, but they told him that was private information, and that they would take care to notify the family. Julian promised himself he would find the information. Somewhere buried amongst his belongings, he would find a clue. Perhaps some crumpled up note or, even better, a number to call.

Julian lay on the couch, staring up at the ceiling. Time trickled by, and Julian agitatedly rearranged his legs, never finding an adequate position. He resigned himself to discomfort, staring off, eyes glazing over. Dancing in his vision, memories of the fire tainted his mind, and he clenched them shut until he only saw darkness.

He repeated Des' words to himself. No matter what happened, he promised himself he would not turn in Des. He could put together a list, but in no world would Des' name be at the top. Though, he knew that was nothing more than kicking the can down the road, and one day their relationship would draw attention, yet to cut any contact at all would do the same. Every time he ran the scenario, altering it slightly, the outcome remained the same. Eventually, Des' name was spat out of Edmund Sands' mouth, and his corpse lay lifeless in front of

Julian. In some cases, he just disappeared. In others, he was executed publicly or murdered on the spot. Julian wanted to push the idea from his mind, but he forced himself to sit with the swirling darkness rising up to his neck, lapping at his chin.

Julian's eyelids drooped with exhaustion, and sleep claimed him- a brief refuge from the chaos of consciousness. In his dreams, Des sat beside him by a vast waterway. Two crows perched on an oak branch, the hum of insects blending with the night. Julian reached out, brushing his fingers over Des's face where a Disc should have marred the skin, but found nothing. Des tilted his head, pressing a larger hand over Julian's. Bathed in the amber light of sunset, Des smiled, and the warmth lingered.

Julian woke slowly, saliva at the corner of his mouth, his blurry vision settling on the stillness of the apartment. The hum of the refrigerator and his shallow breaths were the only sounds. A glance at his watch—ten o'clock. Dread churned as time slipped away, but he shoved it aside, forcing himself to his feet.

In the bathroom mirror, he caught sight of his patchy, unkempt facial hair. Razor in hand, he cleared away the wiry stragglers, then brushed his teeth meticulously, scrubbing his tongue until the taste of sleep faded. A gray jacket and scarf completed his preparation, and he stepped into the night.

The warming weather did little to dull the wind's bite. With his jacket held tightly, Julian kept his head down, trudging beneath the dead glow of streetlights. As he left the residential area, cars passed, and distant sirens and laughter reminded him of the city's pulse. He passed business people smoking beneath a red awning, their faces shadowed by the glow of their cigarettes, and continued along alleyways past shuttered businesses with glaring neon signs.

The city's artificial lights formed a cosmos of their own,

a world where looming buildings and the electric glow surrounding him hid the stars. But that sunset lingered in his thoughts—trees swaying in the breeze, birds perched like silent gods. It felt impossible, a dream too vivid to ignore.

He cut through an alley reeking of rot. When he emerged on the other side, he wiped his palm on his pants and sniffed against the chill. He pulled open a door, stepping inside.

The room was dimly lit, smoky, and alive with murmured voices. He counted six people: two engrossed in cards, others scattered. At the bar, Des sat hunched over a glass of amber liquid, swirling it idly. From across the room, Julian felt the weight of Des's presence—the way he seemed to glow in the curling smoke, magnetic and unshakable.

Julian pulled a stool noisily from the bar and climbed onto it. Des glanced over, faintly smiling, as he raised the glass to his lips. Their eyes locked, the silence between them louder than the room. A grim-faced bartender shuffled over, wiping the counter with a stained rag, but Julian's attention stayed fixed on Des, his heart thrumming.

"What can I get for you?" he asked.

"He'll take rum," said Des before Julian spoke. The bartender nodded and turned around.

"Rum?" questioned Julian.

"Rum," repeated Des. "Seems fitting."

"Sure," agreed Julian.

The man returned with his drink, setting it in front of Julian. Des looked over with a somber smile, the light of the sign on the window catching his eyes and reflecting orange against his gray irises.

"It's too stuffy in here," remarked Julian. "Would you like to go for a walk?"

Des finished his drink, dropping the glass back down onto the bar without care. "It's still early," he said. "Are you sure?"

"I've thought about taking a walk for the past few hours," said Julian hesitantly, "and yes, there are plenty of things outside I'd like to avoid. I might be hit by a car, or mugged, or stabbed. He paused, taking another sip, letting it settle in his stomach before continuing. "But in here, I could just as easily end up in a fight or someone could slip something into my drink. I guess… what I'm saying is that I don't necessarily want to stay here or go on a walk, but I will go on a walk."

"I won't hold it against you if you'd rather stay inside," said Des.

"I've made my decision," he said, finishing his drink and gently setting the cleared glass on the scratched wooden counter in front of him. "Will you walk with me?"

"Only if you're certain."

"I've never been certain about anything in my life," replied Julian, "until now."

Des nodded, stepping down from the stool. He swayed on his feet slightly, but once he regained his footing, he gestured for Julian to follow. The frigid air had only worsened since Julian's walk, or perhaps he'd become too comfortable indoors, accustomed now to a life of cars and convenience. Gently taking Julian's hand, Des tugged him towards the alleyway beside the building. Julian glanced over his shoulder for any prying eyes or knowing looks, but the street appeared empty. Beneath the dim lights, Julian traced the contours of Des' face with his eyes. He reached out, gently brushing his hand against the other man's cheek.

Des grabbed Julian's shoulder with a firm hand, pushing him up against the alley wall, knocking the wind from Julian's lungs.

The man gasped- electricity coursing through his body.

"I don't know what's going to happen next," said Des, "nobody does anymore."

Des pressed Julian against the wall, his hand firm on Julian's chest as he leaned in closer. Julian's breath hitched, his body tense under the weight of Des's touch. A faint whimper escaped him, his face flushing as Des's lips brushed against his neck and jaw, soft yet deliberate. Des' hand moved from Julian's chest, trailing to slip beneath his waistband as he pinned Julian with his weight.

"Quiet," Des murmured near Julian's ear, his voice low. He traced his fingers along Julian's stomach, then lower and lower. Julian bit his lip, stifling the sounds threatening to spill.

The air between them buzzed in the cold alleyway. Julian's fingers dug into the wall behind him, trying to ground himself. Des's movements were slow and deliberate, his touch both reassuring and overwhelming. Julian lost all sense of time in the haze of pleasure. As Julian's head fell back against the brick, he felt a sudden, sharp clarity mixed with the haze of sensation, his breaths coming unevenly.

Des pulled back slightly, his hands still steady, his gaze locked on Julian's flushed face. Even as Julian trembled, Des remained calm, his presence grounding yet overpowering. The city hummed faintly in the distance, but here, in the dim, shadowed corner, the world felt narrowed to just the two of them.

Des buried a hand in Julian's hair, gripping tightly at the roots as he kissed the other man. Julian tasted himself bitterly on Des' lips. He pulled Des into an embrace, burying his face in the other man's chest. He inhaled deeply; his mind glowed pale white. When he pulled away, Des grinned, his lips red and cheeks flushed. As Julian looked down, he could make out the silhouette pressing through Des' jeans. Des gripped Julian's chin with his hand, pulling his gaze up until their eyes met. They stood like statues of glowing angles in the streetlight, praying to an old God, long abandoned.

"Should we take that walk?" asked Des.

Julian stammered, "I—"

Des nodded, taking Julian's slim fingers in his own. With his thumb, he drew small circles on the top of Julian's hand.

"I think I'm ready," said Julian quietly.

Des held Julian's hand as he gently guided him out of the alley. He led the way towards the industrial sector of the city where the factories stretched in length rather than the height. The grime of the city was evident on the discolored walls of the buildings and the slight scent of burned material in the air.

Des halted. Julian stopped with him, casting a questioning glance at the other man until he pulled out a black bandana from his pocket. Julian's stomach lurched.

"You can't know where I'm bringing you," said Des.

Des folded the bandana until it created a strip of fabric only wide enough to cover Julian's eyes. Looking at the other man for confirmation, Des draped the fabric over Julian's eyes, tying the bandana at the back of his head. With a slight tug on the bandana, he double knotted the fabric, taking Julian's hand in his own.

Des guided Julian across the uneven pavement, and Julian trusted Des wouldn't let him trip and injure himself. Des kept a steady pace, never yanking Julian forwards, but gently tugging him to the right or left. The city air filled with the clattering of machinery and a high-pitched droning. As they passed a building, warmth emanated from what Julian assumed was the metal wall of a warehouse.

Des held Julian's shoulders steady as the two stopped. After the turns left and right over the past twenty minutes, Julian tried to visualize where he could be, yet he found himself hopelessly disoriented. Des maneuvered Julian to the side before he heard a knocking. Four raps on the door made dull thuds on what Julian deduced was a thick metal door. A squeak blended into the rest of the dull noise as a handle turned and the door groaned open.

Without notice, he heard a whoosh. A sharp pain shot through his temple, and he brought up a handle to cradle his head. His knees collapsed from beneath him, and the world behind the bandana somehow felt darker.

CHAPTER NINETEEN

Julian gasped. Opening his eyes, he frantically blinked, yet his vision blurred in and out with pulsing pain radiating from his temple. He raised his head, his chin having fallen limply against his chest in his slumber. The surrounding room was dimly lit by an exposed strip of lights, the plastic cover shattered and jagged where it remained. As he looked down at his aching body, he found himself positioned on his knees, legs bare beside his gray boxers. His arms were maneuvered above his head, wrists bound with a rope that pinched his skin, and the rest of the line was strung over an exposed beam above to hold them in position. Even as he squirmed in his restraints, he could not gain a better position. With every slight movement, sharp pain shot through either his shoulders or hips or legs. The hair on his arms stood on edge, and he thrashed against his bindings. Screaming through the consequential pain, his throat burned, and his voice grew hoarse.

Loud music blasted in the room, drowning out any of the thudding or scraping sounds of the city. Metal walls and an unfurnished room amplified the noise, projecting it around the room. Trapped in the deafening eye of the hurricane, Julian pressed one ear up against his bound arm to block out the sound. Yet, the other ear was still assailed by unforgiving noise. He surveyed the room; he was unguarded. His heart pounded as he ran through the possibilities of his captivity.

He lowered his head. No windows allowed the light to shine

through, and he couldn't say how long he had been trapped. He attempted to relax the muscles in his shoulders, but it proved useless in easing the aching pain. The floor beneath him dug with cold teeth into the balls of his feet, and his legs trembled.

Julian raised his gaze as he heard the clattering of a door and the thud of heavy boots against the concrete. Slowly drinking up the menacing form, he traced dark battered boots double knotted at the ankles up onto worn gray cargo pants. The man wore a baggy black short-sleeved shirt. As he met the man's chestnut eyes, he immediately recognized the man.mask. Without sleeves to cover his arms, Julian could make out the defined ridges of his muscles and the smudges of dirt and debris on his skin. Scattered tattoos marked his flesh, some jagged, as if someone sliced into his skin and then dumped the ink in. With the toe of his boot, he gently tapped on the healing wound in Julian's thigh. The one that he inflicted.

"The worst kind of traitor," spoke the man. "Willing to kill your own people just to get a leg up in society."

"I refuse to be complicit anymore."

"Anymore?" the man laughed. "Took a bit too long, don't you think?"

"I didn't mean for any of it," Julian gasped. "I… I didn't want this. I'm sorr—"."

The man struck him in the stomach with his boot. He winced, gasping for the air forced out of his lungs.

"You're so sorry? You think you won't be held accountable for your crimes just because you feel bad now? I've met plenty of sorry people. Real sorry people. But," he said, crouching down until he was eye to eye with Julian, "I don't pity you in the slightest."

"I hate Lancut. I hate them," managed Julian, still struggling to gasp air into his lungs. "They've taken everything from me."

The man shook his head, "But you took the poisoned the apple, didn't you?"

The looming figure leaned into his captive's face until Julian hung close enough to jerk at him in his restraints. He thought about lashing out and biting the man.

"I did," he admitted, "to save myself, but I didn't want to hurt anyone."

Julian didn't process the slap that came next until his face snapped to the side. His cheek throbbed as he slowly returned to look his assailant in the eyes.

"But you did. Do you think you don't deserve punishment just because you regret what you've done?" he taunted, landing a matching blow on the other side of Julian's face.

"I-I," Julian stammered, "I didn't actually do anything. I didn't betray anyone. I left."

The next slap rang out in the empty warehouse.

"Do you believe that? That you didn't do any harm by contributing your ideas. Feeding into their ideology? Did you not make suggestions? You were weak while other people have given their lives to fight the monster you fed," he growled, standing up to glower down at Julian.

"I was afraid to die. Everyone is afraid to die," Julian fought back.

"If you think that, you're a coward," he spat, turning his back to stroll away from Julian.

"I wanted to make my way up; make things better from the inside," he croaked, his voice straining desperately as he pulled at the bindings.

The man turned on heels.

"How many people were you willing to kill? How many

corpses were you willing to climb over to get there?"

"I didn't kill anyone," he pleaded, cursing the pleading lilt in his voice. "I want to help. I have things to tell you. I have access to the people you need. That's why I came."

The man grabbed a metal bucket by the handle, carrying it over to Julian.

"So, you don't think you did anything wrong?" he asked.

Julian felt the panic tightening his lungs until he barely whispered.

"I know I fucked up, but I did what I needed to. You're no better than I am."

He gasped as the icy water poured over his head. Sputtering, he shook his head, his wet hair clinging to his face. He gasped for air.

"I don't think you understand," said the man. He dropped the bucket, letting it clatter to the ground and roll out of Julian's sight. "Do you think you're a good person, Julian Harper? Or are you just as bad as the rest of them? All the sellouts who whore themselves out to Lancut?"

"I'm not one of them," he spat. "I never was, and I never will be."

The man circled him, disappearing from his view for a moment. "Lying to me and yourself won't get you very far. It won't get you anywhere, for that matter."

His footsteps fell, echoing further away. Julian unleashed a scream, tearing into his throat. "I'm not dying here."

Julian gasped for air, his teeth chattering violently. In a sudden jerk to avoid slipping, he bit his tongue, tasting blood as it mixed with the icy water. He shrieked through it.He earned no response beside for the squealing of a hinge and the slam of a door. Thrashing, Julian screamed until he gargled through the blood coating the back of his throat. Julian ceased his struggling, letting himself hang in position. His body trembled with the frigid breath coming out with small puffs of vapor dissipating before his eyes. He wondered if they would slaughter him, already hanging him like meat to cure. They'd burn his body or perhaps drop it into a sewer before anyone noticed him gone. By the time Lancut tracked him down, his mangled corpse would prove too decomposed to identify if not for his Disc.

Harnessing a last burst of terror, he swore into his dim surroundings until his throat stung and he gasped for breath. Julian wasn't sure how long he shrieked for before his raw throat no longer produced a sound. In the creeping darkness, he held his mouth wide, choking on the agony he tried to manipulate into cries of anguish.

Julian shut his eyes. Julian's eyelids weighed heavily despite his chest thrumming, and he breathed raggedly. Julian cursed himself. Did Des know this would happen to him? No, he couldn't have. Unless it was all a rouse. All the affection, the intimacy, a lure to draw him into a trap. He imagined a look of disgust on Des' face as he glared down at Julian's pathetic face. Julian refused let himself believe that—believe he fell head over heels for a lie.

In one last attempt, he tore at the rope binding his wrists. When the rope bit into his wrists, he gritted his teeth. He remained on his knees, stripped and now silenced from his own screams of desperation.

A faint shuffle behind him made him freeze. He snapped his head toward the sound, startled. While his wrists remained pinned together, the tension in his shoulders released as the rope padded to the ground, winding itself into a pile beside him. The man looked down at him, nudging him in the rib with the toe of his boot. Julian struggled, losing his balance. Unable to catch himself, he toppled to the ground, slamming his shoulder against the concrete. A hand dug into his bare forearm, dragging him back onto his knees. The man didn't say a word to him before landing a kick to his shoulder. Once more, Julian could not pad his landing, slamming the back of his head against the ground. As he dug a boot into the center of Julian's chest, the man forced the air from Julian's lungs. He struggled beneath the growing pressure, squirming pointlessly beneath the other man.

"Did you have time to think, or were you too busy dozing off?" asked the man.

Julian sputtered desperately, still struggling against the heavy tread digging into his chest.

"Do you think you're going to die?" asked the man, flipping open a silver blade. He let up his boot enough for Julian to gasp.

Julian shook his head, "No," he said. "I'm not ready to die."

"You don't get a choice," he remarked, cutting through the tape wrapped around Julian's ankles. "You're going to walk with me, and if you so much as look at me funny, I'll slit your throat and leave your body for your friend to find."

"I don't want to run," said Julian with a hoarse voice. "I want to be here."

The man huffed, gripping Julian's wrists and yanking him to his feet. Julian stumbled, wobbling on as the man tugged him forward. He followed the man's quick pace, his hands still bound. The concrete burned his feet with the unforgiving cold seeping through his bare skin. Still in damp underwear, he shivered, forcing one foot in front of the other as the man hauled him through the room and towards the door. His captor fidgeted with the handle before shoving Julian into a bright room. Letting go of his wrists, the man let Julian tumble to the ground. His knees collided with the concrete, and he hissed.

His hair fell in front of his eyes as he looked up. Fingers threaded through his hair, tugging his head up, and four figures loomed before him. Each face was hidden behind a plain gray mask, featureless except for narrow slits for eyes. A porcelain tub stood at the center of the room, smudged with grime and cracked around the edges. The light glinted off of the surface, the discolored water swishing around as if someone had only just finished filling it. Eyeing each of the figures, he stopped on the last face. Julian couldn't mistake those gray eyes for belonging to anyone else.

"Are you ready to accept your death?" asked the man with the blade..

"I will not die," Julian cried. "I've made it too far."

Julian stared up through dark lashes at Des, desperately searching for any remorse in those bright eyes. Des removed his mask, letting it clatter to the ground.

"I guess it doesn't matter if you see our faces," said the leader of the group, pulling off his scarf and dropping it to the concrete. The man gripping Julian grinned with amusement. "Peterson, get over here," the man ordered. "Show me what you're worth."

Des walked forward, stopping in front of the man. "Cam," he said, acknowledging him. "Whatever you need."

"I'll keep him in place, but you're gonna do the important part," said Cam to Des. He turned to Julian. "Get into the tub, and don't make a mess."

Julian glanced over at Des, who gave a subtle nod, and Julian took a deep breath. He swung one still-cramped leg over the side of the tub, slowly lowering his foot into the icy water. He flinched when his skin hit the murky surface, but after a warning glare from Cam, he let his leg fall until his foot brushed against the bottom of the tub. Struggling on one foot, he swung over the other leg until he stood in the tub with water lapping at his shins. There was no verbal order, but Cam pressed down on his shoulder, and Julian bent his knees, lowering himself into the water. Once he squatted fully down in the water, Cam pushed his shoulder back, urging him to lie back in the tub. The cold porcelain cradled his back and shoulders as he slid down, and he tensed his body against the frigid water. Shivering, he couldn't so much as wrap his bound arms around himself for reprieve.

"Des," barked Cam, who quickly came to his side. "Have you ever wondered what it was like to drown?"

"No, sir," responded Des.

"It's awful. At first, you try to hold your breath. Eventually you gasp for air, but there's no air, and you just drag water into your lungs. Sometimes it takes a while; really just depends on how much you struggle," he said with a lilt of excitement in his voice. "It's so much quicker to just put a bullet through someone's head. But that doesn't suit our purposes."

Julian thrashed against the hands on his shoulders. "No," he shrieked, "no—"

"Freedom through death," declared Cam.

Des cast him a final look before his hand pressed down on Julian's forehead, shoving him beneath the water. As Julian screamed, all that came out were gurgles while he struggled against the hands pushing down. A firm grip clamped around his ankles as he thrashed. Des' hand slipped down on his face, jamming Julian's nose into his face. Julian seized the chance, opening his mouth to clamp his teeth down on Des' finger. Gasping to the surface, he craned his neck up, taking frantic breaths as a voice that sounded miles away swore and muttered.

Chest still heaving, Cam ripped Julian's head back by his hair, submerging him completely before he managed to gasp in another full breath.

He kicked his feet, one of them breaching the surface. Soon, a new set of hands gripped both of his ankles, pinning them against the bottom of the tub. The hand on his forehead dug into his flesh, gripping his skull through his skin. He tried to shake his head to loosen the grip, but the hand only followed him, gripping onto his hair to force him back down. Another hand found his neck, choking him against the bottom of the tub. His chest burned as he held his breath. He opened his mouth to scream, letting water rush into his mouth and down his throat.

Coughing, his entire body convulsed, only dragging more water into his aching lungs. As he squirmed against the hands, he opened his eyes. He looked up through the rough water at the distorted faces above him. Even through the water, he unmistakably made out those gray eyes. He opened his mouth to scream out for his friend, choking on the dirty water once more.

His chest burned, lungs screamed, heart shattered.

Julian's vision speckled with black as agony enveloped him. The darkness moved in from the edges. He could not move his body even as he begged his arms or legs to kick or struggle. With terror, he realized his body had given in before his mind. White-hot fear engulfed his vision, dulling his thoughts to a throbbing pain. As his vision faded, he stole one last glance at the man above him. At least Des would know where what happened to him. He saw the man through the star of light, and for a moment, he understood. Then there was nothing.

CHAPTER TWENTY

Pain stabbed through his chest as he heaved on the ground, choking up water mixed with blood.

"He's back," grumbled a muffled voice directly atop him.

The man removed his hands from Julian's sternum, peeling something sticky from his chest. Without the pressure holding him in place, he convulsed, hacking up liquid onto the ground beside him. His full body contracted in with each retch as he dribbled out a pool. Saliva, blood and water gathered beneath his agape mouth. He curled in on himself, shaking as he uncontrollably gagged, shuddering.

As he gasped, drawing in ragged stunted breaths, he struggled to form any thought in his mind over the sharp pain radiating out from his chest and ribs. His head spun as if he were strapped to a spinning wheel on the ground. When he forced his eyes open, Des kneeled above him, other figures blurry and looming over his body. As Des reached down, Julian jerked away from his touch, desperately scrambling to gather his feet beneath himself. He slipped on the wet concrete, collapsing back down. Even with his hands freed, he clumsily handed on his back, knocking his head against the ground.

One of the other figures, a woman with black hair pulled back from her face, leaned down with a familiar device. She pressed a button, then watched him for a short count. He anticipated the freezing of his muscles, but nothing happened. As she repeated the action, she nodded as if satisfied. Managing traction on the ground, he inched himself away, choking on a scream trapped in the back of his battered throat. The faces came into focus, and he froze in place, heart pounding.

"Keep moving," said the woman, playing with the device.

As Julian watched her, he waited for his limbs to seize up, rendering him a helpless statue amongst his captors. Yet, as she continued to fiddle with the remote, he managed to sit up, clutching his chest. With any more than a shallow breath, the pain brought tears to his eyes. He lowered himself back down onto one arm, taking rasping breaths.

"We're clear. First go," she said. "He's lucky."

"Of course he got off easy," huffed Cam.

"Wha…" croaked Julian before exploding into another fit of coughing. He wrapped his arms around himself to brace his own body.

The coughing eased, and muscular arms lifted Julian's limp body. He didn't have the strength to care about his nakedness or the shame of being carried like a doll. His head lolled back as metal beams blurred past, replaced by the crisp night sky. Each breath stung, his raw lungs protesting the cold air.

Murmured voices surrounded him, a low hum that dissolved as someone gently placed him onto the floor of a van. The confined interior came into focus, and then he saw Des. Hope surged weakly. He tried to call out, but his throat betrayed him. Des hesitated, then turned away into the night. Julian managed a faint grunt, and Des looked back, stepping closer until his face hovered just above Julian's.

"I can't go with you," Des murmured, his hand warm against Julian's chest. "But soon. We'll be free." Before Julian could respond, Des disappeared. Someone draped a blanket over him, tucking it securely around his body. The sudden warmth chased away the cold's sharp edge.

A woman slid into the van, shutting the doors. Her presence was steady. Slim brown eyes met his, and she brushed his hair back. "It's going to be alright," she whispered, her touch soft against his cheek. He wanted to believe her.

The van jolted to life, its vibrations rattling his body. The dark streets blurred past, and Julian's sense of time dissolved. A sharp turn rolled him slightly, but the woman held him steady.

"Please," he croaked. "What's happening?"

"You're free," she said, cradling his head in her lap. "We shorted out your Disc. They can't control or track you anymore. You 'died' in that warehouse."

His mind reeled. "I died?"

She nodded. "When the Disc loses power—like when your body shuts down—it becomes useless. We brought you back. CPR, a shock. You're alive, and the Disc is nothing more than a dead chip now."

"Des?" he rasped.

Her hesitation was brief. "He stayed behind. He's more valuable where he is, but he wanted to be here for your rebirth. He insisted."

Julian fell silent, absorbing her words. "What happens now?"

"I don't know," she admitted. "But you're safe. We'll take care of you while you heal. Focus on resting. We're almost there."

The van slowed and stopped. She carried him, still wrapped in the blanket, into a gray concrete building, up staircases, and through dim halls until she set him gently on a padded surface. Blankets cocooned him, and she pulled a hat over his head.

"Someone will bring clothes when you wake up. For now, sleep," she said, holding out a small pill.

"No pills," he whispered, weak but firm.

"It'll help you rest," she coaxed.

A red light shone in through the doorway of wherever he was, drowning the woman in a pulsing glow.

"You're safe now. Trust me."

Reluctantly, he opened his mouth. The pill went down dry, and drowsiness crept over him. Within minutes, sleep claimed him. For the first time in over a year, he sank into true rest, free of fear, pain and the weight of control.

CHAPTER TWENTY-ONE

The compound was unremarkable. The building blended in with the surrounding concrete, with cracks and worn walls leaving floors above the thirteenth inaccessible. Bitter wind slipped through the gaps, and this industrial end of the city had little besides government buildings and warehouses. It was a hideaway; discreet and sturdy, protecting the Reborn and their supplies. The only entry was under lock at night, keeping out vagrants. Inside, cold hallways lined with dim lights hinted at the place's true purpose, yet voices bouncing through the compound gave a false warmth, creating the illusion of a communal home.

Julian sat on his narrow bed, wrapped in a patchwork of worn blankets. A threadbare quilt, the warmest of the lot, lay draped over his lap, and he wondered who might've made it. He saw familiar clothes folded on a nearby chair; his green sweater hung on the back. Relief swept over him as he slipped the garments on, wincing at the pain radiating from bruises that mottled his skin in purples and blues. When he ventured out, he encountered only pale corridors with closed doors, as if the compound was an endless maze.

He took cautious steps down the cold concrete stairwell, hugging his chest to minimize the ache in his ribs. Wandering through another deserted hallway, he heard muffled voices behind a door, but continued on, feeling lost in the vast, barren space. He'd hoped to see a clock- some sign of the hour, but the boarded-up windows muddled all sense of time.

He thought back to the van ride and remembered the woman's promise that he was free, no longer under Lancut's control. Questions roared through his mind, too many to ignore, and he was determined to find answers.

"Who are you?" a voice demanded behind him. Julian turned to face the same man he'd seen earlier, who now raised a pistol to his chest.

"I—I just woke up here," Julian stammered. "I don't know where I'm supposed to be or what time it is."

The man's grip on his arm was unforgiving, jostling his injured ribs as he dragged Julian toward the stairwell. Julian stumbled, his knee scraping painfully against the edge of a step. They descended in silence until the man knocked forcefully on a door. Eventually, it creaked open, and Cam's disheveled figure appeared, looking Julian up and down with clear irritation.

"For fuck's sake," Cam muttered, rubbing his face in exasperation.

"He says he's new here. Figured he was one of yours," said the man holding Julian in a vice-grip.

Cam yawned, nodding, then gestured for Julian to follow him into his room. The man loosened his hold, and Julian stepped forward, flinching slightly as Cam shut the door. Julian's gaze wandered, lingering on colorful illustrations of people in dramatic fights and, strikingly, of a man lounging in a bed, illuminated by lightning. As he spotted sketches strewn across the floor, Cam hastily covered them with a sweatshirt.

"You're awake," Cam observed.

"Not even sure what time it is or where I am exactly," replied Julian.

Cam gestured to a chair, where Julian took a seat, while Cam wrapped a blanket around himself on the bed.

"There's an entire group here, anyone free from control. We organize, make decisions, right here. We have conference rooms below, old office rooms above," Cam explained.

"This is The Reborn?"

Cam sighed. "Guess that's the name sticking. It was way less organized at first, under different names. Des said you'd be useful."

"He's not here?"

"Because he's activated. Can't risk coming here; they can track him. He can only interact with members in places he won't look suspicious."

"This is real," Julian muttered.

"Not as glamorous as you'd think," Cam replied dryly.

"More than I ever dreamed," said Julian, voice low.

Cam huffed. "You'll tire of it soon enough. Can't trust anyone, anything and if you slip up, everyone here's dead. You'd better have something useful. I didn't want anyone else connected to Lancut here, but I was outvoted. You're a hazard, a ticking time bomb. And Lancut, they'll want proof you're dead."

"My disc though—"

"They'll want a body. And they won't find one. They'll pick you off like the others."

"What—"

"Doesn't matter now."

"I…where am I?" asked Julian.

"A building on the south side of the city. Another shitty piece of concrete, but it serves its purpose."

"How many people are here?"

Cam glared at Julian with unease.

"Depends on the day. We were up to sixty at one point, but we're back down to twenty-three."

Julian considered asking the unnecessary question before dropping his gaze to the ground.

"What am I supposed to do here?"

Cam fiddled with the edge of a moth-bitten blanket.

"Maya will send you on missions. Retrieve supplies, cause unrest, or try to find others. Other than that, we just sort of wait."

"For what?"

"To die."

Julian's stomach twisted in his stomach.

"You won't make it more than a year. Nobody does."

"How long have you—"

"Two years."

"Oh," muttered Julian. "Uh, how did you end up here?"

"Doesn't matter," said Cam. "I'm sure Maya will want to see you. She'll give you the welcome tour."

Cam stood, waving at Julian. He stood up, clutching his ribs as a sharp pain radiated through his body. He followed Cam through the gray concrete hallways, eyes darting as if someone at any moment would turn around a corner with a gun in hand pointed between his eyes. When Cam stopped at a door, he tested the handle, pushing it open. Julian did not know how Cam knew where his room was, or whether this was a temporary arrangement, but he did not complain.

"Stay here until someone comes to get you."

Julian sat uncomfortably on the edge of the mattress, hands resting in his lap. He ran through the events of the last two days, his mind swirling. Slowly, he sank back onto the mattress, wincing. He could have laughed at the absurdity, if not for the crackle of his ribs with every breath. As he traced the cracks in the ceiling above, his vision blurred, and tears gathered at the corners of his eyes. Clenching them shut, he failed to fight away the overwhelming sensation.

He awoke to the screech of a door. Julian clambered to grab hold of the wall or anything to pull himself upright.

"That's not necessary," said a familiar voice.

The woman with the graying hair stood above him with a man behind her as if no more than her shadow.

"Take off your shirt," she ordered.

Julian's stomach dropped, but he struggled to pull the material over his head. The man approached, unzipping a backpack on the edge of the battered cot. He removed a stethoscope, fitting the ends into his ears and pressing the cold metal plate to Julian's exposed chest. Julian breathed as normally as he could manage.

"He has a lot of bruising, but I wouldn't be worried," said the man. "Painkillers and a heating pad, if we can dig one up."

"No," started Maya, "I need him sharp. Painkillers dull the pain and the mind."

"Yes, ma'am," said the man, tucking his supplies back into his bag.

"Return to your quarters and alert the others that we will meet at eight."

He slipped out of the room, shutting the door behind him.

Maya smiled down at Julian as she towered above him with arms crossed over her chest.

"I heard you talked to Cam this morning," she said.

"Oh, uh…yeah. He's—"

"Abrasive at best, and an asshole at worst. But he's strong, and he's one hell of a fighter. He's currently working closely with me to formulate our next strategy. After our video, we weren't sure what the next move was, but that's where you come in. You're going to be a very useful asset."

"Oh."

"Please, we're a family here. Speak your mind freely and understand that you are part of something so much bigger than yourself. You have been reborn. You are free."

Julian smiled.

"Feels good to be free."

"You have no debts here," she said warmly. "I'd like you to come with me, so I can introduce you to the others. We have much to discuss."

"Okay."

He held his chest as he followed her out of the room. Once the door shut, it was identical to any other. There was no distinguishing one from the next in the bleak place.

Julian took the stairs carefully in the dim light. Dirt collected in the cracks of the concrete, as if no one ever swept the place. He questioned how high up they were in the building, if it was one of Lancut's towering structures or a stout industrial building, but the answer came as they continued seemingly endlessly down the twisting stairwell. A flickering light cast intermittent shadows of the two figures as they made their way down.

Before they reached the bottom floor, Maya pushed open a heavy metal door. Inside, another wide open room lay before them, sparsely decorated with furniture, none of which matched. Wooden chairs sat beside plastic ones, and a scratched metal table occupied the center of the room. As she flipped the light, it glinted off of the scratched surface with a single thick notebook set at the head.

In the corner of the room, a figure slumped against the wall with a ratty baseball cap pulled over his eyes. He wore stained gray pants with one blown-out knee, and leather boots laced up and tied in a double knot.

"Montero," called Maya.

The figure shifted, grumbling.

"Did you sleep here?"

"You took too long to get here," he chided, flipping around the baseball cap.

His boyish face and bright eyes caught Julian, setting a sense of unease in his stomach. Whoever he was, he was young. Not so young to be a child, but younger than Julian. He pushed shaggy hair out of his face, hobbling from his corner to a chair.

"Julian, this is Montero," said Maya.

"It's Romeo Antonio Montero-Hernandez. But yeah, Montero."

"We'll start calling you Romeo when you prove it," came a voice from behind.

Cam sauntered in, pulling a chair out with a screech against the concrete floor. He leaned back.

"I've more than proved it, but if you're talking about documents, I guess you'll never know," he said with a sly grin. "Good thing I didn't die, or else you would have put some bullshit on my tombstone."

"You're not getting a stone," scoffed Cam.

A woman in a deep purple head wrap walked through the door. She wore a hooded sweatshirt that pooled around her neck, and she carried a tablet that she set down on the table. A crew wandered in as the time passed. Maya took her place at the head of the table, and Julian took an uneasy seat on her left side. He caught Montero massaging his calf with gritted teeth as he propped it up on his thigh. A dark patch blended with the other stains around it, but the fabric clung to his skin.

Some sat at the table, and others took places with crossed legs on the ground. A man with deep wrinkles across his face and gray stubble on his chin rested against the far wall with one leg pulled up to his stomach. The woman with the tablet tapped away at the screen, projecting a bright blank page onto the cracked wall. Julian lost himself in the trickling group of people until the stream ceased, and the empty room still could have echoed.

"JulianJulian Harper," started Maya, staying seated, "has come to join us. He worked as an intern for Lancut working on the Vision project before choosing the path of rebirth. Please make sure he feels welcome here."

Twenty sets of beady eyes fixed on him with glassy gazes and gaunt faces. He forced a smile. They stared as if waiting for something, but he choked on the surrounding air.

"Julian, would you like to speak about the Vision program?"

"Uh...yeah, so the Vision program is intended to increase surveillance everywhere in order to eliminate any rebellion at all. Lancut will store and monitor all the data to ensure that there is no resistance. They would like to install the implants as soon as possible. I was told within six months we need to have the majority of the population taken care of. I can, uh, get into details of how they want to do that..."

Maya nodded.

Julian continued, glancing down at the table beneath him. He caught his own reflection, and he had no basis to judge any of the souls around him. As he finished, he crossed his arms over his chest, glancing back to Maya, who smiled coldly.

"We have reached a breaking point," said Maya. "We don't have nearly as much time as we thought. There is no time for more building and growing out forces. Our focus is not on recruiting so much as creating a way for us to survive, and there is no survival under this regime. We need to gather the resources we need for a final stand- whatever that means for us."

"There aren't enough of us," said Cam.

"We don't need numbers," piped in the woman with the tablet.

"Then what do we need, Dia? Are you going to storm the Lancut building yourself?"

"Every time there's growth, we come closer to being exposed. We lose people," she said, glancing around the room. "We need to move now, and quickly."

Maya stood.

"And that's why Julian is the final addition to our team. We will make our last stand, and soon. Now we need to prepare."

"Are we not gonna talk about Vinny?" asked a man in the corner.

"He's gone, Jon," said Maya. "He's not coming back."

"Well, let's just talk about what a mess that was," started Cam. "Montero got shot. We lost Vinny altogether. They know where we are before we know where we're going. Before we make any plans, we need to figure out where loyalties lie."

"Bit cynical," scoffed Dia.

"We need to entertain the very real possibility that there's someone who isn't who they say they are. And every time we bring another fucking Lancut intern in here, we risk making it worse. Are we gonna bring Edmund Sands in here himself?"

"Sit down," said Maya. "We all mourn Vinny. He was a good soldier and a loyal friend. Any time we leave this compound, we risk our lives. They outnumber us, and they are everywhere. In order to prevent needless loss, we need to act quickly, and we will. If you'd like to complain to someone, I'm sure that Lancut would love to hear from you, Cam."

Cam sat down, his face growing red.

"There's a store of weapons in a facility on the west side of the city. We need to arm ourselves more heavily if we're going to stand any chance," said Maya.

"Chance to do what?" Julian asked cautiously.

"To kill Edmund Sands. To end this once and for all."

"This is happening too quickly," said Cam.

"What choice do we have?"

CHAPTER TWENTY-TWO

Julian sat in the back of an old car with a pistol tucked into his waistband while Montero buckled himself in behind the wheel of the rust-bucket. Julian realized, as he glanced around, that he'd never actually seen anyone drive a car before besides Lancut staff. Intelligent computers steered the buses lumbering through the city, and he usually walked wherever he needed to go. He supposed people could still get licenses; Enforcers drove special vehicles that could manually chase down anyone wanted by the state. Still, he'd never considered a random person off the street behind the wheel.

Cam leaned his head against the window, staring into the stormy night. City lights reflected off the wet blacktop beneath them as the car came to an abrupt stop, jolting Julian forward.

"Jesus," Cam hissed.

Montero scoffed.

"You don't even know how to drive."

"I could do better than that."

"No, you couldn't," Montero said, slamming his foot down on the gas.

The car jolted over divots through the city streets.

Their objective was clear: go in, pay a dealer for a stash of weapons, load up the bin beneath the seats, and leave. Julian didn't couldn't fathom why they had chosen him for this mission. He'd never fired a gun or taken part in a proper fight, and the bruises still littering his body left him wincing with every breath.

Montero hummed, and Cam clenched his eyes shut.

"Quiet," he snapped.

Montero continued, unfazed.

"Shut the fuck up."

"You're so uptight," Montero said, glancing back at his passengers. "Don't you want Julian to feel at home?"

Julian hesitated, then admitted, "I'm not sure why I'm here."

Montero spoke, "It's good to jump right in."

"You'll learn as you go," Cam added. "We don't have formal training, if that's what you think this is gonna be."

Julian shifted uncomfortably. "I thought the group was…I thought there were more of you."

Cam shook his head. "No. It seems that way, though. The video we put out made us look like a real threat. For better or worse. Sam sacrificed himself for the greater good."

"How did you decide who…"

"Maya picked him. Loyalty was the main reason."

Julian looked down, uncertain. "I thought you all voted on that kind of thing."

Montero snorted.

"She runs a tight ship."

When the car came to a stop, Cam wrapped a jacket around himself and opened the door. A gust of frigid winter air flooded the car. Julian wrapped his arms around himself as he set his feet down on the cracked concrete. Montero wriggled out, but Cam shoved him back into the seat with one hand.

"You're staying."

"I'm fine," Montero muttered, but Cam slammed the door in his face, leaving Montero rolling his eyes through the foggy glass. He dragged his finger through the condensation on the window, drawing a frowning face.

They stood in the industrial sector, where machines whirred and metal ground against itself, emitting sharp, clattering noises through the night. Julian followed Cam and the others down a dark alley beside an old warehouse with towering, ridged metal walls.

Cam consulted a small projection from his watch, halting at the corner and craning his neck around. Julian kept close to the wall, staying on the balls of his feet. They stopped at a metal door wedged open with a stone. Cam pressed his open palm against the door, widening the gap to slip inside, and Julian followed, his hand gripping the unfamiliar gun's handle tightly.

Inside the warehouse, a strange sense of familiarity washed over Julian. A single strip light dangled from rusted chains, casting a dim glow over lines of shelves caked in dust. At the far end stood three figures. The first, bundled in a scarf and hat with only his eyes visible, extended a gloved hand as he stepped forward.

"Who am I dealing with?" the man spoke in a gruff voice.

"Romeo," Cam replied smoothly. "Who am I speaking with?"

"Ted."

"Our car's parked close by. I'll transfer the funds as soon as you've loaded the weapons," Cam said.

Ted eyed him warily. "Transfer all of it first."

Cam held up his hands in a show of good faith. "Sure." He tapped his watch, and Ted glanced down, nodding after a moment.

"Third aisle from the South side. Crates are under a blue tarp."

Cam turned to Julian. "Go find the crates while Ted and I finish up here."

Julian glanced between the two men, then made his way

through the aisles, a shadowy figure trailing him. The man, wearing a blue surgical mask and a baseball cap with the brim shading his eyes, took the lead, prompting Julian to jog to keep up. Once he pulled back the tarp, Julian spotted three large plastic bins. After breaking the seal on one, he saw a long black rifle inside.

Julian hefted one of the crates, wincing as he braced it against his sore chest and staggered back to the others. Cam inspected the contents, counting items aloud before picking up a weapon and examining it closely.

"Where are these from?" Cam asked.

"My superiors wouldn't like me to disclose that," Ted replied.

"Want me to test one of them on you?" Cam retorted.

Before Ted could respond, the door slammed open, and Montero stumbled inside, gasping.

"Enforcers!" he cried.

Cam shot Ted a cold glare. "You—"

"No, this isn't—" Ted stammered, backing away, but Cam kept his weapon trained on him. After a moment, he lowered it, and Ted stumbled backwards before bolting.

Footsteps echoed as Montero cracked the door open, slipping out of sight. Julian hesitated, then followed, with Cam close behind. They ran for the pavement outside, Cam leading them along the building's perimeter.

"Get down!" Montero yelled, grabbing Julian's wrist and yanking him to the ground.

Julian collided with the pavement hard, scraping his elbow. He barely had time to react before Montero and Cam raised their weapons, aiming at a figure illuminated by a streetlamp. The Enforcer's badge gleamed against his crimson uniform in the light.

"Drop your weapons," the Enforcer barked.

Julian lay still, tense and silent. Cam's gaze was icy as he stared down the Enforcer, while Montero took a careful step forward.

"Don't move," the Enforcer ordered, his gun now trained on Montero.

"It's two against one," Cam said, voice steady. "You're the one who should drop your weapon, or I'll put a bullet between your eyes."

Julian moved instinctively, crawling closer to the Enforcer in the shadows. Cam's gaze flicked to him, offering no sign of approval, but Montero didn't look away from the threat.

"I have backup coming," the Enforcer warned. "Drop your weapons now, or they'll shoot."

Julian's hands shook as he neared. With a deep breath, he raised his gun, stumbling over the basic instructions Cam briefly grumbled at him.

He aimed and fired.

Three shots echoed as in succession as Cam and Montero let fire, and the Enforcer crumpled to the ground, blood pooling from a gushing wound in the center of his forehead. Julian gasped, scrambling back as Cam kicked the weapon away from the dying man.

"We need to go," Montero muttered, staring at the body. "Those shots will bring more."

Julian clambered to his feet, and they dashed into an alley with Cam and Montero guiding the way. Sirens blared in the distance, but they slipped into the shadows, unnoticed.

Cam threw open a dumpster lid and nodded at Montero, who climbed in first, followed by Julian. Cam joined them, easing the lid shut. The air was thick and stale, the scent unbearable.

"Fuck," muttered Cam. "We're in a fucking dumpster."

"We're alive," Montero replied, though his voice shook.

"Yeah, alive in a fucking dumpster," Cam grumbled.

Montero caught his breath, panting. Julian leaned back, trying to avoid touching the walls, as the events replayed in his mind; the chaotic the shots, the look in the Enforcer's eyes.

After a long silence, Julian spoke. "Who… who killed him?"

Cam's voice was crisp. "Doesn't matter. He's dead, and we're not."

Montero added, "You clean missed him, but you sure as hell startled him. I hit him in the chest, and Cam got him between the eyes. You didn't kill him, if that's what's bothering you."

"Still," Julian murmured. "I don't know what I'm killing for, who I tried to kill for."

Cam's gaze hardened.

"I think you do."

Rain pattered on the dumpster lid and the city buzzed around them as they waited, hidden in the shadows.

CHAPTER TWENTY-THREE

Julian lay in bed, staring up at the ceiling. The blond man with the buzz cut hovered in the forefront of his mind, no matter how bleak his surrounding or the pressing weight threatening to further crush his bruised chest. He never appreciated how Des dozed off and snored, filling the entire room with a rattling noise. Yet, in complete silence, he ached for a warm figure beside him. He felt warm arms wrap around him as he closed his eyes. He trailed his hand under his thin shirt, rubbing his thumb in a circle over the bruised flesh there. Working his way down, he fiddled with his waistband, pressing into the sensitive skin.

With a knock on his door, he yanked his hand away, crossing his arms over his chest.

"Come in," he called.

Maya stood in the doorway with dark eyes and a creased smile.

"How are you feeling?" she asked.

"Tired. Still healing, and all, I think."

"Yesterday," she started, "Cam informed me you took your first shot."

Julian nodded.

"How are you doing?"

"Fine."

"Nobody is completely fine the first time," she said.

Julian hesitated.

"I didn't even hit him," he gritted out, pushing the bright

flash to the back of his mind.

She smiled, sitting down on the edge of his bed. He squirmed back before he realized what he was doing.

"Why me?" he asked.

"What?"

"Why did you send me there?"

"You need to understand what this is," she said. "We have to collect resources. Half of the time, we're just finding more food and supplies to make it through the cold months."

"I guess. You could have taught me to shoot a gun- trained me."

"But you were just fine. Sometimes it's best to learn as we go."

He nodded.

"You were meant to be here," said Maya. "You're a very valuable asset to us. To all of us."

"So is Des."

She sighed gently.

"Yes, and he will join us soon. We need to be patient."

"What's the wait? Things are coming to a head so quickly."

"He's still on the inside. He's doing his work there while you do yours here," she said.

"He and I could leave- do our work from beyond the border. We could get out of here."

She shook her head.

"It's never that simple."

Julian hesitated.

"I want to see him."

"You can't. It's not safe for either of you."

"Could I get him a message?"

"No. You will see him when it's time. We can't have anyone

with connected devices without risking signals tracked back to us."

She stood, smiling down at him, and Julian shivered beneath the unwavering gaze.

"I need you to report to the meeting hall at two. We need to discuss our next steps after the arms failure."

"I'm sorry," Julian managed.

"It's not your fault. Somebody's fault, but not yours."

CHAPTER TWENTY-FOUR

Later that afternoon, Julian wandered through the halls. He checked behind him before trying another door.

Locked.

One after another, he tested them before taking the stairs down another floor. Wandering through the dim concrete fortress, he grazed his fingers over the cracked walls. He knew the place was abandoned long ago. This sector was once a bustling place, but since Lancut pulled their facilities to the center of the city, the building slowly fell into disrepair. He considered the ruins outside the city, and he yearned for anything other than the concrete pillars looming over him. No matter the state of the outside world, he figured it could not be as oppressive as whatever his current fate was. Lancut told them the rest of the world was in ruins, plagued by war and famine without the strength to enforce order. Julian supposed he was tired of order.

As he stumbled down another flight of steps, he wondered where everyone else stayed. He supposed there must be rooms that people called their own, and so far, someone had brought him a warm bowl of oatmeal for every meal. There had to be a kitchen somewhere, and he supposed he would learn that location, too, with time. He stopped at a metal door with an unlit red exit sign dangled above from a frayed wire. A hesitant hand outstretched, he hovered his fingers over the bar. He nudged it open, peering out into the sunny afternoon. The light poured in, drenching in face in bright warmth.

A sharp tug yanked him back, and he nearly stumbled over his own feet.

"What the fuck do you think you're doing?" asked a woman with two blonde braids tightly knotted down the back of her head.

"I—I wanted—"

"You cannot ever leave the compound without express permission. That means not so much as opening a door or window without permission directly from Maya. I should report you."

"I'm sorry," stuttered Julian. "I didn't know."

"That won't fly here. You're gonna get us all killed. What if an Enforcer drove by and saw you poking your head out?" she barked.

"I—"

She yanked him down the hall, knocking on a door with a long scratch down the metal. Julian's heart pounded as they waited. When the door opened, Maya peered out.

"I know we have a meeting shortly, but this one was trying to leave the compound," said the woman.

"I wasn't. I just wanted to see the sun," started Julian.

"Thank you," said Maya coldly, gripping tightly onto Julian's upper arm with nails that dug into his tender skin.

"What were you thinking?" Maya hissed.

"I—I don't know."

"There are consequences to all actions here."

Maya turned over her wrist, checking an old watch with hands that pointed to written numbers. Julian had never seen anyone wear one except in older films.

"I know you're new here, but you will not speak during the upcoming meeting. You need to understand that this is not

Lancut's regime, but we still must maintain order. Future offenses will be met with more severe repercussions. Follow me."

Julian hesitantly followed Maya down the hall, trailing behind her into a familiar room. Inside, Cam and Dia were already sitting at the table. Montero sat the far end with his fingers laced behind his head. The blonde who still glared him down stood against a wall, leaning with her arms crossed over her chest. Julian pulled out a seat, but Maya pointed to the edge of the room. He took a seat on the cold concrete with his back pressed up against the wall.

As the people trickled in, Julian let his eyes fall shut. His head swirled, and his heart ached. He nearly drifted away before a voice snapped him to cruel awareness.

"The weapons deal did not go as planned," spoke Maya. "There are a multitude of explanations for this. Based on Cam's report, I do not believe that the dealers set us up. I have reason to believe that Enforcers already knew about this event. That puts into question everyone in this room right now."

"It's possible they've been watching us," added Cam. "If they know where we're hiding out, and they're waiting, that could offer another explanation. Or if they were following the dealers."

"Oh, come on," spoke up a woman in a stained gray sweatshirt "This happened to the last extraction mission. There's a mole here, and we need to figure out who it is before we lose anyone else."

"Let's not assume everyone is out to get everyone else," spoke Montero.

"It's the truth, though. You think someone wouldn't sell us out for a cushy apartment and real food?" snapped Cam. "Someone here is a rat, and we need to sort this out before we can do anything else."

"How much have you been telling the Peterson man?" asked a slim figure.

"He's given us consistent information," said Maya. "I trust him. And we need to get him out sooner than later. They're gonna figure out he's playing them. Whether that's tomorrow or next month, we can't know.. There's only so long before they track it all right back to the Peterson family and then to their only son."

Julian bit his tongue as the words threatened to pour from his lips.

"How do you want to get him out?" asked Cam.

"We'll keep it simple. Have him meet us at a designated location and take care of the affair within the next few days. Cam, you can work out the details and then inform me what you believe the best course of action is."

"I don't want him here," said Cam blankly.

"I don't care."

"I know, but I don't want him here. You're bringing a ticking time bomb."

"Quiet," snapped Maya. "I don't need anything else out of you here. Why don't you retire to your quarters?"

"No," he said.

"Cam," hushed Montero.

Cam stood, and his chair clattered to the ground behind him. Tension hung heavily in the air as he stormed out of the room, his heavy boots echoing through the halls. Maya smiled as if that were a default- her body returning to its programmed position like a mindless machine.

"When we apprehend Desmond Peterson, I imagine we will have limited time to act before even more attention is pushed our way. We will need to work quickly after that if we are going to weed out evil at the source. Julian, please speak. Where do you believe the ideal place to eliminate Edmund Sands would be?"

Julian's voice caught in his throat as he looked over the grimy faces staring at him as if he held some authority.

"Um, well, I was invited into his home. I don't think too many people know about that place. There were guards, but it wasn't as secure as I would have thought. I think his office inside his mansion would be the place."

"In his home?" scoffed Dia.

"But I want Des first. I want to be certain he's safe."

"You don't make that call."

"I won't help you until he's safe," blurted Julian.

A flash in Maya's eyes pushed him further against the wall before she reset to that eerie smile.

"Once Desmond Peterson is returned to us, you will give us the information needed to infiltrate. We already have a good idea of Sands' comings and goings. After all, we've been watching him for long enough. Montero, I want you to consider how this operation would take shape. I will speak to Cam directly. You are all dismissed."

CHAPTER TWENTY-FIVE

Julian threw down the three of hearts. He glanced back up at Montero, who perched on the balls of his feet, crouched down and rocking back and forth slightly. His hair swung in his face, and his breath puffed out small clouds even indoors. Portable heaters plugged into outlets around the compound warmed the concrete building, but the power source was centralized on the bottom floor. Advanced pipes ensured that they would not freeze and burst no matter that external temperature, but it left no motivation to heat the upper levels for anyone looking to conserve their limited energy. For a moment, Julian missed the confines of his apartment where, at least in the small space, he could stop himself from shivering. With shaking hands, he held his cards in a fan in front of his face.

"Shit," muttered Montero, drawing cards until he placed down the nine of hearts.

"Does it ever get warm in here?" asked Julian.

"In the summer. Then, God help us all."

"You were here over the summer?"

Montero nodded. "Been here nine months."

He smiled.

"And you know what that means…" Montero trailed off. "That I'm about to give birth, or I'm gonna die in the next three months, give or take."

"Are you scared?"

"Are you?"

Julian nodded.

"Yeah, I am too. But it's better than the alternative. Before this, I was registered with the repayment program. I have a rich uncle who sponsored me. Lancut had me working in one of their plants. Sixteen-hour shifts; shitty deal. Anyone would have left. It was all medical debt, too, you know."

Julian nodded, "Yeah, I get that."

"Cam, though, he had it cushy. He'd kill me if he found out I told you, but he was living nice. His parents had Civs. He graduated from university and all. Just really believes in the cause, I guess."

"I guess that's admirable. He's probably a better person than I am," said Julian.

"You never got the chance to figure that out for yourself. Sometimes life just makes those decisions for us. You do what's right because it's the only thing to do."

Julian put down the nine of clubs.

"I'm still not sure I'm doing the right thing," admitted Julian. "Killing Sands doesn't destroy what's already built. I'd be doing just as much good running for the border."

Montero spoke softly, "You can't say that."

"Just, if I'm free, maybe I could do something from the outside."

"Don't. Do not ever say anything like that again. You're repaying your debts to the Reborn for freeing you."

Before Julian could respond, a figure dressed in dark green pants and a black sweatshirt sauntered through the doorway with a pistol noticeably poking out of the front of his waistband. Cam slumped against the far wall, pulling his hood up and closing his eyes.

"Thought you were in the doghouse," shouted Montero.

"Oh, shut the fuck up."

"So, you're not? I just want to know who's in charge tonight."

"It's not you," said Cam. "It's not me either, but at least it's not you."

"Who?"

"Maya's new favorite."

"Dia?" asked Montero, to which Cam nodded.

"Fine with me," responded a man Julian recognized from the meetings, but who never spoke up.

He put out a hand, offering Julian a smile.

"I'm Mikey. I'll be helping you get your friend here safe and sound."

Julian forced a smile.

"Thanks," he said.

"Friend?" asked Montero.

"Yeah," choked out Julian.

Montero packed up the cards, stretching a rubber band around them.

When Dia entered the room, she wore a gray jacket and a pair of faded jeans. A tight black wrap held her hair in place, revealing only the edges of her dark curls. She glanced around at the group. Mikey slung a backpack over his shoulder, joining Dia and taking her by the hand.

"Let's go," she said. "We'll travel by foot north as a group. Maya has disclosed to me the location where we will meet him. I will carry out the initiation myself. Once we have completed our task, we will bring him back immediately. Understood?"

Nodding heads and looks of acknowledgement greeted her. Julian hung at the back of the group. The air stung the exposed skin on his face as they navigated through the narrow alleyways of the city. As Julian passed by a ripe dumpster, he held his breath.

The night was quiet, aside from the caw of a crow perched on a slanted street sign. It called into the night, pointing its beak up towards the cloudy winter sky. Its cries echoed, bouncing between the concrete buildings until it faded into nothing.

Julian's heart raced as he thought of drawing Des in for a hearty embrace. Maybe they would leave together. It was just a fairytale, but they could leave in the middle of the night, slipping away and never seen again. They could face whatever lay beyond the borders together, free from debts to Lancut or anyone else. Julian considered the documentaries that showed the outside as an uncivilized place, mostly wilderness after heavy bombing, but that could not deter him. He could picture himself hauling a deer carcass back to skin in a cabin made from fallen logs. Julian understood it was all oversimplified- nothing more than a fantasy in his mind, but supposed even if he succumbed to the elements, it would be better than any other fate. If he did not survive the wilderness, it would be with a pair of familiar arms around him.

As they neared an abandoned storefront, Dia put up a hand. She pulled out a small device, holding it up to the door. A click rang out in the night, and she swung the door open. In the darkness, they walked over shattered glass across the stained linoleum. Julian carefully stepped between the shards on the thin soles of his shoes.

"Hands where I can see them," barked Dia.

A broad figure shrouded in shadow held its hands up, stepping forward slowly. Shining her bright flashlight forward, Dia directed the beam into Des' eyes, and the man squinted, crumpling his face.

"Des," cried Julian.

A tight hand gripped his bicep, and Cam held him in place.

"Mikey, Montero, I want you two to hold him down," ordered Dia. "Des, slowly lower yourself to your knees."

Dia dropped the backpack to the ground, spreading supplies onto the ground. She picked up a small glass vial, holding it up into her flashlight to read the label.

"Cam has a certain belief about how these things should go, but I have to disagree. He's convinced that just because his initiation was traumatizing, that everyone needs to needlessly suffer- that it proves loyalty or something. But I'm going to inject this into you, and it will stop your heart, and once your Disc is no longer transmitting, I'll administer another injection to bring you back," she explained, plunging a needle into the side of Des' neck. Julian caught his wide eyes as he opened his mouth, perhaps to scream.

The man slumped forward, held in place only by Montero and Mikey's grips on either of his arms.

"Lower him onto his back," said Dia calmly.

She kneeled over him, preparing a second injection. Dia glared at a watch around her wrist. Julian's heart leaped, and he yanked against Cam's grasp.

"Stay still," barked Cam, but Julian thrashed against him.

Julian glanced up at Cam, and for a moment, the clamp faltered, and Julian pulled free. Falling to his knees beside Des, Mikey hauled him back by his shirt.

"It's fine," said Dia.

Julian's fingers hovered above Des' chest, tracing a hesitant path where his heartbeat faltered. His breath hitched, dry and uneven, as Dia plunged the second injection into Des' neck. Without thinking, Julian latched onto Des' hand, squeezing it three times in quick succession. The silence pressed down on him, sharp and suffocating.

Des convulsed. His body jerked as though lightning had struck him, arms flailing wildly before his chest heaved in a desperate search for air. His hands scrabbled against his own ribs, clawing for relief. Julian stayed frozen, his throat dry as dust, until Des' glassy, unfocused eyes locked onto his.

A flicker of recognition broke through the haze. Julian's lips twitched into a smile—weak, forced, but all he had to give. The room felt suspended in time, the air itself weighted and thick. As he knelt beside Des, Julian's chest tightened with each shallow breath the man dragged in. His gaze stayed fixed, counting each fragile rise and fall, until the soft pressure of a hand on his shoulder pulled him back to the moment.

Mikey crouched beside him, his voice barely above a whisper. "We've got to move."

Together, they hoisted Des to his feet. His legs buckled, and Julian took his weight without hesitation, wrapping an arm tightly around him. The icy air outside bit at their exposed skin, but Julian's focus stayed locked on Des. His breaths puffed out in faint clouds as he adjusted his grip, steadying the man as they stumbled forward.

Snow crunched underfoot, muffled and slow, each step a struggle. The distant outline of the concrete building grew clearer with every labored step, its blocky silhouette looming like a promise- or a threat. Julian's muscles burned under Des' weight, but he pressed on, glancing at the man's face. Des' eyes fluttered closed, and Julian gave him a gentle nudge.

"Stay with me," he muttered, his voice rough but steady.

When they reached the metal door, Julian sagged against the frame, his chest heaving. His breath puffed against the cold Peterson, swirling into the night before fading into nothing.

Dia's voice cut through, sharp and measured. "Cam first. Then me. Montero, Mikey. Julian and Des, you're last."

Cam slipped inside, his shadow swallowed by the dim light beyond the door. Dia followed, her movements sharp and precise. A shrill commotion erupted before the door swung shut again—a burst of shrieking that sliced through the night like a knife. Montero shoved the door open a crack, enough for a sliver of light to spill out. Mikey darted inside, vanishing into the chaos.

In the room, Cam kneeled, hands laced behind his head.

"-gotta believe me. Why the fuck would I do anything like that?"

"You've been here longer than anyone else," said a woman with ginger hair pulled up into a bun.

"What the fuck would I have to gain?"

"I bet they offered you something good. Told you that you could have your old life back," said Maya, stepping out into the open.

"What?"

"I bet your parents would forgive you for all of it. You got tired of the slop for every meal and the cold nights. All you had to do was get back into Lancut's good graces, and then you'd be free to move on with your life without us. You'd kill us all for a hot meal, wouldn't you?" spat Maya.

"I left because I hate them, hate Lancut. They're evil. I won't be complicit—"

A slap rang out, and Cam raised his head back up in defiance, a pronounced handprint stamped on his right cheek.

"We relied on you," cried Maya. "You've been so outspoken about a leak, and when I assign the mission to someone else, give the information to someone else, there are no Enforcers, no anything. I know you've been talking to your sister. I found the device."

"Read the messages," said Cam. "Read them. I only ever sent them on my own time, far from the safe house. I never told her anything, just that I was safe. Nobody else in the family has any idea."

"I should put a bullet between your eyes," scoffed Dia.

Montero hesitated, glancing over at Julian.

"No, we'll make sure we get all the information we can out of him. He'd do the same to us. He's the one who got Vinny killed. We'll only put him down once he finally does some good for us. Montero, Mikey, take Cam to the holding cell. I expect everyone to follow so we're all clear what happens to traitors."

Des slumped against Julian. Maya's fiery eyes and sharp words stung him as if he were the one slapped across the face.

"I'll walk," said Cam. "I'll take whatever you give me, but I'm not a traitor."

"Then walk," Maya replied. "Dia, take Des upstairs. He can share quarters with Julian for the time being. Julian, I want you to come with me."

"Can I…" started Julian softly, stopping himself and forcing himself to silence.

Des cast him a dazed expression before the woman hauled him away. Julian jogged to keep up with the group as they wound down the stairs and into the basement of the building. While the upper levels were cold, the basement chilled to the bone anyone who dared venture beneath the concrete structure. Julian wrapped his arms around himself, squeezing until he pressed against the aching bruises around his battered body.

In a corner, a chain hung from the ceiling, rusted with thick links. The dim light sputtered, as if struggling to consume the small surges of energy it was allowed. Cam walked steadily, as if ready to stand in line for a coffee. A man in a stained green sweater threw open an old locker, pulling out a set of cuffs. The captive man offered his wrists up, and Maya locked them to the chain above his head. With a tug on the other end of the chain, Cam teetered on the toes of his boots, gritting his teeth.

"I'm not a traitor. I have never betrayed the Reborn, and I will never, no matter what anyone does to me."

"You're gonna hang here a long time," muttered Maya.

"I have nothing to tell you. I messaged my sister, and I will take my punishment for that because I deserve it."

A faucet ran in the far corner, and the water clattered into a faded red bucket.

"Montero," she ordered, "You know what to do."

He picked up the bucket, walking hesitantly towards the hanging figure. Cam looked past Montero, his face expressionless and but head raised defiantly.

Montero stumbled, dropping the bucket and sending it clattering to the ground. He gripped his thigh, gritting his teeth as he hissed.

"Fuck," he muttered.

He went to grab for the empty bucket when Julian took his place. In the far corner, he refilled the bucket, hands trembling as he plodded through the small crowd, eyes fixed on him. He looked at Cam, and for a moment, sharp anger surged through his veins for all the things he said, that he'd done, but a pit in his stomach twisted. Drawing back the bucket, he splashed the contents into Cam's face, and the water soaked his hair, dripping into his face and down his body. Cam shivered as the water left his shirt soggy, traveling down to his pants and leaving puddles in his boots. Cam let out a hitched breath but kept his eyes up.

"I will take my punishment for putting the Reborn at risk with my messages to my sister, but I am not a traitor."

"Who's your contact? Sands himself?" hissed Maya.

"I have no contact with anyone," he managed through chattering teeth.

"Strip him," barked Maya.

The group moved around him as if one, controlled by their queen in their concrete hive. They cut away his shirt, pulling it off him as it clung to his body. When they finished, they left him in a pair of faded boxers. His exposed muscles trembled as he struggled to steady his feet beneath him as he swung from the chain.

"I'll deal with you later," said Maya. "You'll tell me the truth,, or you're gonna rot down here, and nobody is coming to save you."

CHAPTER TWENTY-SIX

Julian lay face down on the cot with a warm presence beside him. He moved towards the warmth, nuzzling his face into the familiar scent, forcing his nose into the crook of Des' neck. The other man grunted, pushing into the motion, and Julian wrapped his arms around the man's chest, crawling atop him to intertwine their legs.

Des ran his fingers through Julian's dark, curly hair, brushing any stray strands from his face. As he traced a finger along Julian's jawline, he flipped Julian's slight form with ease, planting a kiss down onto his chapped lips. Julian moaned into the other man's mouth, heat traveling down his body until the ache was low in his stomach. He ground against Des, a slight whimper escaping his lips. Des smiled.

"I missed you."

"I was so scared," whispered Julian. "Scared of what's coming next, too. I want to run away with you so we can be free."

"We can't," hushed Des. "There's too much to be done here."

"It's not right. Things aren't right here either. We don't belong here."

"We're building a better tomorrow."

"At what cost?" Julian muttered into Des' parted lips, planting another rough kiss. "I want to be safe together. We could get out of here and live a life. We deserve that, don't we?"

"We owe the Reborn our lives."

"I'm not in debt to anyone. I am a free man; *we* are free. Don't you think we should run away while we can? We could build a proper life. There have to be more people out there. You can't put a fire from inside the house."

"Maya has given me a new purpose-"

"I don't trust them."

"Who?"

"Any of them," stated Julian. "Lancut, the Reborn. None of them. I want to get out of here before it's too late."

"We'll deal with it when it comes," he said, trailing a hand down Julian's bare torso and towards his waistband.

Julian whimpered, his hips bucking as Des dipped lower.

A knock echoed through the room, and Julian scrambled off of Des, pulling on a shirt strewn beside his cot. Des rolled over, cocooning himself in a blanket as Julian stood, cracking the door open. A shaggy-haired man stood in the doorway, leaning against the outer wall.

"Can I come in?" he asked.

"Sure."

Julian adjusted himself as he turned around, sitting down on the base of the cot and throwing a blanket over his lap. Montero took a seat at the desk chair, staring down at the seemingly unconscious figure curled up beside Julian.

"Why did you to Cam?"

Julian hesitated.

"I had to put up an image. Why didn't you?"

"My leg is fucked up. I stumbled."

"No, you didn't."

Montero smiled faintly.

"You don't think it's him?" asked Julian.

Montero shook his head. "There's something going on, but it's not Cam. He's an egotistical asshole, but he's loyal. Too loyal."

"What do you think is going on?"

"I'm not sure. People trusted him; they followed him. Someone is seeding mistrust from the inside."

"Who?"

"I'm not sure, but we need to be more cohesive than ever," said Montero. "No time for infighting or whatever. We'll deal with this issue later, but I don't agree with what's going on. I don't think it's right. How long before we're just as bad as them?"

"Probably already are."

"Maya wants to finish this once and for all. She sent me to tell you we're meeting at three, and she wants Des there as well."

"Okay," said Julian. "Whatever is right or wrong, we'll do what we need to do."

"Yes, yes, we will."

The other man softly shut the door behind him, and Des rolled over.

"What's going on?" he whispered.

"I'm not sure anymore," Julian admitted.

While Des dozed, Julian could not shake the looming weight. He paced around the small room until he wandered into the hall. He couldn't shake the feeling that he needed to speak to someone; one particular person. The vague directions he had been given helped him little, and he lost track of time within the identical halls and doors in the cold, gray structure.

Julian stood outside of the plain door. Hesitantly, he knocked twice before standing back. When the occupant opened the door, Julian noticed the vast space. She smiled, gesturing for him to follow her into a sitting room with two leather couches situated into an L. They faced an old television screen. He stole a glance around a corner. A hallway led to a bathroom, and Julian assumed somewhere within the maze lay a bedroom.

Maya sat down on a stool in the small kitchen, gesturing for Julian to join her. He climbed onto the adjacent stool, perching himself on the edge as he shoved his hands into the pockets of the tatters pants the Reborn supplied him with.

"Would you like coffee or tea?" she asked him.

He hesitated. "Only if you're having some. I don't want to be a bother."

"Smart man," she replied. "Matilda," she called, and a tall slender woman emerged from one of the further rooms. "Could you make us a pot of coffee? The strong stuff I like."

The woman nodded, and Julian caught her eyes. She dressed in the same garb as anyone else in the compound. As he averted his eyes from the woman, he looked down at his stained sneakers, legs dangling from the tall stool.

"Is there anything else I can do for you, ma'am?" the woman asked.

"That will be all," she said. "And when you're done, the glass in the bathroom is awfully smudged."

"Of course," the woman replied.

Maya smiled. "You seem uneasy. I know this must be quite the adjustment for you."

Julian nodded, "I am," he admitted. "I, um," he started, "I didn't think there were any waitstaff here."

Maya's smile faltered.

"Not waitstaff. Some people here make amends for something they've done. Service to the compound strengthens loyalty while helping us to get the necessary tasks done."

"What did she do?" asked Julian.

"What?"

"What did the one working for you...what did she do?"

Julian inquired.

"Doesn't matter," she dismissed. "I must ask you why you came to visit. Is there anything you need? You're a valuable asset here, and I want you by my side when it's time. We need you."

"Will Cam get a second chance?"

"That… is to be decided. That's not your concern. Ask me what you want to know."

Julian mulled the proposal over.

"Before The Reborn, who were you?" he finally asked.

She hissed slightly as she pulled in a quick breath.

"That matters no more than your past does," she said.

"My past matters. It's what makes me valuable," he said hesitantly, studying Maya's twitching face.

She no longer hid behind a smile.

"I will tell you how the Reborn came to be."

The woman taking care of the house poured the two mugs of coffee. She set a shallow cup of cream between Julian and Maya and gently presented a bowl with finely ground sugar and a small spoon sticking from the mound like a flag. Maya took her time, carefully measuring two spoonfuls of sugar into her coffee. After pouring a few drops of cream into his dark coffee, Julian watched as it danced, sinking like smoke before dissipating.

"I know multiple rebel groups came together to form one," said Julian. "I want to know how you rose up through the ranks."

Maya let out a long breath, any smile she wore before wiped away. She looked Julian in the eyes as she started.

"It wasn't so much that multiple groups came together to form one; the Reborn are just the last ones standing," she said. "Before the Reborn, there were dozens. We'll never know how many. Just little sparks, fires Lancut could easily put out, scattered. People in disorganized factions with stolen weapons and limited rations. I worked for Lancut, in intelligence, but I left. I couldn't stand by anymore. I knew about a small group of rebels through Lancut channels, and I went to find them myself."

She lifted her coffee, staring down into the dark abyss, but she didn't take a sip. "These groups start the same way. There are patterns to all of it. There are a few angry idealists, someone who knows how to get weapons and operate them, and someone willing to fund the effort, at least for a little while. There was always infighting. We argued constantly over strategy. How public should we be with our efforts and how much we were willing to risk. Some thought laying low and gathering supplies would work, while others thought a swift attack before Lancut caught onto us would be best. The separate groups were fragmented, but even within our own factions, we couldn't keep order."

She hesitated. "The first group I joined was just six of us camped out in an abandoned factory. One of our people was shot by an enforcer, and the others turned themselves in. Not me. I said I would die before ending up in custody. I was taken in by another squad who were sympathetic. We had worked together in the past. But they were destroyed in a single night raid. There was no warning and no chance to run. I was out gathering supplies, and when I came back, they were all gone. Most disappeared like that," she lowered her gaze. "By the time I had my own followers, most other groups stopped answering calls. One by one, the radios were silent. Empty camps with no bodies."

Julian paused. "How? How did you survive when so many died?"

"I survive everything," she said plainly. "I see the patterns. I see the shifting, and I hear the whispers in the wind. Every time a group grows, gains real numbers or momentum, it collapses or disappears. Someone is always listening. Someone always knows exactly where to strike. The Reborn is the last one left with enough manpower to matter. It has been for years now, and we've even been picked off one by one. Picked off when people leave for supplies or go out on missions. Our time is limited, and I know that." She tapped her fingers against the table in measured rhythm. "I didn't mean to lead anything. I was just the last one standing."

When she met his eyes, her pupils were pinpoints, steady and sharp. "I've always known how to stay standing, and I think you have too. That's why you're still here."

"You worked for Lancut?" Julian hesitated.

"Same as you," she replied bluntly. "I was ruthless enough to work with them. It's the same ruthlessness we need to work against them."Julian nodded, taking another sip of his coffee. "Do you have survivor's guilt?" he asked bluntly.

"Every day," Maya replied. "There's not a person here who hasn't lost someone in the fight."

"I don't intend on losing anyone," said Julian.

"Maybe you'll be the lucky one," she scoffed. "I expect you'll do great things with us. You have something that Cam doesn't. He saw the world as black and white, and that was his downfall. You understand that sometimes we have to do things that we don't necessarily agree with for the greater good. That's why you agreed to work for Lancut, isn't it?"

He nodded.

"I know you're prepared to do whatever you need to," she said. "You're a fighter, Julian. You and Montero make a good team. You work far better with him than Cam did."

"You're right," said Julian. "And when it's time to do what I have to, I'll do it."

"Yes, you will."

CHAPTER TWENTY-SEVEN

"You aren't worried about guards?" asked Dia.

Maya shook her head. "That's what the first team is for. The first team, which you will lead, is going to knock out anyone externally. You will send back any information you have about increases in security. You will also disarm the security system before retreating back to the nearest safe house. The second team will do the rest."

"I want to see it happen," grunted Dia.

"And you will," she assured. "This will all be recorded, so the world knows exactly what happened. When the second team enters, they will address any security inside of Sands' residence. Half of the secondary team will be led by me, and the other half by Montero. We will take alternative routes through the mansion in order to fully surround Sands. Based on information from Julian, there is limited internal security, and it appears that Sands spends a large portion of time in an office central to the structure.

"This is all happening so quickly," spoke Mikey.

"We don't have time to waste anymore. We have no idea how much Cam told Lancut, and we cannot remain idle anymore. With the Vision project becoming a greater barrier every day, we can't afford to waste a second. Our time is now."

Julian and Des were ushered to Montero's group with three others. He regretted to admit that in the short time he had been at the compound, he had learned very few names. After all of this, he supposed it would not matter. Surely, some would not make it, and his mind still drifted to a place beyond the border where he could live his life with interference from anyone, no matter who or what they fought for.

Dia and her group departed in a gray, scuffed van. While the rest waited in the large conference room, a deadening silence set over the space. Des kept his eyes down, fiddling with his shoelace. Julian realized the great absence originated from one person, and he clenched his eyes at the thought. As he imagined Cam dangling from his wrists somewhere in the labyrinth below them, he tried to flush the image from his mind. As he glanced back up at Maya, his stomach twisted.

A warm hand snapped his attention away. Des wrapped his hand around Julian's slender fingers, gripping tightly. Julian offered a strained smile.

"I'm not sure why I'm going," whispered Des.

"What do you mean?"

"I don't even know how to fire a gun."

"It's good to just jump right in, I suppose, or at least someone told me that."

"Are you scared?"

Julian hesitated. "Yeah."

"Me too."

"It's not too late…" Julian stopped himself.

Des smiled sadly. "Yeah, but it's our duty, isn't it?"

"I'm not sure anymore."

"Let's go," barked a voice, and Montero stood above him.

Julian stood, dragging Des up with him. They followed the small group outside towards a small moving van. Montero hauled open the back on its tracks, and the members filed in. Julian climbed to the back, bracing his back against the wall.

The door slammed down, and they pulled away in complete darkness. A sharp movement jolted him into Des, and he clung on as the truck rattled down the road. As the time passed in the stuffy truck, he closed his eyes, letting his head bob with the small jerks and bumps.

For a moment, he imagined himself in his nook. In the corner of his apartment, he could wrap himself beneath blankets. The cold seeped in from the concrete beneath, but if he insulated himself well enough, he could ward off the dark presence ever watching over him. If he had only spoken to Des sooner, perhaps they could have curled up in the space together. He nearly laughed at the thought of the man laying in the dirt, but Julian was sure he would have insisted.

The van stopped once more, and the rumble of the engine died. Julian covered his eyes as the bright streetlights beamed into the back of the truck in the night. With a last squeeze of the other man's hand, Julian let go, following the short line of people out onto the pavement. As they emerged into the open, the night was silent. Even the cars that would have passed through the area had abandoned them. The quiet of the night would have been peaceful any other time, but as he stood before a familiar structure, he shuddered.

"Dia and the others are on their way back to a safe house. Locks are disarmed. No casualties," stated Maya. "We'll enter in through an emergency exit in the garage, and from there we'll take separate staircases with teams divided between Montero and I."

Julian fiddled with the handle of his pistol, the surface now slick with sweat. Under the cover of night, they may have crept through the city, but beneath the abrasive streetlights, every feature of his face was illuminated, cast in a distorted shadow behind him. He stayed close behind a woman with a shaved head.

Maya halted, testing a door handle before slowly twisting the knob and pulling it open. Inside, Julian could have mistaken the place for Des' garage. The white walls gave the place a sterile appearance, and if not for the lines of cars, the echo of their feet would have echoed endlessly. Even with the garage teeming at its capacity, the soles of their shoes pattered softly against the ground, bouncing through the room until it sounded like an army approached.

Montero waved his hand, and the group split off, heading left. He stopped at a white door that nearly disappeared into the room. When he cracked open the door, Julian held his breath. He imagined armed guards on the opposite side, ready to put a barrel to his temple and pull the trigger without a moment of hesitation.

"We're heading to the eighteenth floor," said Montero. "We will wait outside the door there until I get a signal from Maya to proceed."

Julian took the stairs on the balls of his feet. His lungs burned, and he glanced up at the seemingly endless stairwell, and he half wondered why they couldn't have taken the elevator. Nobody in the team dared complain or stop to catch their breath. Julian's throat stung, and his lungs ached as he kept the swift pace set for him. He brushed his fingers against the railing. Sweat settled in the center of his back. Des kept pace, though his face reddened, and he wondered how the other man was recovering from the trauma of just days ago.

When Montero put up a hand, Julian could have collapsed. He leaned against one of the white walls, awaiting any word from Montero. Though just a man- younger than himself, deep creases drew cracks through his face as though he could crumble at any moment. The cheeky grin from the first time he met the man was gone, replaced by a solemn expression and a knit brow. He held his weapon in its holster, holding his watch to his ear with the other hand. Julian glanced over at Des. His mind raced through a million things he could say, yet none of them fit the moment. In the utter silence, he could not risk muttering even a few words, but they burned in the back of his throat as if he would choke on them if he could not force them out. Yet he held them down, fixing his gaze on his tattered shoes and double-knotted laces.

"We've lost all connection. We're going in," ordered Montero.

Julian's heart leaped, and he stole a final glance at Des before following directly behind Montero. The door opened into a familiarly dark space. In the dim lighting, they walked over hard wood stained a deep shade of burned umber. The velvet curtains he recalled from before draped from ornate golden rods above tall windows that he imagined overlooked the city from the most stunning perspective. Julian wondered if Sands kept the skyline hidden away in shame, as if looking down on what he had created, looking down at his sins, was like peering at a rotting portrait of himself meant to be hidden away in some locked closet.

Julian trudged behind, lingering at an amber vase on a stark white pedestal. As he leaned in, he could make out a deformed version of himself on its warped surface. The hall stretching before him might as well have been mirrors in a fun house as his head swam.

Julian gritted his teeth, jogging to catch up to the disappearing team.

As they rounded the corner, Montero checked his watch once

more. He held up a hand for the group to stop. The surrounding footsteps silenced, and Montero threw open the door.

There was a moment of complete stillness as he stood in the doorway.

"Run!" Montero managed before the words caught in his throat, and a gunshot rang out.

Julian spun on the polished floor, struggling to gain his footing. As he lunged forward, his legs froze beneath him, and he tumbled to the ground. He struggled to force his arms out in front of him, but horror stabbed through his stomach as his limbs were not his own, and his cheek slammed against the ground, splitting open the skin. Blood gushed out onto the floor around his immobilized face.

In the corner of his vision, he spotted Des as a figure in a crimson uniform grab his ankle, dragging him down the polished floor and further into the maze. Julian struggled to choke out a scream as a hand cinched around his wrist, and he could only watch the white ceiling as his skin squeaked as it caught on the wood.

When the hand released him, he shifted his gaze to spot a painted cardinal. One of its wings was smudged as if someone hand dragged a bloody hand across it and hung it on the wall. Tears welled in Julian's eyes as he struggled against his invisible bindings.

No help would come.

"I thought you were brighter than this," said a figure above him. Edmund Sands loomed tall with an expression that Julian could have mistaken for pity. "You believed any of that? That you could short out a Disc that easily?

"What a shame. When I picked you, I thought you had the drive that I had. I saw myself in you. But then Maya let me know exactly who Desmond was. I found out who he was to you, and I had to accept you were a lost cause. You were head over heels for a criminal, ready to bring down the system that sustained him; bite the hand that fed him."

Julian felt the muscles in his face release.

"What's going on?" he blurted.

"You've met the fate as hundreds before you."

"What?"

Maya stood over him with crossed arms beside Sands.

"Tomorrow morning, the news will come out that a rebel faction tried to invade my home, but they were eliminated. Only their leader escaped, and the Reborn will continue to recruit the radicals and the enemies of the state—"

"And they'll disappear one by one," said Maya.. "They'll die or someone will drag them away on sabotaged missions—because nobody lasts more than a year…Except for Cam."

"He knew he couldn't last forever, but he stayed. So loyal," said Maya. "He'll die in that basement. Anyone who cares that he's down there will be dead by dawn."

"What do you get out of this?" sputtered Julian.

"You know the answer to that," said Maya. "And one day, I'll be captured by Enforcers. The rebels will watch them drag me away so I can live out the rest of my days somewhere other than concrete."

"Just imagine how disappointed Dan Peterson will be in his son, and, of course, the man who he'll blame for pulling Desmond into this mess," said Sands.

"Lock him up," pleaded Julian, "put him on house arrest forever, but don't hurt Des."

"I have my own arrangements. Julian, you're going to continue to be an asset to us," said Sands. "You have a bright future ahead of you."

CHAPTER TWENTY-EIGHT

Julian flipped over on his cot, staring blankly at the gray wall. His cell was never dark. Around the clock, a humming light above him pulsed like a sickly heart. There were no other prisoners to give him trouble, and besides food deliveries and his weekly meetings, nobody at all bothered him. Julian always considered himself a reserved man without the need for excessive human contact, but he thought of what he would do to be able to feel the embrace of another person or to feel the warm breath of someone who saw him as more than an insect under a microscope.

He sat up in bed, wrapping his arms around himself. The thin orange fabric he wore offered little protection from the cold seeping through the concrete walls around him. The loose scrubs hung from his boney shoulders. Julian rubbed his eyes. He stumbled across the room, no larger than a closet, sitting down in a metal chair bolted to the floor beneath. The cold rungs stung the exposed skin on his arms.

They allowed him a pad of paper and a felt-tipped pen. As he glanced through the thick glass barrier between himself and the hall, he wondered why they bothered at all with the precautions. Unless he were to slither through the small delivery slit barely tall enough to slip his rations through, he was useless. He could spend the entire day scratching at the impossibly strong glass barrier with any of the useless instruments in his cell and not leave a scratch.

A small clock sat on the wall across from his quarters. As the time crept forwards, he readied himself. He carefully stacked the few books he was allowed on the corner of his desk. As the clock struck the hour, he laced his hands together on his desk as instructed of him.

He heard the familiar footsteps before the man came into view. Sands smiled at him, dressed in a navy suit with a gray handkerchief tucked into his breast pocket. A woman dressed plainly in a loose brown dress followed him, setting down a padded stool. He waved her away as he sat down, smiling at the man in front of him.

"The board loved your ideas."

Julian sat silently.

"I always knew you'd make a great intern. I hoped it wouldn't be under such circumstances, but I was speaking with some colleagues, and I decided that if you keep up the good work, we could grant you a bit more privacy; larger living quarters and all. There was even discussion about getting you a tablet."

"I don't need that," said Julian coldly.

"What do you want?"

Julian gritted his teeth.

"Why don't you hand over your work for the week?" said Sands.

Julian grabbed the manilla folder from his desk, sliding it through the slot. Sands snatched it away, opening of the folder and quickly riffling through before shutting it with a smile.

"You must get lonely," said Sands.

"No. I'm just fine."

"You wouldn't want a roommate? Or at least visitation?"

"With who? There's only one person I'd want to see."

Sands smiled.

"Cam has been very cooperative as of late."

"I want to speak with Des," said Julian.

"I'm afraid that's not possible."

"Can you tell me what happened to him? That's all I want. I don't need anything else." Julian hesitated before he weakly spoke. "Please."

Sands dropped his gaze, shaking his head. He glanced up at Julian, opening his mouth before shutting it again. When he spoke, his words were soft.

"I need you to do something for me first, Julian."

Julian stared through the glass with a clenched jaw.

"Take off the bandage."

"No," said Julian.

"I'll tell you where he is, but first, you need to show some cooperation."

"I didn't want it."

"I won't have you handicapped so long as you're in my care," replied Sands. "Let's see it."

With trembling fingers, Julian reached behind his head, struggling with the knotted fabric. He held his breath as he unwound the makeshift bandage from his healed eye. The light blinded him as he struggled to meet Sands' gaze.

"Much better," said Sands.

"Tell me," managed Julian through gritted teeth.

"As a show of my appreciation, I'll tell you. Desmond Peterson was declared dead two months ago after state sanctioned decommission. His father offered a large sum to spare him, but his crimes were too great, and we did not believe he had enough to offer as an asset to keep him alive."

Julian stared through the glass with glazed over eyes and a blank expression. "Why don't you think about my offer? I'm sure Cam would appreciate it. In the meantime, here's your next assignment," said Sands, producing a new, identical folder.

He slipped it through the slit, and Julian grabbed it, dropping it onto his desk.

"Until next week," said Sands.

The man stood, flashing a blindingly white smile before disappearing down the hallway.

Julian sat back in his chair, clenching his both of his working eyes shut beneath the abrasive lights. Time passed slowly, wherever he was. He asked when he first arrived where he was, but nobody told him anything other than he was underground. With no natural light, his skin had grown gray and pale. His scrawny form had grown weaker, and with nowhere to walk, his muscles had quickly deteriorated.

A knock on the glass snapped him to attention. He smiled at the woman in the brown dress. Julian held open the delivery slit.

"How are you managing?" she asked.

"Just enjoying the sunshine."

"They authorized the book you asked for. I read through it last night, and I bookmarked a Chapter that I thought really stood out."

"I appreciate it. Really, I'm in your debt," said Julian.

He nearly laughed at the words.

"Would you like me to collect anything from you?" she asked.

"Not today, but once I finish this one, I'll give you a few books and make room for the new ones."

"Of course," she said.

She grabbed the stool, carrying it away with her.

Once she was halfway down the hallway, he flipped through the book until he found the dog-eared page. They would not allow him any electronic books, but Julian didn't mind. He couldn't suppress a smile as he pulled the thin piece of paper from between the pages. As he unfolded it, his fingers trembled, and his heart raced. He smoothed it out with the palm of his hand against his metal desk.

Things are getting warmer. The work is still hard, and the hours are getting longer with the sunlight, but it's not so bad. We had another execution. One worker in my squad tried to make it out in a shipment truck, but they caught him, and they put him down on the spot. We all heard the gunshot. My dad sent a message saying that he would try to get me out of here, but I'm not sure I want to come back. This is the closest to freedom I think we'll get. I promise I will get you out here.

They think they've stripped everything from me. They think they've taken my life in every way that matters.

But I'll find you, and we'll live for the first time. Reborn together.

-Des